Praise for Lynn Messina's first novel, *Fashionistas*

"*Fashionistas* is quietly hysterical, a stealth satire of magazine and celebrity culture."

—*The Star-Ledger* (New Jersey)

"*Fashionistas* has genuine style, plus wit and wisdom. Messina is an acute observer.... The premise—indeed, much of the book's affectionate satire of the magazine industry—is frighteningly believable.... Displaying a light touch, Messina has written a book that captures the idiocy and humor of the fashion-magazine world. Perhaps she's even succeeded in raising the stakes of jealousy—by proving that imaginative flair is clearly more important than wearing the latest Jimmy Choos."

—*Time Out New York*

"Messina's tale is a hip and funny parody of trendy magazines and the people who toil at them."

—*Booklist*

"Delightfully witty."

—*New York Daily News*

"Wickedly entertaining.... Messina's prose is witty and assured (she's read her Austen, her Wharton, her Noel Coward), and her novel is an irresistible frolic."

—*Publishers Weekly*

"Get the inside scoop on the scandalous world of fashion magazines..."

—*Elle*

"Well-written, funny and sharp."

—*Pittsburgh Post-Gazette*

tallulahland

lynn messina

RED
DRESS
I N K
™

First edition January 2004

TALLULAHLAND

A Red Dress Ink novel

ISBN 0-373-25044-4

© 2004 by Lynn Messina.

Author photograph by Chris Catanese.

Visit Red Dress Ink at www.reddressink.com

Printed in U.S.A.

For Mom

Thanks again to: my father, my brothers,
the Linwoods, Chris Catanese, Deena Rubinson,
Roell Schmidt, Jason Robinette, Dawn Staub,
Donna Levy, Meredith Steinhaus.

As well: Susan Ramer, Farrin Jacobs, Margaret Marbury.

Plus: Jennifer Gibbs and Helene Ige for their fabulous
Giig and Iggi designs (yes, they were completely pilfered).

The Picasso 2.0

1

Nick tells me to stop being ridiculous as he hands me a gin and tonic. He says it sharply, with impatience and a fair amount of disgust, but he's wearing the bland smile he usually saves for bank managers and car rental agents. Then he turns to my father, who is now only a few feet away, and offers his hand. "Congratulations. It's a lovely party, sir. So kind of you to invite me."

My father shakes Nick's hand enthusiastically. He likes this treatment. He enjoys fielding compliments and being called sir. "I'm glad you could join us, Nicholas. Tallulah never brings friends home," he says. There's a touch of fondness in his voice that you could mistake for affection, but I know better. Dad isn't affectionate and he isn't fond. He's dutiful. Like Cordelia, he loves no more and no less than his bond. "Carol and I wish she would do it more often."

"I'm sure it's just an oversight," says Nick, lying outright in his smooth way that throws you off and lulls you into trusting him. Nick knows how much I don't want him to be here. He also knows how much I don't want *me* to be here. My ungracious presence is the result of a knock-down, drag-out, kicking-and-screaming, pull-your-hair-out-at-the-roots fight that left me wounded and bruised. Nick doesn't pull punches when he thinks something important's at stake—in this case, my future—and he relentlessly pursues his end until you yell uncle and plead for mercy and throw up your hands in surrender. It doesn't help that he gets you drunk first before taking the offense.

I laugh politely. There's only a thin thread of mockery in the sound—a considerable accomplishment given the circumstances—but Nick picks up on it and disapproves with a look. I ignore him. "Yessir, an oversight. That's exactly what it is."

Nick narrows his eyes at me angrily. He doesn't want me undoing all his good work with my sourpuss expressions and my unchecked scorn. "Lou was just saying that she thought she might go out to the Hamptons for Labor Day weekend."

Dad looks taken aback by this. He knows very well—or at least he thinks he does—that this isn't the sort of thing his daughter says and for a moment I think that

Nick has overplayed his hand. I think he's revealed too much and given Dad enough clues to piece together the truth: I'm a weak country being bullied by the large nation I border. But he hasn't. Dad rushes in to do the fatherly thing and within seconds I'm invited to a barbecue with Carol and her daughters. "And please bring Nicholas. That is, of course, if he doesn't already have plans."

Dad says this with a sly look in Nick's direction. He thinks Nick and I are dating. He's convinced my claims to the contrary are subtle pleas for space and privacy, but they are not. Nick and I aren't an item. We're just a pair of single hopefuls who waste weeks and sometimes months in relationships with the wrong people. We make bad choices and do stupid things, and when it all ends in a bout of tears or disgust, we run to the other for comfort. We find shelter in the other's apartment and spend hours dissecting seemingly insignificant moments. And we are good at this. We know each other so well that we can always pinpoint the exact second when things turned sour. We can always outline the other's mistakes and draw up "do" and "don't" lists for the next time around, but this doesn't matter. We make the same mistakes over and over. Sometimes it feels as if we should pledge our dysfunctional selves to each other, but it's not that simple. Despite our compatibility, we aren't each other's solution. The strange and complex formula that makes up a romance doesn't equal Tallulah and Nick.

Nick says something noncommittal and vague about the barbecue just as my father's being called away by his new wife to greet another guest. The wedding reception is in full swing, but Dad is still making the rounds. He's still shaking hands and accepting compliments and working his way through the crowd of well-wishers. There are so many people here that the party has spilled out onto the gardens. It has overrun the small patio and commandeered the rosebushes and the lily pond. Most of the people trampling the hydrangea—congressmen, museum directors, publishers—don't belong here, but the bride has turned her wedding into a coming-out party. This is Carol. She's ostentatious throngs and velvet ropes and social registers.

"I'm not being ridiculous," I say, watching Dad shake hands with a Broadway producer. There it is again: the I'm-happy-to-see-you smile. I turn away abruptly and glare at Carol's two daughters. "They *do* look like evil alien bunnies from hell."

But Nick isn't paying attention to me. He's still focused on my father. He's still looking at a problem and trying to solve it. My future is a Rubik's Cube to Nick—there are a million combinations but only one that's right.

"Look at them," I say, pointing rudely at Carol's buck-toothed twin daughters, who are oblivious to my attentions. "When was the last time you saw smiles that wide outside of a Miss America pageant?"

"Lou, you agreed to be on your best behavior," he says,

as he replays the scene in his head: Was he too obsequious? Should he have accepted the Labor Day invitation? This is the problem with Nick. He has tunnel vision
and an awful stubbornness to follow it up. He never aban-
dons a project midstream. And that's what we Wests are
to him right now—a project that must come in on time
and under budget.

But I'm stubborn, too. I'm impervious to reason and
set in my own ways and on the side of the angels. This
time I have the advantage of the high moral ground.
"Come on, Nick, just look at them," I insist. "Cammie and
Sammie are not human. Their glued-on beauty pageant
smiles haven't wavered once all day. That's"—I look at my
watch and do some fast calculating—"seven hours. Even
a game-show host can't smile for seven hours straight. And
have you seen their eyes? They're completely devoid of
expression, and notice how huge their pupils are." I lower
my voice and lean in. "I think they're taking commands
from the mother ship. No," I say, when Nick finally sub-
mits to his weaker impulses to take a look, "act natural.
We don't want them to get suspicious. For all we know,
they could be watching us on their holo-scanners right
now."

Nick forgets that he's annoyed with me and laughs. It's
a nice sound, cheerful and strong, and several people turn
around to get a glimpse of its source. Then Nick remembers why we're here. He recalls my waywardness and
my refusal to be led where he leads and starts coughing

to disguise his amusement. "Lou, when you agreed to come, you promised to be polite."

The promises I made that night are fuzzy. They're tattered photos with faded images. "I *was* being polite," I say defensively.

Nick stares at me unblinkingly. "No, you weren't."

"I congratulated him, didn't I?"

"Actually, no, you didn't. I did."

This is Nick. He likes to split hairs and be right all the time. "Yeah, but I brought you along. So it was like I congratulated him. What else do you want from me?" I say, my voice dropping to a pitiful whine. I've had several drinks and very little of my dinner, and my victimhood is starting to leak out of me. It's starting to seep out of the holes in my facade. This wasn't supposed to happen. I had every intention of getting through this evening with my dignity intact. "I'm not like you, Mr. Diplomat's Son. I haven't spent my whole life perfecting mild good humor."

I see anger in his eyes and for a moment I think this has worked. But Nick isn't easy to pick fights with and he isn't easy to distract. That mask of mild good humor is hard to pierce. Most of the time it's like galvanized steel and I never have a blowtorch on hand.

"Lou, we've already had this discussion," he says calmly. "You have to talk to him. How else are you going to get seed money?"

This is a very good point. I don't have many options left. The banks refuse to give me a small-business loan, winning the lottery isn't as easy as it sounds, and I don't have anything of monetary value that I can bring to an antiques dealer and hock. Despite the number of dead relatives who surround me, including a mother, nobody has ever left me something of value. I have costume jewelry and stacks of letters and a heart-shaped locket that my great-great-grandmother wore, but nothing you can start a business with.

"By selling my body," I say now, because it's the only solution I haven't explored.

"Lou," he says dangerously.

"What? I'll use condoms. It'll be perfectly safe and tax-free."

But he's not in the mood for prostitute humor. He's trying too hard to broker peace. "You will march right over there, you will congratulate your father on his nuptials, you will kiss your new stepmama on the cheek and then you will talk to your father about a business loan."

This course of action sounds reasonable and anyone else would have little trouble falling in line. But not me. I know the subtext. Despite the jump-to-it practicality of Nick's order, this isn't a straightforward venture. It's riddled with land mines and quicksand. "But he'll find out."

"What?"

"He'll find out what I need the money for," I explain. "He's bound to ask."

Nick's doesn't grasp the significance of this. He doesn't

understand why divulging the money's purpose should have any bearing on his West loan scheme. "So?"

"If he knows what I need the money for, it'll make him happy," I explain calmly. "I can see the headline: Daughter Goes into Family Business—Father Swoons with Joy."

Nick wrinkles his nose. He's still in the dark. "Is that so bad?"

"Swoon with joy, Nick," I say, speaking slowly so he'll understand. "Swooning is happier than thrilled or ecstatic."

"And your point is?"

I sigh heavily. Sometimes the people who know you best are the ones who understand you the least. "Nick, he's my father. I can't bear to make him happy."

Nick finishes his drink and asks a passing waiter to bring him another. While we're waiting for the man to return, Nick doesn't speak. He gathers his thoughts, examines the crowd and wonders what he's gotten himself into. The waiter returns quickly with a fresh scotch and soda. "Let me see if I understand the situation," he says, reinforcements in hand. "You are willing to make yourself miserable so that your father won't be happy. Is that what's going on?"

"Well, duh, Nick. Where have you been for the last four years?" I finish my drink and look around for the waiter but he has disappeared. I hold my empty glass in one hand and ball up the napkin in the other.

Nick stares consideringly into his drink. "I thought you liked your job."

"I work as a personal assistant for a man who designs second-rate, mass-produced garbage cans with names like the Desdemona and the Picasso. I have a master's degree in industrial design from Parson's. How can I *like* being someone's girl Friday?"

Nick is startled and he stares at me for several moments without saying a word. This isn't what he signed on for. When he stumbled across the pile of sketches among the clutter on my kitchen counter, he thought he'd discovered the perfect excuse. He thought he'd found an excellent pretext for putting me in touch with my father. Nick assumed that a loan would bind us together. He figured that a common goal would provide us with opportunities to talk and to mend fences that had long been left in disrepair. This is what Nick does. He sees a gulf, measures the distance across and starts building a bridge. The need to tinker with chasms is innate and compulsory— he comes from a long line of social engineers. But the diplomatic corps doesn't teach you how to deal with self-destruction on my level.

He's appalled and shocked and a little bit dazed by the wounds I've inflicted on myself. I can see it in his eyes. I've managed to pierce his mask of mild good humor but that wasn't my intention. This confession wasn't supposed to be a blowtorch. I was just stating a fact, but somehow there's something harsher about words spoken than words thought. Suddenly I'm appalled, too. Although I know that the last four years haven't been completely wasted, suddenly I'm shocked by bad decisions impulsively made.

"May I have another drink?" I ask, holding out my glass with the crumpled napkin inside. I want Nick to leave. I want him to go away and stop looking at me with that horrified expression. Something has changed. Something has altered dramatically but I can't put my finger on it. Uttering the words has somehow expunged me from the garden and now I feel naked and exposed and painfully self-conscious.

Nick hesitates. He's not sure what I need right now. He's not convinced that gin and tonic is the best cure for masochism, but he takes my glass and wanders off.

After he disappears into the crowd, I close my eyes, take a deep breath and wonder how I got here. I took the job with Marcos Medici to spite my father—imagine: Joseph West's daughter working as a gofer for an obsolescence-monger—but there were things to learn. Marcos is a master at what he does. He's a genius at making trash cans and credit cards and coffee cups and shopping bags for well-known designers on Fifth Avenue. He knows all the cutting-edge technologies and can easily manipulate them to his will, producing plastic chairs and garbage cans so cheaply and efficiently that he can change their shape and color at the drop of a hat. With inexpensive silicone molds at his disposal, Marcos can bend to market forces. He can wet his finger, gauge the direction of the wind and redesign accordingly. In Marcosville, everything is disposable and seasonal and easily replaced by a newer model.

Wests don't subscribe to the ethic of fast-moving consumer goods. We don't believe in short life spans. My father is an old-fashioned modernist. He believes in permanence and classics and products that will stick around forever. He's still Bauhaus. He's still making good designs for the masses, and even though every modern art museum in the world has something of his on display—a chair, a vase, a clock with hands that run backward—he doesn't rest on his laurels. After thirty-five years, he's still creating new, ground-breaking designs that are wholly unlike anything he's done before. Marcos can only produce variations on a theme. He even has a formula, which he follows faithfully: Exhume a classic from the fifties; then add swoopy amoebalike flourishes. He's a fashion editor pinning an ivory cameo to the lapel of last year's suit to make it fresh.

I like some of Marcos's designs. The Desdemona, with its sweeping curves and wide handles, is a great garbage can, even if it is just an adaptation of an Alvar Aalto vase. But I've maxed out on disposability. I've had my fill of planned obsolescence. There are no great leaps forward at Marcos Medici Associates, and this is what I'm pining for. This is why I took out my drafting table and my sketch pad and my charcoals and started designing again. It had been a long time in between—more than three years—but some things you don't forget. Some things are so basic they're encoded in your DNA.

My work isn't a great leap forward, either, but it's a baby step in the right direction. I've mixed Medici technology with West ideals. The results are sleek and simple designs with a small presumption of permanence that can be produced easily and cheaply. This is what I learned at Marcos Medici Associates: how to bring a product to market. The recent grads who litter his office don't know the first thing about this. They're like movie directors who include dangerous, difficult jumps across twenty-foot gorges in their scripts and expect the stunt coordinator to work out the details. But I'm not a designer with illusions. I have a clear, practical understanding of what it takes to produce a design at a reasonable price. Blueprints are relief maps of complications to me. They are navigational charts with islands marked "too impractical," "too intricate" and "too expensive."

Years of liaising with manufacturers and making Marcos's problems go away have brought me here. They put the pencil in my hand and turned me into a mild-mannered employee with a secret identity and superpowers. Every day I sit at my desk smiling blankly and answering to self-important apprentices whose work isn't one-tenth as interesting as mine. It's not a comfortable feeling. It's a painful constant ache that tightens your muscles and destroys your peace of mind. I didn't know this would happen. When I decided to take a menial job to spite my father, I didn't know that I would continue to grow as a person or an artist. People talk about the maturation process but you never really think it'll happen to you.

I take a deep breath and wonder what I'm going to say to my dad. It's obvious now that I have to say something. Epiphanies are one-way streets and I can't leave this party the way I came in.

I'm avoiding eye contact with my great-aunt Dorothy and thinking about the future when Nick returns.

"Cammie asked me to give you a five-minute warning," he says, smiling endearingly at Dorothy. Nick is a suck-up. He's compulsive and incurable and has a constant pathological need to be liked. At his hot molten core, he's a politician kissing babies and shaking hands with constituents.

I look at Carol's daughters wrapped in champagne-colored satin polyester. Even though Carol is fifty-six years old, she's having the fairy-tale wedding. Even though this is her fourth shot at till-death-do-us-part, she's wearing a long white dress, walking down the aisle to "Here Comes the Bride" arranged on the organ and releasing soaring white doves at the foot of the church. But at least this time she's hedged her bets. My father has only fifteen good years left in him—a respectable clip, of course, but hardly a lifetime. "How do you know it was Cammie and not Sammie?" I say, to distract myself. This line of thinking won't produce humble requests for money. Only happy dad thoughts need apply.

Nick shrugs. "They're not completely identical. Cammie has a beauty mark under her right eye."

I glance briefly at the evil alien bunny twins. "That's poorly applied mascara, not a beauty mark."

He's disconcerted but practical. "Still, it serves its purpose. A rather thoughtful improvement."

"I suppose it does have its uses, although why you would want to distinguish between the two is a mystery to me. They're equally awful," I say. Then something he said earlier strikes me. "Five-minute warning for what?"

"Your toast," he says. "Although I imagine it's four minutes by now."

"What toast?" I ask, alarm growing. "I'm not supposed to make a toast. Nobody mentioned anything about a toast."

"Perhaps I misunderstood," he says, not at all convincingly. "Maybe they're going to serve toast in five minutes."

I can feel my palms beginning to sweat, and I ball my hands into fists. I don't want to make a toast. I don't want to stand in front of a crowd of people and say a few words about Dad and Carol's happiness. Their joy is just a mirage. It's a rainbow that will disappear as soon as the sun goes behind a cloud.

The band, which had been lingering on the final chords of a fifties doo-wop tune, stops abruptly, and the microphone screeches loudly as Carol picks it up. She talks over the noise while the bandleader plays with the amp. "Hello. Thank you all for coming to share this special day with us. It's traditional for the father of the bride to make the first toast. However, since my father is no longer with us, I thought a new spin on an old custom was in order. Therefore, Joseph's daughter, Tallulah, will be making the first toast."

"That bitch," I whisper to Nick, smiling tightly as everyone on the patio turns to look at me. "She didn't even give me five minutes to think of something on the fly."

"Give me paper and a pen," Nick says.

"What?"

"Paper and a pen," he says again, more emphatic this time. "Quickly."

I'm carrying a bag but it's only filled with lipstick and a card for Dad and Carol. I pull the card out and hand the envelope to him. I borrow a pen from a passing waiter.

Onstage, Carol is still talking. She likes the spotlight, and despite her plan to embarrass me, she's reluctant to give it up.

Beside me Nick starts scrawling furiously.

"What are you doing?" I ask. I have more important things to worry about but I'm too distracted. My nerves are too jangled for me to focus on any one thing.

"I'm writing you a toast," he says.

I try to read it but his hand is blocking the words from view. "Don't make it mushy. I'm not getting up there and making some maudlin speech about happiness and love."

Nick doesn't respond. He's too busy scribbling.

Carol makes a joke and the audience laughs. She's

winding down now. She's thanking us again for being here. Seconds are ticking away and I fight the urge to tell Nick to hurry. He's already writing as fast as he can.

"Here," he says, just as Carol introduces me.

I take the envelope and walk up to the stage, skimming the toast with my eyes. I'm not looking where I'm going and trip over the microphone's wire. The crowd "oohs" collectively. I regain my balance and take the microphone from Carol. Then I suffer a hug and a kiss on my cheek. She is all affection and sentiment, but it's only for the benefit of the crowd. Carol doesn't like me. She doesn't trust me and treats everything I do with narrowed-eyed suspicion. Her relationship with my father is a tower of chairs balanced on the back of an unruly mare and she's afraid that I'm going to spook the horse.

With my heart beating furiously, I stare out at the sea of faces. Only a few are familiar. I'm an only child of only children, and our family is threadbare on both sides. All that are left are second cousins we haven't lost touch with yet and some elderly relations on their last legs. Most of the four hundred guests here are business associates of my dad's or friends of Carol's or glitterati who the new Mrs. West wants to lunch with.

"Hi," I say as the microphone screeches again. Rather than talk over it, I wait until the noise stops. My eyes scan the speech, checking for words I can't read easily. But Nick's penmanship is always neat, even when the only surface he has to lean on is the palm of his other hand.

Nick's toast starts with a pleasantry. "Hello. Thank you all for coming. And thank you, Dad and Carol, for getting us out of our sweltering New York apartments. I have an air conditioner, of course, but it doesn't feel nearly as lovely as this cool mountain air."

There are a few shouts of approval and I unbend enough to smile. "Also, Carol, thank you for giving me this opportunity. In the last couple of years, I've been in a few wedding parties but nobody has ever asked me to speak. You know what they say: always the bridesmaid, never the well-dressed young woman with a clever toast." This gets a laugh. I wait for the titters to stop before getting to the substance of the toast. "Duke Ellington once said, 'Love is indescribable and unconditional. I could tell you a thousand things that it is not, but not one that it is.' This is true, especially for my father and his new wife. Love *is* the world's greatest mystery and it doesn't matter how it works or why it works—only that it does. So please, raise your glasses. To Dad and Carol, the most beautiful mystery of all."

The guests comply. They raise their glasses and drink champagne and say "hear, hear." I give the microphone back to Carol, who air-kisses my cheek. She's not pleased with me. I've handled myself too well. I haven't mumbled or stuttered or flushed painfully from the attention.

As I walk by my father, he puts his hand on my shoulder. "That was very nice. Thank you, Tallulah."

This isn't what I want from him. His thanks are useless

to me, but I tell him he's welcome and go in search of
Nick. He's standing at the edge of the lily pond, clapping.

"That was brilliant," I say, giving him a hug. "Thank you
for saving my life."

He shrugs. "Anytime."

I'm tempted to take issue with the word *beautiful* but I
restrain myself. Not everyone could have churned out an
almost perfect toast in less than two minutes. "What's
happening now?" I ask as I turn to face the stage.

"Carol's introducing her daughters. They're up next."

One alien bunny from hell—I'm too far away to distinguish if she's wearing a painted-on beauty mark—takes
the microphone from her mom and prattles on about love
and family for several aimless minutes. Although she's
had more than a hundred seconds to prepare a toast, her
thoughts are unorganized and random. The Shelby twins
don't have the advantages of Nick's upbringing. They
weren't raised in a household that valued public speaking
and well-turned phrases; they weren't expected to remember epigrams from Dorothy Parker and Oscar Wilde.
But the audience is chock-full of sentimental fools, so this
isn't a problem. As soon as she finishes welcoming my father into her family, the crowd cheers loudly. Alien bunny
from hell number one gets a nine on the clap-o-meter.

I can see Carol standing on the corner of the stage. She's
smirking. This—the triumph of sentiment over elo-
quence—is a minor victory. It's a small success she will
relive several times before the evening is over.

As soon as the applause fades, a waitress wheels out the wedding cake. It's a three-tiered white confection with a fondant version of one of my father's most famous designs: the Peterhoff chair. Plastic bride and groom figures are sitting on the recliner. It's cute. Too cute.

The band strikes up "Celebration" as Dad and Carol retake center stage. Then Carol takes a knife to the cake, cuts a piece and holds it up. "Oh, God," I say with a glimmer of suspicion of what's coming next, "don't tell me they're going to feed each other cake."

"Okay," Nick says agreeably, "but you're a smart girl. You'll probably figure it out on your own."

I want to avert my eyes but I can't. This is a train wreck. This is something that you can't turn your head away from, even though you're horrified to the pit of your stomach. I watch and wait and wonder how in the world I'm going to be able to ask my father for a business loan after seeing him stuff a piece of cake into Carol's plump red mouth.

Carol takes the thick slice of seven-layer cake, puts it on a plate and gives it to the waitress. Spectacle averted.

"The waitress is carrying away the slice," Nick says, providing unnecessary play-by-play. I can see what's happening for myself. "I bet she's putting it in the freezer for them to eat on their first anniversary,"

"Ha!"

"Ha?" Nick looks at me perplexed. I don't often respond with guttural one-word exclamations.

"Like they're going to make it to a year," I say. My voice is louder than I realized and Aunt Dorothy and several strangers in pin-striped suits turn sharply. "With... that...cake in the fridge," I add haltingly. "Yes, indeed, Dad sure loves to eat his cake."

Aunt Dorothy purses her lips, but she returns her attention to the happy couple on the dance floor without comment. I was never her favorite.

"And that, ladies and gentleman, concludes act three. Thank you for coming out tonight and please exit through the doors on the side," I say, when the wedding planner in her black Chanel dress wheels the cake off the dance floor. "We can go anytime we want."

"No, we can't."

My parents weren't diplomats. They weren't dignitaries who attended ribbon cuttings with kings and sultans, but they knew a thing or two about etiquette. "It's okay to leave a wedding after the cake is served. Our social obligation ends here."

He shakes his head. "You haven't spoken to your father yet about the loan we talked about," Nicks says pedantically, as if reminding a child to look both ways before crossing the streets. This treatment is unnecessary. I haven't forgotten why we're here. I haven't forgotten for a single moment why I'm standing at the edge of a lily pond in the Adirondack Mountains watching a father I hardly know marry a woman I can't stand.

"I'm going to do that on the way out," I explain, scan-

ning the crowd to see if anyone is making a mad break
for freedom. Nobody is. Instead of dashing to the parking lot, guests are sitting down and drinking coffee.
"There's always that awkward moment when he and I are
not sure if we should hug, kiss or just shake hands. I figured I could fill the gap nicely with a request for a loan.
Then we could shake hands like gentlemen. See? I have
a plan. I know you rarely credit me with any planning
whatsoever, but in the right circumstances I'm a regular
secretary general of the United Nations." Waiters and
waitresses are starting to bring out plates of wedding cake
and guests are returning to their tables. I don't want to
return to mine. I don't want to sit down next to Cammie
and Sammie and their dates and make more small talk.
Dinner was enough pain for one evening. It was enough
penance for all the awful thoughts I've ever had about
Carol.

"Do you know what the secretary general does?" he
asks.

"Makes a lot of plans," I say as Carol and my father sit
down. Getting a moment alone with Dad will be chal-
lenging—Carol sticks close to her investments—but if
Nick helps it should be doable. If he compliments her on
her gleaming white dress or the band, he should be able
to keep Carol away for a few minutes.

"Be that as it may," Nick says, unaware of his sudden
usefulness, "you're not going to ask your father for a loan
in the middle of his wedding reception."

"But I thought that was the plan," I say. "Remember, you said I should march right over there, congratulate my father on his excellent choice—do note that I am using invisible air quotes around *excellent* out of deference to Aunt Dorothy, who has eyes in the back of her head— kiss my new stepmama on the cheek and then ask dear, old dad for a business loan. Also note that I'm using invisible air quotes around—"

"Dear and old. Yes, I know, Lou. You're hardly subtle."

"Actually, just around 'dear.' He is pretty old. No irony there."

Nick sighs. "I know I said that but I was only making a point. You can't do it right now. You'll have to wait until tomorrow. Until after brunch."

I narrow my eyes. "What brunch?"

"What brunch?" he repeats almost exasperated. "Didn't you read the invitation at all?"

I roll my eyes. "Well, duh. I threw it away unopened. You're the one who fetched it from the recycling bin and insisted we come."

The events replay themselves in Nick's mind—my refusal to come, the ugly fight, the drinks at the bar, the stupid bet—and he moves on. He doesn't linger over the invitation. "Brunch is tomorrow at eleven."

I try to think of some sort of pressing engagement that I have tomorrow but come up empty. Nothing presses on Sundays in the middle of the summer. At least not in New York. Everyone is out of town. "I suppose this means we should get a room." Although I'm resigned to my fate, there is nothing gracious about it. I resent the added expense and time. I'm not completely poverty-stricken but my budget—a loose flow chart that lets me break even at the end of each month—can't easily accommodate fancy hotel-spas in the Adirondacks. There will be many brown bag lunches in the coming weeks to make up for it.

"I've already—"

"Don't say it. Just give me the key." Nick has already booked us a room. He's already called the hotel and reserved a spot for the night of July 4. This is what he does. Even when I'm at my secretary general of the U.N. best, he still outplans me.

Nick pats his pockets in a pathetic display. "Hmm, where did I put it?"

I narrow my eyes again. By now they're mere slits. "I'm sure you'll find it if you just apply yourself."

"You're probably right," he says, making no effort to look. Nick is the give-no-quarter type. He's merciless and indifferent to reason and he'll make us stay here until the band belts out "Last Dance." "But in the meantime, let's eat cake."

I don't object to the cake so much as the company it keeps. I look over to where the alien bunnies from hell are licking chocolate frosting off silver forks. Even though they're eating cake and drinking coffee, their lips are curved in smiles. "Can't we just stand here and look for the key?"

Nick is silent for a moment. He's considering his next words carefully. He wants to finish what he's started. He wants to play the part of carefree wedding-goer until the curtain drops, but he doesn't want to push me too far. He's too smart to sacrifice his main objective—peace with Dad—for some lesser goal of complete and total compliance with wedding protocol. "Tell you what, you sit at the table with Cammie and Sammie for ten minutes—just sit, you don't even have to talk to them—and then you can hide in your room for the rest of the night without any objections from me."

"Five minutes. And I get to hold the key."

Nick shakes his head. With anyone else, he would negotiate. With any other friend, he'd flex his meditative muscle and offer a compromise. But he knows I'll buckle. He knows I'll take the path of least resistance. "Ten minutes and the key stays with me."

Cammie's and Sammie's dates are handsome professional men from the city. They're stockbrokers or lawyers or accountants, with no discernible personalities but plenty of manners. They stand when I approach the table.

Although our parents have been dating for almost four years, the Shelby twins and I never interact. We avoid one another's company and decline invitations when we know the other will be there. This wedding is an immovable object. It's an irresistible force that we've all succumbed to with something resembling grace.

As I sit down, Cammie makes eye contact with her sister and their twin smiles dim. They flicker and fade for a brief moment and then return to a blinding one-hundred kilowatts. Cammie and Sammie have been on their best behavior all day but snide remarks have slipped out. They know my menial admin job is where I'm most vulnerable. They know it's the soft fleshy beating center, and this is where they aim their arrows. But I recognize Carol's poison. It leaves traces, like arsenic in the nail beds and hair follicles.

Conversation fails to resume after we sit down. The alien twin bunnies from hell smile brightly, but they don't say a word. Their dates look on, mystified by the silence but uncertain how to change it.

"That was a nice toast," I say, deciding to be gracious. The next ten minutes are going to pass slowly enough without a thousand pounds of silence weighing them down.

Cammie dips her head in acknowledgement. "Thank you. And yours was…" She pauses a moment to find just the right adjective. "Short."

The word drips slowly from her pursed lips like an insult. In Shelbytown, brevity is not the soul of wit. I turn to her sister and try another topic. "Sammie, how was France? You were there for two weeks?"

I'm only being polite—I really don't care about her trip to Europe—but I have my facts wrong, and rather than tell me about the sun setting over the Mediterranean Sea, she explains in detail why an indispensable person like herself can only be away from her job for five days at a time. She rattles off an inventory of her accomplishments—lead on the Pepsi account and the Sony account; team coordinator on the General Electric and the Citibank—but I'm not impressed. The list sounds like the Standard and Poor's index from the newspaper and is just as meaningless to me.

"I've always envied people with less responsibility who can get away for weeks at a time," she says. "It must be a wonderful relief to know that any dropout from the temp agency can keep the seat warm while you're gone."

She's looking at Nick but her dart gun is pointing at me. Under the table, Nick hands me the key card. Peace in our time is one thing, but these thinly veiled comments are petty jabs. They're insults tossed over the back fence of feuding neighbors and not worth the effort of a Townsend. At least not now, when there are landmark treaties to be signed. I take the key and slip it into my purse. I'm released from our agreement but I choose to stay. This is now a test of endurance and I refuse to cry mercy until the ten minutes are up.

2

The next morning is perfect. It's sunny and warm and breezy and the air is tinged with honeysuckle. Everyone is happy to be here. Everyone is pleased to toast the newly-weds with mimosas and eat dry French toast and runny eggs except me. A full night's sleep has done nothing to improve my temper. It's only given me time to rehearse and rerehearse the conversation with my father. But this is a waste. We never get to recite the speeches we've prepared.

Breakfast is being served on the veranda, and Nick and I sit at a small table for four surrounded by woven bas-kets dripping with lilacs and azaleas. Vines of ivy cling sinuously to bright white trellises. Dad and Carol are here but their table is around the corner and out of sight. This is where I'd like to keep Dad and his wife. I'd like for them to always be just beyond my line of vision, but I'm familiar enough with the workings of fate to know that my preferences are meaningless. Any second now Carol will rise from her seat and start another round of lady-of-the-manor. She will walk from table to table, laying a hand on men's shoulders and asking if there's anything they need. This might seem like the typical sort of hostessing that brides do, but it's something more. Carol wears an intolerable air of triumph. She's a society dame now. She's the wife of an important, respected man who gets invited to gallery openings and movie premieres and fabulous parties on fifty-foot schooners. This is what Dad offers her: the chance to take her small life in Massapequa, Long Island, and magnify it. My mother never felt the need to live her life on the international stage but Carol is a different breed. She didn't get married to Joseph West to play mahjong in the suburbs.

"How are you doing, Tallulah? I haven't seen you in ages," says Ann Harris, the fifty-something wife of my dad's business partner, Charlie. "Are you still in London?"

I haven't been in London for years. When Mom got sick, I transferred to Parson's in Manhattan and spent the rest of her life within handholding distance. I went to dialysis with her every Tuesday night. I got her ice cubes when she was thirsty, piled blankets on her when she was cold and stood by helplessly as her body spasmed and cramped in pain. Nancy knows this. We talked about it at the funeral, but I'm not surprised that she forgot. Nobody remembers the details of your life as well as you. "No, I got my master's a few years ago," I say simply. "I'm working in the city now."

"Really? Charlie didn't mention that you were in the office," she says, making the assumption that everyone makes. The one that I myself had made.

"No, I'm not working with Dad. I'm at an Italian firm," I explain, knowing she won't ask why. Nobody ever asks why I'm not working with Dad. They assume it's a touchy subject best left to family members and therapists. They are right.

"Italian, really?" She can't conceal her disapproval. WW II ended more than fifty years ago but I'm still working for the enemy. But that's all right. As far as Charlie's wife is concerned, anyone who isn't Joseph West is the enemy. "How interesting. Which firm?"

"A small one," I say evasively. I don't want to mention Marcos. Ann will recognize his name, think about it for a moment and then look at me differently. It has happened a million times before and I usually enjoy the moment. It's like a little piece of performance art: the disclosure, the surprise, the polite smile to smooth everything over. But suddenly it feels petty and embarrassing and too revealing to share with another person, especially one whom I haven't seen since the week my mother died. In the wake of yesterday's epiphany, I'm more than the accumulation of bad decisions.

Ann nods and switches gears. She knows the score. After twenty-five years of making small talk with her husband's business associates, she knows when to leave a subject alone. She hasn't abandoned it completely, though. She'll simply wait until Nick and I leave the table and then ask Charlie all about the small Italian firm I work at. "Where are you living?"

I name a few streets in the West Village, and Ann, on terra firma, quickly lists her favorite restaurants in the area. The conversation isn't engrossing—half my mind is firmly rooted elsewhere—but it flows naturally with no awkward pauses and it passes the time. Before I know it, the waiters are clearing the table and offering another round of coffee. My cup is empty and I'd like more, but I forgo the pleasure. I'm jittery enough without the help of artificial stimulants.

I dart an angry look at Nick but he fails to respond. He isn't oblivious. He isn't unaware of my rude glances and impatient jabs, but blocking out distractions is another one of his diplomat's-son skills. Talking to heads of state while rioters picket in the streets is par for the course.

The waiter interrupts to ask Charlie if he'd like a refill on his coffee, and I take advantage of the break in conversation. "Let's get this over with," I say, leaning over to speak softly in Nick's ear.

Nick responds instantly, tossing his napkin onto the table, and my heart flips over. Despite my impatience, I don't want to get this over with. Despite my brave words, I don't really want to be mature and practical and a responsible grown-up who swallows her medicine in one gulp. I'd much rather sit at the table surrounded by dripping azaleas and talk about the warm chocolate cake at Tartine. I'm thinking of ways to back out when Nick stands up. He says "excuse us" to the Harrises and pulls out my chair with an air of expectation. Here it is: the point of no return. Either I go forward or stand still.

We walk around the veranda, skirting waiters and waitresses, until we arrive at Dad and Carol's table. The newlyweds are sitting with another couple, whom I don't recognize. The woman is sporting a wide-brimmed yellow hat with dried flowers that wave whenever she moves her head. The man is wearing khakis and a blue polo shirt.

Nick takes charge and I follow his lead. My social graces aren't finely honed skills. They're not muscles that I exercise regularly, so I follow him around the table with a large, fake smile on my face. Nick apologizes for interrupting, introduces himself to the pair, compliments the lady on her bold choice, comments on the idyllic setting and arranges for me to have a quiet moment alone with my dad. Although I'm wrapped up in my own nerves, I can't help but admire the smooth way Nick moves everyone around as though they were pieces on a chess board.

When I leave, he's reclining comfortably in my dad's chair while Carol orders him a fresh cup of coffee and the woman in the hat waves a croissant under his nose.

The hotel is crowded with more than just West wedding guests and as soon as we step inside the lobby, we are accosted by the noise of people checking in, checking out and making plans for the day. Bellboys in blue uniforms with gold buttons and tassels drag by squeaking carts filled with luggage, while parents trail behind, yelling at little Johnnie to stop pulling his sister's hair. It's not the quiet out-of-the-way place I had in mind for this exchange but the chattering voices and squeaky wheels serve a similar function. We are surrounded by people, but I feel completely alone. The din is a filter. It keeps everything out.

We find an empty couch and sit down across from a young couple trying to decide what to do with this perfect day—sailing or shopping. The couch is not the ideal arrangement. I don't like occupying the same space as my father. I want him farther away from me. I want him on the next chair, not the next cushion. I take a deep breath and wonder how I'm going to start. The words are in my head and while they stay there, this whole scene is simple. I say: "Dad, it's high time I started taking my talent seriously. I have sketches—I found studio space. All I need is a little start-up capital to get the whole venture off the ground." He says: "Sure." Then he takes out his checkbook, which he somehow has on him even though few bridegrooms have the reasonable expectation of writing checks on the morning after their wedding, and scribbles a generous amount. After I fold the check and stick it in my pocket, I thank him for his generosity and with an awkward display of affection—a handshake preferably, but a peck on the cheek possibly—we return to the party as if nothing had happened.

But reality is a choppy ocean. It's a tempest-tossed sea with one-hundred-foot waves, not the calm waters of daydreams. Here, money will not be exchanged without conversation and questions and an Inquisition-like interrogation. Only infidels choose to worship in someone else's workshop.

In the end, Dad will give me the money. This is what he's always wanted—an heir to follow in his footsteps, a successor to make the name West a little more immortal. I should be flattered by his faith in me. I should be complimented by his high regard for my talent but I'm not. It's just another reflection of himself. When Dad looks into the Tallulah mirror he sees his own bright future shining back at him.

While the silence stretches, Dad grows increasingly uncomfortable. He doesn't want to be here. He doesn't want to do this. A father-daughter tête-à-tête in the lobby of the Adirondack Hotel and Spa terrifies him. He thinks I'm going to give him grief. He thinks I'm going to sob and scream and assault him with my dislike of Carol, but he's wrong. The grief well is dry. It's nothing but sand and pebbles. "Tallulah, you wanted to talk to me about something?"

"Yes, I wanted to ask you…" But I trail off. Despite my intentions, my voice weakens and dies.

The words won't come out. I can't get them out. They are no longer arranged neatly in sentences like soldiers in formation. Rank has been broken and numbers are now flying through my head. But they are the wrong numbers. I'm not thinking of the cost of studio space in New York or the price of adonized aluminum from the distributor in Minnesota. No, my mind is filled with old resentments. Twenty-six: the number of days after Mom's death that Dad went on his first date with Carol. One thirty-one: the number of days after Mom's death that Dad left me alone in the Long Island house to sleep over at Carol's on Christmas. Three forty-eight: the number of days after Mom's death that Dad gave Mom's car, a car she'd left to me but Dad kept for himself, to Carol.

Dad is looking at me with impatience and confusion, and I can do nothing but close my eyes to shut him out. This was a mistake. This was a gross miscalculation. I can't ask him for help. I can't ask him for anything. I can only look at him and see betrayal of me and Mom. But no, just me. You can't betray the dead.

My clearest memory of my mother is from her last month. We are in the Sloan Kettering cafeteria trying to eat lunch under the cold glare of fluorescent lights. Mom is pale, and in this awful lighting she looks as if she were already dead. She takes my hand, grasps it tightly—a surprising accomplishment given that most of her strength has been sapped—and tells me I'll be all right without her. Her voice is firm and bathed in conviction. I will be all right without her.

The memory asserts itself now and I can hear Mom's voice clearly in my ears, loving and comforting and so incredibly ephemeral it breaks my heart all over again. I open my eyes and stare at my father. He's still a handsome man at sixty-eight. He has dark intelligent eyes and a round friendly face that's quick to smile. In many respects he's a good man—generous with his employees, thoughtful of strangers, willing to go out of his way to help out a friend in need. But he's an awful father. Two ninety-three: the number of days after Mom's death that Dad told me he doesn't miss her anymore.

I will be all right without him.

"It's not important," I say now, determined to do this on my own. Money, a key component up to a few split seconds ago, doesn't seem very important anymore. I have talent and skill and a willingness to work hard—people with fewer advantages than I have built more on less. "I thought I needed help with something but I've managed to sort it out myself. We can go back to the party now."

Another parent might have pressed the issue. Another parent might have sensed this was an evasion and asked a question or two. Not mine. Mine stands up, relieved, and gestures toward the veranda. My impulse is to hang back, to stay right there on the couch listening to the happy couple discuss their day, but I sweep by him and he follows me outside.

Nick is exactly where we left him, only now he is drinking coffee and eating croissant. He glances up as we approach and there are questions in his eyes. I can read them easily enough. He knows I haven't asked my father for a loan. Without my saying a word, he knows that I haven't even broached the subject of money with my father.

Nick pushes his chair back and gets to his feet. "Lou, I'd hate to be the party-pooper but we've got to hit the road. We have theater tickets for later," he says, explaining why we have to run off to my father, my brand-new stepmother and the unknown couple at the table. This isn't true. We don't have tickets to anything but it's a good excuse and I'm grateful to Nick for making it.

The car ride back to the city is five hours long. We spend the time arguing over radio control and playing twenty questions. The subject of me and my father never once comes up. This is Nick being diplomatic. This is him demonstrating the difference between pushing someone in the right direction and shoving her off a cliff.

3

I'm only home a few minutes when Hannah rings. She tells me she's coming to New York and hangs up. An hour later she calls again, this time to let me know that she has a bus ticket in hand and will be getting on board in two minutes. In this way she keeps me apprised of her movements, and when she arrives on my doormat at two-fifteen in the morning, I'm hardly surprised. Twenty-seven minutes earlier she had called to say she'd arrived at Port Authority.

"I'm going down to the subway now," she said, the sound of an approaching train nearly drowning out her words. She doesn't say good-bye as she rushes to catch the downtown A.

While I'm waiting for Hannah to disrupt my life, I piece together what has happened. I take the small hints and dropped clues and draw a conclusion: Someone she went to high school with is more famous than she. Hannah has been dreading this moment for her entire life. She's been tense and ready for this blow for almost thirty years, but she's still not prepared for it. Despite the Eastern philosophies and the soothing morning chants and the carrot shakes with just a touch of ginger, seeing Adam Weller on *Entertainment Tonight* in his French blue shirt and his wild curling hair sends her into a tailspin.

For a moment everything stops. Life stands still, and the only things moving are the wheels in her head, which are madly grinding out plans and schemes to the tune of the *Entertainment Tonight* theme song. It's hardly the sort of inspiring music that suits the epochal moment and she flips off the TV with something like disgust, packs her bag and starts the five-hour migration north. She hasn't chosen north. North chose her. This is where Adam Weller is.

Her journey is so unexpected and unplanned that she has to call her sister from the Peter Pan bus and ask her, over the din of *Mrs. Doubtfire* playing from ten television screens suspended by metal arms from luggage racks, to please remove the pot of boiling water she'd left on the stove.

When Hannah arrives she's exhausted. She's only covered two hundred miles in a gasoline-powered bus but she lies down on my couch as if her journey were far greater. She tosses herself onto my small squeaky couch as if she's just crossed the great plains on a wagon train. This is Hannah. Every thought, feeling and action is exaggerated, like a shadow on a wall.

I consider her for a moment in her pose of exhaustion—her black shoulder-length hair on the arm of the couch, her large brown eyes closed, her olive skin stretched tight—before offering something to drink.

"Water would be great," she says. Now that she's here, the drive is leaking out of her.

"Tell me about Adam Weller," I say, handing her a glass, which she drinks greedily. If anything, her fatigue is mental, not physical—seven hours of plotting the downfall of an unsuspecting man takes a lot out of you.

"Adam Weller," she repeats with a sigh, her head falling once again against the arm of my IKEA couch. She looks comfortable and at home there, as if she plans to never leave. But she has to leave sometime. The Homestead Act isn't about pitching your tent on someone else's couch and it doesn't apply to Village apartments in the twenty-first century. "Adam Weller was my year. In many of the same classes. He was very quiet. Participated in no activities. Wore argyle sweaters with matching socks. I never paid any attention to him. Oh, how could this have happened? He wasn't even on my watch list."

The watch list is made up of outgoing, gregarious types from her graduating class, the people everyone expected great things of: the captain of the cheerleading squad, the quarterback of the football team, the ingenue who always got the lead in the school play, the class president. There are no introverts among the two dozen names. There are no shy quiet geniuses who will one day take the world by storm. This is the list's great weakness. It doesn't account for the Adam Wellers, who walk quietly and carry big sticks.

Not that accounting for Adam Weller and his ilk would have prevented this moment. Some things are inevitable. Turning life into a race to the finish line only guarantees that someone else will get there first.

"What's he doing?" I ask, hoping that Adam Weller is notorious, that he's broken up J. Lo's latest marriage or he's embezzled millions from Brad Pitt—anything but an actor. Hannah's recovery time will be much shorter if she hasn't been beaten at her own game.

"He's a director," she says, her voice sinking still under the heartbreak of it all. "An up-and-coming director. He's just signed a three-picture deal with a major studio. And get this, he already has an Oscar, a friggin' Oscar. Can you believe it? *I* was supposed to be the first person from Poolsville, Maryland, to win an Oscar. They were supposed to erect a sign at the city-limit line with *my* name on it."

An Oscar is impressive, but I'm not convinced that Adam Weller was awarded one. Hannah has a tendency to stretch the truth. She has a habit of embellishing details in order to make her own suffering seem more acute. He was probably handed the Poolsville Academy Achievement award by a man named Oscar. "He won an actual Academy Award? One of those statuettes they give out in the Dorothy Chandler Pavilion in front of a billion people worldwide?"

She purses her lips and admits that it wasn't quite an *Oscar* Oscar. "But it was a student Academy Award," she concedes. "They use the same criteria for greatness."

"Oh, well," I say, as if this proves a point. And it does. "Oscar Junior."

"But it was gold and shiny," she said, with a drawn-out whine, "and Steven Spielberg handed it to him."

"Still, it's nothing you announce on a sign out on Route 44, is it?"

Hannah sits up and tilts her head, willing to look at the problem from this angle for a moment or two. Blinded by the shiny gold of the statuette and the glare reflecting off Mr. Spielberg's superwhite teeth, she hadn't thought about it in quite this way before. But it makes sense. What town erects a sign bragging about a student Oscar?

"There's still the three-picture deal," she reminds me. "Three shots at greatness—three shots more than I've been given. Which is why I've moved to New York. I've taken D.C. are far as it will go. It's over. Behind me. I can't go back now."

Other people would have done it differently. They would have terminated the lease on their apartment or found a subletter; they would have put all their belongings into taped-up boxes for UPS. Some might have found a new job or informed their employer that they were quitting their old one or even told their parents about the drastic lifestyle change. Not Hannah. She just throws T-shirts and eyeliner into a duffel and moves. It might sound strange, but it's not. This is New York. This is where you come with your life in a bag to start over.

"All right," I say, fighting a yawn. I don't usually stay up until 3:00 a.m., and although my job is the sort you could do in your sleep, I prefer to be fresh and alert. I learned early in my tenure that time creeps by on turtle legs when you're exhausted. "Let me make up the bed and we'll talk more about this tomorrow. I've had a very long weekend."

Hannah sits up and looks at me, horrified. "This weekend was your father's wedding, wasn't it?" she asks, waiting for me to deny it. I can't deny it and she taps herself repeatedly on the forehead as she mutters, "Stupid girl, everything isn't about you." This is Hannah's form of self-flagellation. This is her way of taking herself to task, but it's not a successful behavioral modifier. No matter how many times she reminds herself that the world doesn't revolve around her, she can't quite bring herself to believe it. "Darn it, Lou, I meant to ask how it went. I was even going to call you tonight. It was on my list. But then the Adam thing exploded and it was all over. I lost my ability to reason. To think clearly. I've been going on instinct for seven hours now. God, you know how much I've been dreading this moment. Didn't I say the first day we met that I wanted to be the first famous person from my high school *and* the most famous?"

I remember the moment. We were in a room surrounded by other freshmen and we were sharing something about ourselves with the group. This is what resident advisors do. This is how they foster intimacy among floormates. Feeling none of the embarrassment that consumed me, Hannah stood up and announced that she wanted to be the most famous person ever to graduate from Poolsville High. She even made the distinction between notoriety and fame. Notoriety is a no-brainer. It's something anyone with a good ass can do.

While Hannah reexamines her principles—for the first time ever she's open to scandalousness, if it's done tastefully—I disappear into the bathroom to get bedding. I return a few moments later with a bath towel, a face towel, a washcloth, sheets, and a toothbrush. This is how I know I'm living my life right, because my towels aren't frayed and I have all the provisions for an overnight guest. These are things that were important to my mother. While she was alive they meant nothing to me—we argued violently over beloved sweaters with stains and pulls—but now that she's gone I find myself caring. Life is a tug-of-war and without somebody else pulling on the other end, you give in. You submit to the rules because nobody on earth cares if you wind up in the emergency room with holes in your underwear. This is what it means to be an orphan.

I put the pile on the table next to the couch. Hannah

is still talking. She's traveled back in time to locate the exact site of her mistake: December 12. "It's so obvious now," she says. "Mr. Beale came into AP English, and without saying a word he drew a circle on the blackboard. But it wasn't a complete circle; it was missing, like, a quarter of an inch. Then he went straight into that day's lesson. *Heart of Darkness,* I think. Ten minutes in, Adam got up and finished the circle. He should have been on the watch list. I mean, how proto-director is that?" She lays her head against the back of the couch again. "I'm like that person who has eyes but does not see."

Although there is nothing biblical about this situation, I just nod and hand her a sheet. I can't make the bed if she's sitting on it. For any other guest, I'd have to take out the air mattress, but Hannah is small and she fits comfortably in the space between the couch's denim arms. This is a relief. The air mattress is large and cumbersome and has to rest against the wall during the day, where it blocks a numbered Matisse litho of Morocco that Mom gave me for my twenty-first birthday. "Why'd he do that?"

Staring at the blue sheets as if not sure what to do with them, she answers, "Because he's an inveterate director. It's been in his bones since the second he was born. I just never noticed."

"No, I mean your teacher. Why'd he draw the unfinished circle?"

Hannah shrugs and stands up. The purpose of the blue sheets is starting to sink in. "I think it was something he'd read in the *New York Times* that morning. It's supposed to be some sort of gauge of personality. To see how uptight or laid-back you—" She breaks off as a truth strikes her. "Of course, it was a test to see who had a natural bent for direction. I bet after class Mr. Beale pulled him aside and gave him a screenplay to read." Hannah drops the sheet onto the couch and begins digging through her red shoulder bag. She tosses out contact solution and CDs and small packages of tissues as she rummages through it. Finally she finds what she's looking for: a black-and-white marble notebook.

"What are you doing?" I ask as she scribbles quickly and silently. Usually when Hannah breaks off conversation abruptly to take rapid notation, it's because she has thought up some movie idea that she doesn't want to forget. Hannah is always looking for a vehicle to showcase her talents and she's not above creating one for herself. In her Washington apartment she has notebooks and notebooks full of detailed plots about four-foot-eleven heroines who save the world from madmen or fall in love with doomed soldiers or discover cures for obscure diseases. The problem isn't ideas; it's backing.

"Making a note to myself to check Weller's bio for mention of the name Howard Beale." She puts down the pen and closes the book. "It never hurts to be thorough."

No, it doesn't hurt to be thorough but Hannah's left it a little late. Thorough doesn't leave a pot of water boiling on the stovetop or relocate to another city without telling anyone. "Of course," I say, fetching an extra pillow from my bed and putting on a clean pillowcase. When I'm done, I toss the pillow onto the couch while Hannah tucks the sheet's corners around the cushions. Next I retrieve a thin cotton blanket from the top shelf in the closet, even though I doubt she'll have much use for it. The night isn't dog-days-of-summer hot—while I was idling in the mountains, Manhattan cooled slightly—but the temperature is still in the mid-eighties. It's pleasant, the air is no longer humid and a faint breeze brushes by every few minutes. I'm relieved I don't have to turn on the air conditioner and watch it sputter almost-cool air.

"Thank you so much for letting me stay," she says when the bed is made. "I know I'm imposing. It's a huge inconvenience to suddenly have a roommate but I swear it won't be for long. Just as soon as I establish contact with Adam and get cast in his movie, I'll be out of your hair. I promise." She smiles to assure me of her sincerity. "It'll probably be, like, two weeks tops."

I return her smile weakly. I don't doubt Hannah's intentions. In the years that I've known her, she's always been reliable and resolute. No, it's her timetable I take issue with. I have little faith that Adam will fall in line with the plan.

Hannah folds her wrinkled summer dress and lays it on top of her notebook. She has been here for less than an hour and already the living room is hers. Stacks of clothes are piled neatly alongside bottles of shampoo, conditioner and moisturizer. Her bags are in a corner, half hiding under a drop-leaf table that is covered with unpaid bills and quickly drawn sketches. They are trying to be discreet. They're trying to seem invisible, as if they don't exist, but they do exist, and you can't help noticing them in my four-hundred-square-foot apartment. One sweep of the eyes and you see everything.

"Good night, then," I say, suddenly desperate for the peaceful oblivion of sleep. The file of things that I don't want to think about is growing thick. Add Hannah's desperate scheming to Dad, Carol, the evil alien bunnies from hell, and my own uncertain future. "I'll try not to wake you in the morning. The walls are pretty thin. My alarm is set for seven-thirty and I usually hop into the shower around eight."

Hannah rolls her eyes. "Please, the last thing you should be worried about is waking me. I'm an interloper and deserve your worst. Besides, I can't imagine it's much louder than those horns." She walks over to the window and stares down at Bleecker. "Is it always this bad?"

The answer is yes but I make some vague comment about traffic patterns and time of day. Even if it weren't always this bad, it wouldn't matter. The only time it keeps you awake is at three in the morning.

I'm climbing into bed when Hannah knocks softly and ducks her head into the room. "One more thing and then I swear I'll let you get some sleep. Do you have plans for tomorrow night? I thought we could hang out."

Monday nights are mellow. I usually stay in, defrost something for dinner and watch TV, but I have a sneaking suspicion that this Monday night will be different. This Monday night Nick will show up on my doorstep wanting to talk about what happened between me and Dad in the lobby of the Adirondack Hotel and Spa. He'll ask questions about my feelings and try to get at the core of my reluctance. He won't push. He won't press. He'll just wait with that expression on his face that says he understands. It's the same expression his father wore when he brokered arms agreements with Eastern Bloc countries in the late eighties.

"Sure, that sounds nice. There's a cheap French restaurant around the corner that makes fabulous crepes," I say, leaning against the pillow. It's always nice to be back in your own bed. "I get off at seven. Why don't I meet you there at seven-thirty? I'll leave the name and address on the refrigerator tomorrow before I leave." Avoiding Nick is not the most mature way of handling things, but I've had enough of trying to be a grown-up for a while. I'm no longer sure where I fall in the child-adult growth chart. Either today was a great leap forward or a giant step back.

"Excellent," she says. "All right, see you tomorrow, Lou."

The door closes behind her, and I listen as she turns on the faucets in the bathroom. The shower shares a wall with my bedroom, and I can hear water running through the pipes. It's a soothing sound, like a waterfall or a cascading brook, and I close my eyes to go to sleep. My muscles are tired and my mind is worn-out, but sleep is elusive. The scene with my father is playing over and over in an endless loop: There I am determined to talk to him like a responsible adult. There I am trying to speak but no words will come out. And there I am saying never mind. It's an inevitable cycle and yet I'm still not sure how it happens.

For a few seconds this afternoon, life had seemed simple. For a few fleeting, precious seconds, life had felt like a quiz show I knew all the answers to. Tallulah, what will you do next? *Bzzz:* become a successful designer. How will you do it? *Bzzz:* without my father. Things that have long been outside my grasp felt within reach. An unprecedented sense of confidence had swooped down like an eagle and taken hold of my heart. But it was just a trick of light. My prospects are dim. They're a faint incandescent candle flickering in the window of the house next door.

I try to block out the memory of this morning. I try to push Dad's impatient look out of my mind, but it persists. There he is—eyes darting, terrified that I'm going to pester him with my emotions. With effort, I focus on something else. I think of Mom. I concentrate on her face—flushed and smiling—as she throws softballs across home plate. It's late afternoon on a warm July Sunday. The sun is setting and Mom is teaching me how to hit. I'm ten years old and clumsy and frustrated from failure but Mom doesn't notice. She keeps throwing softballs and fixing my stance as if this is something I can do. I recall the feel of her hands on my shoulders and her clear, firm alto as she tells me not to give up. I fall asleep with my mother's voice in my ear.

4

When my alarm goes off four hours later, I ignore it. I've lowered the volume out of deference to my houseguest, and the irritating beep is no longer an unrelenting jackhammer that digs into my skull. At this gentler decibel level, it barely penetrates my unconsciousness.

I climb out of bed at ten o'clock, not the least bit concerned that I'm already late for work. I'm usually the first one there in the morning. I'm the one who turns on the lights and makes coffee and retrieves messages from the voice mail system and strews Marcos's path with rose petals. The thought of Marcos fending for himself makes me smile. He probably won't find the light switch. In all likelihood he won't remember that it's in the women's bathroom behind the door, but he has options. Marcos can sit in the dark or he can go to the Starbucks in Astor Place.

Once in the shower, I stand under the stream of cool running water for several minutes, willing myself to wake up. I have gotten by on less sleep before but there's something new about this languidness. There's an element of indifference mixed in with the lethargy and exhaustion that is nurtured by the sudden lack of an escape route. This is my life. It is Marcos Medici's drawings of trash cans, endless color copies of the Picasso, purchase orders, memos, and calls to the messenger service, and there's no invisible jet in my closet to take me away from it. I have no secret identity. This is me: Tallulah West, doer of insignificant things. I'm not Icarus standing on a chair to change a lightbulb.

I emerge from the bathroom wrapped in a robe that depicts frolicking blue dolphins swimming in a green sea. The robe is old and worn. Its cuffs are frayed, its hem is falling, its belt loops are hanging by a thread and there's a three-inch tear in the armpit that I keep meaning to sew. It's on life support, but I cannot throw it away. It's the last thing my mother ever gave me.

"Hey," says Hannah, a spatula in hand as she stands over the stove, "I couldn't remember whether you like waffles or pancakes, so I made both."

Set up on the counter next to the frying pan is a long-forgotten waffle maker. Hannah lifts up the cover, extracts a waffle in the shape of Mickey Mouse's head and adds it to the plate keeping warm in the oven.

I reach for the Arabian mocha java and Hannah waves her spatula at me. "Uh-uh. You're running late as it is. Get dressed and I'll put on the coffee. How do you like it? Strong and black?"

This is exactly how I like it and I return to my bedroom with a smile. The smell of cooking pancakes has had an unnatural effect on my stomach. Ordinarily just the thought of food early in the morning causes my gag reflex to kick in but today I'm hungry. Today I'm looking forward to sitting down and eating breakfast. It will throw off my schedule even more but I'm languid and indifferent and don't care if Marcos sits in the dark for hours.

Although my kitchen is larger than most in New York City tenement apartments, it is still too small for a table and Hannah has set up a makeshift dining arrangement in the living room using chairs. It's a welcome change. I usually eat with a plate on my lap and a glass of water balancing precariously on the cushion next to me.

She hands me a cup of coffee. "Which would you like? Pancakes or waffles?"

I prefer pancakes but since she has gone through the trouble of preparing both, I insist on having one of each. "You really didn't have to do this," I say, unfolding a napkin and putting it on my lap before taking a deep sip of coffee. It tastes wonderful.

"Yes, I did," she says quite seriously. There's isn't a glint of humor in her voice. "It's my part of the guest–host relationship." She lays the plate down on the chair and holds out margarine and butter. I'm impressed that the fridge is so well stocked.

"The guest-host relationship?" I ask, taking the butter.

"Yeah, you know, the social contract that governs the way guests and hosts behave. I am a lone and weary traveler, so you have to take me in. But you're a kind and generous host, so I have to earn my keep. The guest-host relationship. It dates back to, like, the B.C.s."

I'm not surprised that it predates Christ. It sounds like something that Odysseus encountered on his way home from the Trojan War. "Well, regardless of the guest-host relationship, you don't have to make me breakfast every morning. Just keep the living room neat and replace the toilet paper and we'll get along fine."

Hannah stacks three pancakes on her plate and sits down next to me. "I have no money," she says, reaching for the syrup, "but I can feed you for weeks on the stuff you have in the pantry. I'm the MacGyver of food preparation. Give me a stick of bubblegum and a paperclip and I can make a soufflé."

This is certainly an impressive feat. "I have a pantry?" I ask, only mildly interested. I'm distracted by the pancakes. They're light and fluffy and remind me of the ones we used to have on Sunday mornings. It's been more than five years since anyone has made me pancakes and I'm swamped by nostalgia. I want the old stuff back—the kitchen table buried under the *New York*

Times, the worn countertop frying pan well greased with Crisco, Mom holding up a spatula and asking how many do I want.

"Not a pantry per se," she explains, soaking her waffles with Log Cabin, "but you've got shelves and cabinets and a lot of basic supplies that should carry you through the first few months of a nuclear winter." She pauses for a moment, then puts down the syrup and looks at me consideringly. "You don't mind my using this stuff, do you? I mean, you aren't really planning for a nuclear holocaust?"

The question pulls me back to the present. "Not that I'm aware of."

She nods. "Do you think it's subconscious? Maybe a lingering childhood fear that the end of the world will happen while you're looking in the other direction?"

"No, I buy whatever I have coupons for," I say, although this doesn't explain why I cut coupons for confectioners' sugar and cream of tartar and rice vinegar. These products are traces of another Tallulah—one who talks to her father, works at a fulfilling job and eats sensible, home-cooked meals.

Hannah dumps a dripping forkful of waffles into her mouth. "I do that, too, except I cut coupons for only the things I use. It's cheaper that way."

I help myself to another waffle. "Speaking of money-saving efforts, what's this about your being broke?"

"I've got a small stash that should get me through the next couple of weeks if I don't do anything extravagant like take the subway but that's all I have in the world," she says this casually, as if it isn't a cause for concern. I don't have much money either but it's something that keeps me awake at night. It's something I think about for hours and hours. "I'm getting my security deposit back on my D.C. apartment, so there's a couple of hundred dollars, and as soon as Adam casts me in his movie, I'll be flush."

This refrain—as soon as Adam casts me in his movie—seems to be Hannah's new mantra, and she repeats it often, as if it were some sort of invocation. I don't think this will work. I don't think the gods respond to pure repetition. "We don't have to go out to dinner tonight, if things are too tight. We can stay in and make soufflés out of bubble gum and paper clips."

She waves away my concern. "Please, I wouldn't have moved here if I couldn't afford a minute or two out on the town. Don't worry about me. I've got it all sussed out."

I nod agreeably but suddenly I'm very worried. Clearly Hannah hasn't sussed out anything. Twenty-four hours ago moving to New York wasn't even a glimmer in her eye. "I should probably get going," I say, shoveling a waffle into my mouth. The crevices are filled with equal parts butter and syrup. "My God, these are fantastic." Hannah reaches for my empty plate but I pick it up first. "No, don't get up. Finish eating."

Letting me put my own plate in the sink violates some tenet of the guest-host doctrine but Hannah lets it slide. "Thanks."

I duck into the bedroom to get shoes and a bag. "You have my number, right?" I ask, sliding into a pair of well-worn brown mules.

I've sat at the same desk for almost four years, and Hannah easily rattles off by rote the correct seven digits. I toss my Filofax into my bag, throw my bag over my shoulder and turn to leave. "See you later."

"Lou," she calls after me. I have my hand on the doorknob. "Do you mind if I straighten up around here?"

I stare at her blankly.

"I've noticed that you have piles and piles of papers in the most unusual places, like in the magazine rack in the bathroom and under soup cans in the pantry."

My cleaning habits are haphazard and unreliable and sometimes it's easier to toss things in a corner than to find a proper place for them. "Do your worst," I say, the languor keeping me here. Ordinarily I'd be rushing out the door. Ordinarily I'd feel the minutes ticking by. Not today. When you don't have a future, it's all the indistinguishable present. "But you really don't have to."

Hannah is bound by chains of obligation stronger than my middle-class good manners. "It's the guest-host relationship."

I shrug and leave the apartment.

5

When I arrive Marcos isn't sitting in the dark. He isn't
half-hidden by shadow or staring out from the inky darkness. His office faces Lafayette, and during the summer,
sun pours in through the eastern exposure.

"Ah, there you are, Lou," he says, when I knock gently
on his open door to tell him I'm here.

"Hi," I say, stepping into his office, which is large and
shiny. The polished wood floors reflect your image as do
the glass cabinets and the high-gloss desk. There is a comfortable sitting area off to one side, with an overstuffed red
couch, a pristine vermilion carpet and two large lamps
with shades the color of fire trucks. The overall effect is
corporate bordello, and I used to marvel once at his flam-
boyant sense of style. I used to wonder how a man with

such overblown tastes could shed personal preferences long enough to create simple products with mass appeal, but then I figured it out. Marcos isn't a creator; he's a tinkerer.

"Busy morning, eh?" he says understandingly, looking up with his eager smile and friendly green eyes that draw you in. Marcos makes a great first impression—outgoing, generous, thoughtful—but he can't sustain it. He's a hotel with a sleek refurbished lobby and shabby rooms. "I can't seem to get the copier to work properly. Can you call the repairman? I need thirty-seven copies of the report I left on your desk."

"I'll give the copier people a call right now," I say. I'm prepared to defend my lateness. I'm prepared to rattle on about a doctor's appointment that ran long but he doesn't question my absence. My being too busy to say good morning is exactly what he expects from his assistant. As far as he knows, the overhead lights are on and I've been running around the office doing odd jobs for hours. "Is there anything else?"

Marcos runs through a to-do list—return telephone calls, renew magazine subscriptions, balance checkbook, make dinner reservations, find a baby-sitter.

"All right. I'll be out here if you need anything," I say obligingly. I'm not usually so amenable but I'm feeling generous because he didn't notice my absence.

Before calling the repairman, I stop by the copier to find out precisely what's wrong. There's always an error code or a maniacally blinking light that highlights where the problem is, and the copier people become irritated if you're unable to relay this information.

The machine is curiously silent. It's not jammed. It's not out of toner. It's not waiting for someone to fill the bottom drawer with 11-by-17 paper. It is simply turned off. I flip the switch, and while it warms up, I glance at the fifty-page report that Marcos left on my desk. It's mostly a collection of figures and charts detailing our economic growth over the last five years, and in recent months, I've copied many versions of this report. It's mating season at Marcos Medici Associates, and we are ardently courting investors who will take us to the next level. I don't quite know what the next level means for the company—the big picture is assiduously guarded—but for me it translates into more busywork. It means more trips to Kinko's and more telephone calls to the accountant and more cups of coffee for potential suitors who sit in my waiting room trying to make small talk. They want to chat harmlessly about the weather and I listen with half an ear, even though I'm misbehaving. I'm under strict orders to talk up Marcos, but I hate name-dropping the awards, commissions and grants he's won. I hate listing his many accomplishments as if they were love poems whispered in the ear of a reluctant sweetheart. It makes me feel like a go-between, like Pandarus procuring Cressida for Troilus.

The copier whizzes and sputters and the steady green

ready light stares expectantly up at me. I put the report in the feeder and hit Copy. The machine complies with hardly a whimper, confirming my suspicion that Marcos hadn't noticed that the machine was turned off. This has happened before. For a man who does most of his work on a G5, he is curiously devoid of any understanding of technology. Whenever his computer misbehaves, he either throws a temper tantrum or sulks. He never tries rebooting.

With the copier running smoothly, I take the fifty-page report and go to Kinko's. There's no point in my standing over the machine as it churns out copy after copy when Kinko's can do it *and* make the document look pretty with a neat plastic binder. Rather than return to the office, I kill time in the Starbucks across the street, drinking a frozen cappuccino and flipping through the *Village Voice*. I'm usually a better employee than this—I always make a point of bringing a trade publication to the café—but the languidness of this morning has only intensified. Despite intentions that may or may not be good, I'm useless today.

When I return a half hour later, Abby, one of Marcos's design assistants, is there. The office is usually crowded with designers but this is the Monday after July Fourth and everyone is away. Marcos himself would be at his house on the Cape if he weren't wiggling his little puffin tail at excited investors.

"Hey," I say, surprised to see someone else here. "I didn't know you were coming in today."

Abby looks up from her computer and smiles depre-catingly. "I'm not really here. I just had something to fin-ish for Marcos," she says, pushing her hair out of her eyes. She has long wispy bangs that are fashionable but impractical. "Marcos gave me the drawings for the Pi-casso 2.0 and I told him I'd have the 2D model ready by the end of the day. But that's it. Once I'm done I'm out of here. I have some face time scheduled with the beach."

The next generation Picasso is very similar to the orig-inal. It's hipper and swervier and comes in brighter col-ors, but its basic structure—round, eighteen inches high, malleable plastic—is the same.

"At Kinko's again?" she asks, eyeing the familiar brown paper bag. "It sucks that you get dumped with all the crappy stuff. Maybe when the new investors come through we can get you some help."

Her voice is sympathetic, and I find myself bristling with resentment. Abby does that to me. She's nice and we get along really well—sometimes after work we go to the Bowery Bar and make fun of well-dressed scenesters in their practiced poses—but she has a way of putting my back up. It's her condescending demeanor, her stick-with-it-kid-and-one-day-you-might-achieve-what-I've-achieved attitude that assumes wrongly that she has achieved any-thing of merit. Her job is creative and more interesting than mine but Abby's ideas and her designs are mundane. She actually consults color-forecasting books for color schemes.

She will never set the world on fire and I cannot envy anything less.

"It wasn't so bad," I say dismissively as I put the Kinko's bag down on my desk. The message light on my phone is lit and I wonder if Nick has called yet. "The mismanaged unorganized ineptness of Kinko's doesn't bother me so much anymore. I think I've entered into an abusive relationship. If they don't ignore me for ten minutes, I feel unloved."

Abby laughs. "You should get out now while you still can."

"As soon as the investors come through I will gladly sever all ties with Kinko's."

"The end is in sight," Abby assures me with confidence.

"Really?" I ask but I'm not really interested in the answer. Marcos's future looks a lot like his past—only with more state-of-the-art computer stations.

"Yeah, Marcos expects to hear something this week."

I'm about to reply when Marco calls me into his office. At his bellow Abby rolls her eyes at me in a show of sympathy—again resentment stirs—and I grab my notebook and headset, steeling myself for the excruciating process of returning telephone calls. Marcos is capable of dialing a phone on his own, but he prefers to have me go before him in the world announcing his presence.

The sun has moved several degrees to the west but shards of light are still illuminating his office. I can see specs of dust dancing in the sunshine.

I take a black leather bear-claw chair—the matching ottoman at my feet rounds out the set—and stare at Marcos across the desk. The sunlight gleaming off his streaky blond head looks almost like a halo, and I'm struck for a moment by how angelic he seems with his brother-can-I-lend-you-a-dime smile and fine Italian clothing. This is Marcos—*enfant terrible* of industrial design, purveyor of kooky shapes and the new amoeba aesthetic. But he's not the real thing. He's not the genuine article. Despite the celestial glow, he's just a cheesy souvenir you pick up a few blocks from the Vatican. I close my eyes to block out the vision. When I open them again, the sun has moved a fraction of an inch to the left.

Marcos's appearance is restored to normal, but the desire to close my eyes and shut him out is still strong. I need to get out of here. This place is suffocating me. This place is squeezing the air out of my lungs bit by bit, and I have to run fast in the opposite direction. I'll begin today. As soon as I leave this room, I'll update my résumé and look for a new job—a proper job, the kind of job I would have gotten if I hadn't been so set on hurting my father. Tallulah Designs can wait. It's not necessary that I start at the top with my own company. I'll find some place to apprentice. I'll take a stab at selling designs to manufacturers. I didn't want to go this route. I didn't want to give up the rights to my designs and forfeit control of their production, but this is a well-trod path. This is a respectable road that people like my father and Marcos have gone down. And it would be a start. It would be an opportunity to build a name.

"Tallulah," Marcos says, leaning forward in his chair. The sun is a thin strip to the left of him now and I have to shift to avoid the glare. "I'm very sorry to say this but I'm afraid we have to let you go."

I stop fidgeting and gape at him with wide-eyed wonder, suddenly terrified that my feelings are so strong that they've flown across the desk and zapped him like X rays. But this isn't possible. Thoughts don't travel through air. They aren't radio waves to be picked up by well-placed antennae.

"What?"

"I'm afraid that we have to let you go. The new investor thinks our numbers are bloated and we need to scale back. I'm sorry," he says, lowering his voice and looking me straight in the eye. This is Marcos being sincere.

"Your numbers are bloated," I repeat, stunned.

"Yes, we have bloated numbers. If we're going to get an infusion of cash, we need to prove to the investor that we know how to spend sparingly."

"Your numbers are bloated and *I'm* the corner you've decided to cut?" I say calmly, just to make sure I have all the facts.

"It's nothing personal." He smiles smoothly and tilts his head at a concerned angle. This is what he looks like in all the magazine articles. "We just have to demon—"

Marcos stops talking because he's disconcerted by my laughter. It's hearty and robust and underscored by genuine amusement. This is not a bout of female hysterics. "Are you all right?" he asks. He's still wearing his sincere face. He's still trying to play the part of good guy in this office drama.

It takes me a moment to answer. "Yes, I'm fine," I say, breathing deeply, but I still can't get my amusement under control. The ridiculousness of the situation is like a feather to my funny bone.

"Are you sure? Do you want a moment alone?"

"No, no. I'm really fine," I assure him but I haven't stopped laughing.

"Very well," he says peevishly. His patience has run out. "I don't see what's so funny."

I look at him. Here is a man who takes monthlong vacations to Bali and charges them to the company, a man who pays his jet-setting wife a weekly salary out of the company's petty cash, a man who lunches every day at Nobu. His company is hemorrhaging money, and I'm a paper cut on his little finger. My twenty-eight-thousand-dollar salary is a scratch that doesn't even require a Band-Aid. "No," I say, as the laughter fades, "I suppose you wouldn't."

Marcos hands me an envelope that has been prepared by his accountant. "Here's your severance information. If you have any questions, feel free to give me or John a call."

John is the firm's accountant. He's a nice man from the

suburbs, and if I need to know something like how much my Cobra premium is, I'll go to him. It's unlikely that I will give Marcos a call for anything. I never have before.

"You'll probably want to pack up your things and leave as soon as possible," he says, his tone abrupt. My response has been out of step with the situation—I'm supposed to be fighting tears, not laughter—and he's no longer inclined to linger in comfort mode. "And don't worry if there's too much to carry. Abby will UPS it to you."

Marcos starts leafing through the pile of papers on his desk. This is his dismissal. This is the way he kicks me out of his office. Now that the blade has fallen, my presence is an embarrassment to him. I'm not surprised. His firing me is a cosmetic solution, a short-term answer that avoids the real issue, and he knows it. I'm the virgin sacrifice to the investment gods, but it won't make a difference. My spilt blood will not ensure a good growing season.

"All right," I say, getting to my feet. There is nothing else to say, and I leave his office without a good-bye or a handshake or a best wishes tossed carelessly at my departing back. He doesn't even take a second to thank me for four years of service.

There is no reason to linger, and I start cleaning out my desk right away. It doesn't take me long, and within forty minutes all my possessions are stuffed into a Jimmy Choo shoe box and a small tote bag with a company logo that I no longer recognize. I've spent four years of my life in this office, more time than I have anywhere else except the house in Bellmore where I grew up, but nothing has been accumulated. The only belongings I take home with me in the end—a Murano glass bud vase, an assortment of design books, an old Sony cube radio and a snapshot of my mother and me—are the belongings I brought with me in the beginning. My desk is buried under magazines and Post-its and 11-by-17 printouts of computer designs, but this is an impersonal mess, like towels on the bathroom floor of a hotel. I was always just passing through.

I pack up my stuff quickly and neatly, placing the books at the bottom of the box and enfolding the vase in bubble wrap. I linger over the framed snapshot before placing it on top. It's sunset on my twenty-fourth birthday and we're in front of the Eiffel Tower. Mom's left arm is around me and her right one is out in front of her as she explains how the camera works to a confused Australian tourist. We look so much alike: same wide grin, same brown curls, same wiry frame, although I have several inches on her, thanks to my father. This is my favorite picture—mother and daughter in the wilds of Paris. Neither one of us spoke French, although Mom had taken it in college and hoped useful bits would come back. I remember her on the plane: excited and impatient and a little bit nervous to be leaving her element. Mom's cloak of parental competence had slipped. A stiff breeze had blown it off her shoulders, and there she was, Emily

West—not someone's mother, not someone's wife, but a tourist, eager and anxious to experience something new. Watching her pretend to read a book, I realized the scales had shifted. They had tipped toward the middle and were balanced perfectly on the head of a needle. For the first time ever we were equals—I would take care of her as well as she had always taken care of me. But this equality was fleeting. This sudden, heady equilibrium wouldn't last. In the space of time it takes for a camera to flash, it would be over. The scales would tip in the opposite direction and before I knew it I'd be standing in a hospital room holding her hand and giving her strength and making promises nobody could keep.

"Ah, a little summer cleaning," observes Abby when she returns from lunch with her Time Café takeout bag and her *Wallpaper* magazine tucked under a ruffle-clad arm. "I've been meaning to do some of that myself."

Although Abby has only been with Marcos Medici Associates for three months—she graduated from Parson's in May—her workstation looks like a well-lived-in dorm room. She's even hung a Klimt poster on the wall behind her.

"Not cleaning, clearing," I say, hunting for a blank disk among the staples and pencils and paper clips that clutter the top drawer.

Abby tilts her head to the side, trying to make sense of this distinction. "Clearing?"

I find a zip disk and stick it into the zip drive to download files. For the last few months I've devoted every spare moment to revising designs of tables and couches and lamps and clocks. These are the first, hesitant sketches of Tallulah Designs and I'm not leaving them behind. They're my future.

"Clearing my desk, packing up stuff and taking it home with me," I explain, while opening files from the disk just to make sure they transferred safely and in one piece. Then I delete the originals from the hard drive. I don't want to leave traces of myself here. I even take a minute to empty my CC Mail in-box. "Marcos fired me about an hour ago."

Abby blinks several times. She looks like some sort of frightened animal but I don't know what she fears more: losing her job or getting stuck doing mine. "What?"

"He let me go to appease some investors." I shrug as if the matter is of the utmost indifference to me. It isn't really but it's hard to gauge how much I care. It's still too soon to tell, like trying to decide if you like the color of paint before it dries. "He said you'd ship whatever I can't carry, but don't worry"—I gesture toward the shoe box and the tote bag—"I've got it all here."

"But we need you."

"Apparently not enough."

"Oh, Lou, how awful," she says, as she envelops me in a bone-crushing hug. Abby is stronger than she looks. "You'll be fine. I'm sure you'll find another job in no time at all. You're friendly and intelligent and so clever with computers. You'll land on your feet, I just know it. And if it does take a little time, you mustn't get discouraged. It's the economy, not you."

There is nothing worse than getting an earnest pep talk from a twenty-two-year-old design grad who uses the D-cipher F.M. catalog to establish color schemes and I extricate myself from her grasp. "Thanks for the lovely vote of confidence, Abby," I say, only a little sarcastic—despite her condescension, she's sincere.

"Let's go get a drink," she suggests. "We'll have a small good-bye party. Maybe we can get the bartender to put a candle in the pretzel dish and you can make a wish."

"It's not my birthday."

"No," she readily agrees, although she has no idea when my birthday is, "but it's the first day of the rest of your life. Isn't that the same thing?"

It's a good argument and I let myself be swayed by it. "All right. I'm almost done here. Just give me a few minutes to finish copying files."

"Not a problem." She sticks her leftovers into the fridge and disappears into the bathroom for a few minutes. When she reemerges, she's wearing shimmering purple eye shadow on her eyelids. She looks like a disco queen.

"Bowery Bar?" I ask, easily reading the signs. The Stila pansy palette only comes out for the high-profile venues.

"Sounds good," she says, as if agreeing to a suggestion rather than confirming a suspicion.

I do one last lap around the desk and computer to make sure I have everything. Then I shut down the iMac and gather my stuff. "Ready when you are."

"Here, give me something to carry," she says, relieving me of the tote bag.

We are waiting for the elevator when Marcos's door opens. My former employer steps out of his office and smiles in my direction. He doesn't say a word but he's radiating goodwill. He's had time to regain his equilibrium.

"I need to return calls," he says to Abby, but her understanding is imperfect. First she's baffled by the fact that he's addressing the statement to her. What does she have to do with Marcos's telephone calls? Next she's disappointed. Not only has she put on her best eye shadow for nothing but she also has to stay here and work instead of getting drunk at the Bowery. But then the truth hits her. Like a tall, frightening wave that crashes on the beach, the truth washes over her. Marcos needs to return calls. Marcos needs *her* to return calls.

He tosses a goodwill nod in my direction—still not a thank-you for all your hard work but a step up from cold shoulder—and disappears into his office. Abby turns to me with a panicked look on her face. This isn't what she signed on to do. She isn't some lackey who takes messages and orders No. 10 envelopes from the Staples catalog.

I don't know what to say, so I squeeze her shoulder in a silent show of support. The elevator dings and a second later the doors open. Abby hands me the tote bag, and I leave to go home to celebrate the first day of the rest of my life alone.

6

When I enter the apartment a half hour later, my new roomie is in the living room sorting out her head shots. She's sitting cross-legged amid a sea of black-and-white Hannahs. Each one is staring thoughtfully and pensively at me, as if I've just detailed the things that haunt me and she's determined to rid me of them. It's just a pose—her head is tilted and resting on her palm—but she pulls it off with aplomb. Looking at the photo, I believe she's capable of exorcism.

I drop the tote bag and the shoe box onto the kitchen counter, which is clean. Hannah has stacked this week's mail into a neat pile. Then I shrug off my pocketbook and leave it lying on the floor.

"Hey there," I call, opening the refrigerator as the first

pangs of the day hit me. Much to my surprise, breakfast has served its function. It has successfully staved off hunger for hours.

"Hi," she says, unalarmed by my sudden appearance. At first I attribute this to typical Hannah-centric behavior, but then I rethink and give her the benefit of the doubt. She isn't familiar enough with my routine to be concerned. For all she knows, I could come home every day at three o'clock and stare into the refrigerator waiting for what I want to hit me over the head. "There's some gazpacho cooling on the second shelf."

"What!" I say, zeroing in on a large soup pot. I remove the lid and inhale deeply. It smells delicious.

"There's some gazpacho in the fridge," she says again, mistaking interjection for question. "I'm not sure if it's cool enough yet."

"It's cool enough for me," I assure her, ladling a healthy portion into a deep yellow bowl. When I'm done, I stand in the entranceway eating soup and watching her work. I'm surprised to find Hannah here. I thought she'd be out on the streets of New York stalking Adam Weller. "What's up?"

"Just alerting the locals to my arrival," she says, putting a thoughtful, pensive Hannah into an envelope and sealing it with a glue stick. "I should be done in an hour or so."

"Is this the first step?" I ask as a mouthful of gazpacho slides down my throat.

She wrinkles her brow as she sticks another version of herself into an envelope. "The first step?"

"The first step in your diabolical scheme to get cast in Adam Weller's movie," I explain, leaning against the wall. I'd sit on the couch but it's covered with envelopes and Hannahs. "This soup is fantastic, by the way. Am I tasting cilantro?"

Hannah shrugs modestly. She's too busy stuffing envelopes to look up. "Just a hint."

"Don't tell me there was cilantro in the pantry." I know my life is filled with ingredients I'll never use but not perishables. I have enough sense to stay away from anything that will rot.

"On the windowsill."

"What?"

"You have cilantro growing on the windowsill."

I look across the room to the window that faces Bleecker Street. There are three terra-cotta flowerpots with green leafy plants growing out of them. "Huh. I thought those were weeds."

"Nope. Parsley, basil and cilantro."

This is a revelation. I've never thought of myself as a person with a green thumb. Growing things has always seemed mysterious. It's always seemed like something that only a few devoted people like my mom could do. But this is interesting. This is worth exploring. When the unemployment runs out and the new job fails to materialize and I begin the slow slide into poverty, I can grow my own food. I can start a victory garden, with freedom cabbage and small brave leaves of baby spinach.

"Anyway," Hannah continues, unaware of my sudden farming proclivities, "steps one and two, if you want to call them that, have already been implemented in my Adam Weller plan, which is not at all diabolical but rather straightforward and completely on the up-and-up. These are just résumés that I'm sending to New York agents and casting directors."

"Steps one and two?" I say, spooning yummy gazpacho into my mouth. It's nice having a cook around.

"I established contact with the office temp who's working for Weller and learned that Sugar Snap Peas is having a small party on Friday for their investors."

"Sugar Snap Peas?"

"His production company," she explains. "I don't know why he chose that awful name. The first thing on my list once I get cast in his movie is to change the name to something less agrarian."

"What do you have in mind?"

She shrugs. "I don't know, something theatrical like Hannah Silver Productions." Hannah smiles to let me know that she's kidding, but she isn't. Not really.

"Of course."

"Anyway, once I found out about the party, I went over to the caterer and got a job with them. I start on Friday."

"You cater?"

She shakes her head. "Never have before, but I've been

serving myself breakfast, lunch and dinner for almost thirty years now. I think I've got the general principles down pat."

"Serve on the left, clear from the right?"

Hannah stares at me as if I'm speaking in tongues. "Bring the plate to the table, take the plate away from the table."

Although I've never catered myself, I know it's slightly more complicated than bringing and taking plates. But I don't say another word. Hannah thinks she has the whole situation sussed out and she won't hear anything to the contrary. She has a wonderful ability to pick and choose which facts she's willing to subscribe to.

"All right," I say, returning to the refrigerator for seconds, "what's next?"

"I use my catering connection to get past security. Then as soon as I'm in, I duck into the bathroom, take off the wig and facial prosthetics, change into my stunning red dress and go mingle."

I look at Hannah. I'm ninety-seven percent certain she said "facial prosthetics," but I need confirmation. Some things are too outlandish to hear only once. "You have a facial prosthetic?"

"Yeah. It's some plasticy-latexy thing I wore for a film short I did last year about an overweight synchronized swimmer trying to make a comeback. It's not the best quality—sometimes I have a hard time keeping the double chins on—but it looks real enough on camera," she explains in her careless way. Hannah doesn't think this is unusual. She thinks every actress gets to keep her fat suit and take it out for special occasions. "Oh, it's not a fat *suit*," she says, rushing to clarify when I make my observation. "The budget wasn't big enough for a whole entire suit. They just filmed me from the neck up."

"If the budget was so tight, why not just hire a fat actress?"

Hannah laughs and tells me to not be so droll. I ignore the condescension and move on. I don't want to hear anything more about facial prosthetics. "How will all this get you cast?"

"Who do you think I'm mingling with?"

Because this sounds like a rhetorical question, I don't answer. But Hannah expects more. She stops putting versions of herself into envelopes and stares at me impatiently. I answer. "Adam Weller?"

"Adam Weller," she says, before I've finished uttering his name. "I'll bump into him by the bar and show shock and amazement that he's in the movie business, too. We'll catch up on old times. What have you been doing since high school? Oh, really? Directing. How droll. Any success? A student Oscar? What? This party's for you? *Très magnifique.* You must excuse me if I seem out of step with the culture at large. Why? I've been out of town. Well, actually, out of country," Hannah says, using her affected cocktail-conversation voice. "Then once he finds out that I'm a sensation in Australia and a duchess to boot, he'll have no choice but to cast me in his movie."

I smile. The plan is ridiculous and naive and reads like the punch line to a long involved joke. "A sensation in Australia?"

"A national treasure. I have a reporter friend typesetting my notices as we speak," she explains.

"And a duchess?"

Hannah shrugs. "It's not my fault. Weller's screenplay is a broad physical comedy about a duchess who thinks she's gay. It turns out she isn't: One of her ladies-in-waiting is a man pretending to be a woman so he can steal the duchess's jewels. Needless to say, he falls in love with her and becomes a duke. But in the meantime there are lots of mistaken identity jokes and pratfalls and hilarious misunderstandings as the duchess tries to deal with an awkward social condition," Hannah says with a trace of scorn. It's clear from her derision that the script is another thing she'll change once she's at the helm of the Sugar Snap Peas ship.

"And you think being a duchess will you get cast as a duchess?" I finish the soup and put my bowl into the sink, even though I'm still hungry. I'm unemployed now and must behave accordingly. Resources, previously squandered or overlooked, must be hoarded and stretched.

"Of course, I already know the language and once I let slip that the very photogenic family seat in Derbyshire just happens to be languishing unoccupied, he'll beg me to take the part."

"What happens when they get to Derbyshire and there is no family seat?"

Hannah's unconcerned by this eventuality. "I'll cross that bridge when I come to it. No use putting the cart before the horse."

"Don't take this the wrong way, Han, but your plan is insane."

"Desperate times call for desperate measures," she says, stretching her legs and back. The area is no longer covered with headshots and she lies down on the hardwood floor. "I've tried it the other way. It doesn't work."

"The other way?"

"I've spent the last six years commuting back and forth between New York and D.C. I've auditioned for every single play; I've sent headshots to every single casting director, agent, playwright and talent agency admin on the East Coast. I've put on my own showcases, became a stand-up comedian and stood outside Madison Square Garden in a bikini for twelve hours to promote the boat show because the producer of *Baywatch* was supposed to buy a schooner. I've had it," she says.

As Hannah rattles off her list of grievances, she grows increasingly agitated and adopts a familiar yoga position. I don't think this is what yoga is for. The lotus pose isn't about venting your spleen and listing grievances. It's about being quiet and meditative, but Hannah has her own version.

"Do you know what it's like to be me?" she says, her

voice now a high-pitched squeak. Her face is flushed from exertion, both mental and physical. "Do you have any idea what's it's like to want something so badly that sometimes it's a physical ache? To expect so much from each moment that you can't relax, even for a split second? I can't take it anymore. The waiting and the hoping are too much for me. Every time the phone rings, I think, This is it. Robert Altman's people are calling me for a screen test. Whenever there's a message on my machine, my heart skips and I think, This is it. ICM wants to represent me. And for that brief second before I pick up the phone or press Play, the moment seems to float with potential, like a bubble filled with possibilities. But then it's just my mom calling to tell me that roasted chicken is on sale at Costco, and I realize how absurd it is to expect anything. Moments are made of lead and they crash around me endlessly. And all I do is stand in the middle like some stupid child in a rainstorm. Well, goddamn it, I've had enough. I deserve more than cheap poultry."

Hannah finishes her impassioned speech and I stare at her silently as she takes deep calming breaths. I know she's frustrated and discouraged and tired of beating her head against a wall that won't budge. I know the career train is supposed to be at the next station by now, but I still find myself growing annoyed with her dramatics. Hannah has assumed an air of suffering, but this isn't suffering. Not really. It's not standing over your mother in the emergency room while the nurse tells you you have to make a decision now. It's not hearing your scared mother cry for her dead parents from a hospital bed. It's not waking up in the middle of the night convinced that she's healthy and alive and living with your father on Long Island.

I'm being unfair. I know very well that one thing has nothing to do with the other, but this is where my mind goes. This is where it always jumps first. Every day something different and unexpected brings me here. It's not something I can control.

"I'm going to go lie down for a while," I say, feeling impatient with myself and with her. Hannah still hasn't noticed anything unusual about my being home and even this announcement—so odd from a working girl in the middle of the afternoon—fails to send up flares.

Feeling limber and lithe, she stretches her legs out in front of her. "All right."

Once in my room with the door closed, I slide out of my mules, turn on the TV and curl up under the covers, suddenly feeling sad and maudlin and overwhelmed by the future. I'm not pining for Marcos Medici Associates. I'm not grieving for a job that made me miserable and dissatisfied and scornful of everyone I worked with, but this sense of freedom is terrifying. Security, for all the shackles it wraps around your wrists, is an alluring notion. It's a pretty cloth that you toss over a scarred and damaged table, and people like me cannot resist the cover it provides. We cannot walk away from it without a backward glance.

This feeling is all Hannah's fault. Hannah, with her outlandish plan that will explode in a spectacular flash of fire, has thrown my inadequacies into stark relief. Hannah is fearless. She's Christopher Columbus, and I'm every other human being on the continent of Europe in the fifteenth century. The world feels flat. It feels like the sort of place where you can slide off the edge; it's so much wiser and safer and easier to stay here than to go tumbling into an abyss.

I close my eyes, determined to banish these thoughts from my mind. I don't have to be an explorer, not today at least. This is my grace period, and all I have to do is seek solace or oblivion or some cozy place where the sting of memory is dulled. The rest of my life doesn't have to be sorted out right now. No, I have the rest of my life for that.

7

When I wake from my nap, Hannah is sitting on the edge of my bed. Her legs are hanging over the side and she's holding out a cup of tea as an offering.

"Here," she says, fluffing the pillow behind me with the cool efficiency of a nurse making rounds, "have a sip and tell me all about it."

I thank her for her thoughtfulness and grab the cup before she can spill tea on my clean sheets. The glass is hot and wisps of steam are floating upward. As I let it cool, I stare at her, slightly amazed. It's not the tea. If she can make gazpacho from the weeds on my windowsill, then she can no doubt make green tea from the mold on my shower wall. It's her insightfulness that has given me pause. It's her recognition, perhaps a few hours late, that something is wrong.

When I don't respond right away, Hannah lays a comforting hand over mine. "There's no need to be embarrassed, honey, at least not around me. I've been fired a bunch of times, and let me tell you, it almost never has anything to do with the firee. In my experience, employers are always looking for a scapegoat, anyone to blame poor performance or low productivity on, and just because you're the one who every so often shows up an hour or two late or makes a few long-distance personal calls or sometimes uses the color copier to make postcards to send out to agents, they settle on you. They might as well be throwing darts at a dartboard for all the thought and scientific methodology that goes into the decision. It's not fair and it certainly isn't right, but it's the way of the world, honey, the way of the awful world, and the sooner you accept it, the easier this thing called life is going to be." Her expression vacillates so smoothly between outrage and wisdom that my bedroom might have been a stage and my firing, fodder for commedia dell'arte.

Although I fully appreciate Hannah's school-of-hard-knocks pep talk for its entertainment value, it's not quite the peppy talk that she thinks it is. But I don't linger there. "I *know* I didn't do anything to earn it. They just needed to save money; it was a purely economical decision."

Hannah envelops me in a hug. She crushes the pillows behind me, which she had arranged so nicely, and knocks the teacup so that the liquid inside sloshes over the edge. "I know, honey," she says, as if comforting a child. "I know. I see you wandering out there in the wilderness with all the sins of the villagers on your head. It's all right." I sigh as she pats my back. "We won't say you were fired. We'll say 'let go.' How does that sound? Much more innocuous, no? Much less you're-an-awful-worker-who-steals-staplers-and-tape-dispensers-and-large-padded-en-velopes-when-you-think-nobody-is-looking. And it's not stealing, honey, not when they give you a key to the sup-ply closet and tell you to take whatever you need."

This is not about Hannah and because I refuse to let it be about her no matter how hard she tugs the rope in her direction, I ignore this misplaced plea of innocence. "I really wasn't fired. I was let go. It had nothing whatsoever to do with job performance," I say, trying to break free of her embrace without spilling more tea. The tea is still too hot for comfort but I resolve to drink it in one gulp the next chance I get. I'd rather burn my throat than have to change my sheets again. I just did it two days ago. "It was straight arithmetic. One Marcos Medici Associates minus one Tallulah West equals the kind of industrial design firm that investors want to throw their money at." This is ut-terly ridiculous, like new math, and as I run through the formula, the bile rises again in my throat. Only this time I don't laugh.

Hannah pulls back first, leaving me free to drink the tea. But I can't bring myself to take a sip. Steam is still swirling up in misty strands and I'm suddenly reluctant to burn my tongue and my throat and my stomach lining. There has to be a way of disposing of it without the risk of personal harm. After a moment's thought I put it on the floor and push it under the bed, away from Hannah's dangling feet.

"Are you sure you weren't fired?"

"Pretty sure," I say with only a hint of sarcasm, "I was there and all."

"All right," she says, although obviously unconvinced, "if you say so. But FYI, Nick is spreading rumors that you were fired. You might want to straighten him out before he tells more people. Your reputation is your calling card. You can't have it soiled."

Even though I don't believe in calling-card reputations, I get out of bed to call Nick. Hannah trails after me with a triumphant look on her face.

"That was much easier than I thought," she says under her breath, as she watches me hunt around the living room for the telephone. Her envelopes stuffed with head-shot-résumés are stacked discreetly in the corner next to the bedding and her bags. Otherwise the room is spotless. Someone has even vacuumed the rug.

"What was?" I ask. The phone is in the last place I'd look: on its cradle.

"Cheering you up. The way you took to your bed, I was sure you were having a breakdown. I was expecting you to ask me to bring the microwave into the bedroom so you could live on Hungry-Man turkey dinners. This is considerably better—your fending for yourself. I'll help in any way I can but don't ask me to be an enabler. I can't compromise my ethics, not even for the guest-host relationship."

I'm about to tell Hannah not to worry about her ethics when Nick picks up the phone. Thanks to the phone system's liberal use of caller ID, he knows it's me before I utter a word.

"I'm on my way," he says. Nick sounds frenzied. He sounds drained and harried and as if too many people are commanding his attention. There probably are too many people, but thanks to the rules of primogeniture, these commanders are not the heads of warring nations. Only first sons have to go into the family business. Second sons are free to explore other pursuits. For Nick that meant Web design and computer programming. "I just have one more thing to finish here. Can you hold on?"

I don't know what he imagines is going on but it bears little resemblance to reality. "I'm fine, Nick. I'm only unemployed, not in cardiac arrest."

"They're practically the same thing," he says. I can hear him frantically typing on the keyboard. It's a steady calming sound. Nick has swift, precise fingers. "Didn't your heart stop for a moment this afternoon when they told you?"

"Paused briefly but it started right up again, the old reliable thing, so don't worry about it," I say, even though

I know I'm fighting a losing battle. This is what the people around you do—worry.

"I'm coming over"—the typing stops for a moment as he takes a deep breath—"and I'll bring dinner."

"I don't want to talk about it."

"Fine," he says. "Then we'll drink wine and eat cheese and stare at the wall in silence."

"Wine and cheese?" I ask. "That's the kind of meal that's going to sustain me through these trying times?"

"I figured you weren't very hungry."

"Why not?"

"Because of the breakdown," he explains. "I'm saving my document to the server right now."

I roll my eyes. This is all Hannah's doing. She's the one who's spreading rumors and soiling my calling card. "I'm not having a breakdown."

"Hannah said you took to your bed," he says, as if he were citing an unimpeachable source. But he should know better. He's been friends with Hannah almost as long as I have. They met at a basement party in Georgetown the summer before our sophomore year and dated a few times. The romance fizzled quickly—they both wanted to be on top—but they stayed in touch and when I moved back home to New York, Hannah hooked us up. She gave me his number and told me to call and transferred the Nick deed from her name to mine. This is how Hannah treats friends. We're apartments whose leases can be taken over by people she likes. "And that's a direct quote."

"I didn't 'take to my bed.'" I say this as much to Hannah as to Nick. Hannah shakes her head sadly, as if my denial is so deeply rooted, not even a jackhammer could dig it out.

"But you were sleeping when I called."

"It was a nap, not a decline."

"If you say so." There is only amusement in his voice—no conviction, no sincerity, no remorse. "I'm shutting down my computer this very second. Expect me there in thirty-five minutes."

"All right, but bring some sushi as well. I'm starving."

After I hang up the phone, Hannah attacks me. She wraps her arms around me again in a bear hug and pulls me close. "I'm so proud of you, the way you're bouncing back."

I have one more protest in me but just as I'm about to make it, she cuts me off with a finger over my lips.

"No, you don't have to say it. Friends help friends. No thanks necessary."

I hug her back and fight the rising laughter. I don't want her to think I've recovered completely.

Tallulahland

1

I'm working at Stark for almost four weeks when my father stops by. We haven't spoken since his wedding, but I'm not surprised to see him saunter through the door in his charcoal-gray suit. One of his assistants had been in three days earlier, and although he showed no outward flash of recognition as I helped him select Baccarat crystal wineglasses, he knew who I was. He'd just seen me stumble through a toast a month before at his boss's wedding.

"Good morning, Mr. West," says Jeffrey, one of seven full-time salespeople and an obsequious little man who sells thousands and thousands of dollars of merchandise each day. His fawning strikes the perfect note with presidents of museums and owners of galleries, and they come to him whenever they need a little pick-me-up. He follows them around the store with his please-Ms.-Desmond–just-one-autograph demeanor, which they soak up while selecting five-thousand-dollar couches and sixty-dollar stuffed leather pigs that are sewn together with thick black string. I understand the appeal. Jeffrey is like a mirror that makes you look ten years younger and several pounds thinner.

From across the sales floor, I watch Jeffrey approach my father with his hand extended. He always makes a beeline for the luminaries. Jeff doesn't have a heart; he has a beeping and whirling global positioning satellite programmed with the coordinates of every famous person on earth. "What a pleasure this is. I'm your biggest fan, Mr. West," he says, the stars that reside permanently in his eyes twinkling.

Dad takes the proffered hand. He's expecting a routine shake, but this is only step one of the famous Jeffrey Klinger greeting. Next Jeff puts his left hand on my father's shoulder. Then he pats him enthusiastically on the back, as if their sons have just graduated summa cum laude from Yale. Dad's lucky he's not the president of MoMA. Agnes always gets an exuberant hug.

Jeffrey finishes off the greeting with a lavish faux-humility dismount with a half twist. He abruptly lowers his arms, turns away and adopts a commoners-should-not-touch-the-robes-of-royalty pose. "Please excuse me, Mr. West. I didn't mean to be so familiar. It's just that I can't believe that I'm actually meeting the man who created the Peterhoff chair. It's the most sublime use of— But, of course, you're not here to be gawked over by the help," he says, as if remembering his manners. But this too is an act. Jeffrey never forgets anything. "You're here to see your daughter. If I may so say, Mr. West, Lou is a pleasure to work with. She's an excellent saleswoman and practically outsells everyone else here."

Although Mr. West is presumably here to see his supersaleswoman daughter, he wouldn't mind hearing more about the sublimity of the Peterhoff. "No need to apologize. It's always a pleasure to meet one of my daughter's friends, especially one so well versed in design."

The door behind me opens, and Marcy steps out of the stockroom with her fingers wrapped around a Lucelli lamp. She takes one look at the scene unfolding in the front of the store and sizes up the situation. "Jeff scoring points with your daddy?"

I don't have to ask how she or even Jeffrey knows that Joseph West is my father. Although nothing is openly discussed among the staff of Stark—the cutthroat commission arrangement leaves too much on the line for interemployee friendliness—everyone knows the minutiae of everyone else's lives. Their methods are secretive and sneaky and on the brink of violating the Fourth Amendment.

"I think Dad's this close to buying a Marc Newson table," I say, watching as Jeffrey's head dips up and down.

The more excited he gets about a commission, the more his head bobs.

"Don't let him get away with it," Marcy orders, the light of fire in her eyes. "What are parents good for if not sure-thing commissions? He tried selling my mom a set of beautiful Mexican salad bowls but she knew the score. She took up twenty minutes of his time vacillating between two colors while I sold ten thousand dollars worth of vases to a sheik of a small oil-rich Middle Eastern country. Then she decided she still liked her reliable old Mikasa and took me out to lunch." Marcy smiles fondly as she recalls the story and walks off to show the lamp to a customer.

I watch Jeffrey do his slick and painfully smooth schmooze for a few minutes more and interrupt just as he's about to close the deal.

"Dad," I say, walking across the gleaming white floor. Everything about Stark is gleaming and white, except its staff. We are dressed in black from head to toe. It's not the most original color scheme but it sells expensive kitchen gadgets.

Jeffrey's head abruptly stops bobbing as he turns to face me. His top lip is curled in a faint sneer. "Lou, I was about to notify you that your dad was here."

"Of course you were. Dad, how are you?" Although I'm not usually demonstrative, I give him a peck on the cheek for Jeffrey's sake.

"Well, Tallulah, very well. Your friend here was just

trying to interest me in this table. It's very beautiful but perhaps another time. Right now I'd like to take my daughter to lunch," he explains before looking at me. "Do you have time?"

"Sure, there's a great brasserie across the street, or do you have somewhere in mind?"

With the introduction of this new topic, Jeffrey sees his sale slipping away. It is sliding out of his grasp and he tries to salvage something from the wreckage. "Do you think, Mr. West— No, I suppose you don't have time. You probably want to beat the lunch rush."

"We have a moment." Dad looks to me for confirmation. I shrug, expecting now the flawless execution of the Jeffrey Klinger recovery maneuver. It's like the Hamel Camel but more slippery. "What is it?"

"I have one of your books in the back," he says, still hesitant. "Do you think you can sign it before you leave?"

Dad agrees. He likes his celebrity and his signature on the cool white of a well-designed title page. Jeffrey runs to the back and returns seconds later with Dad's book that came out several months ago. It's a large coffee-table edition with color photos of his most famous works and thoughts and recollections of the works' creation. That Jeffrey had the book in his locker is not a coincidence or proof that he worships at the altar of West. Stark has a well-stocked book section in the back and Jeffrey is always dipping into it to increase his personal wealth. After getting my dad's signature, he will sell the autographed copy on eBay for five times its cover price.

When the book signing is over, we head across the street to have lunch. Although I don't know why Dad is here, I naturally conclude that it has something to do with my working at Stark. But we don't get into that right away. First we talk awkwardly about the wedding. I mumble tepid words like *nice* and *pleasant* and he tells me how happy he was with the catering and the band. I don't ask about Carol and her daughters and he doesn't tell me.

"Jeffrey said you're an excellent saleswoman," he says, approaching the topic of my employment from a side street.

This is untrue. I can make a sale when the person who comes into our store has already decided to buy something. But I have no patience for browsing yuppies, and it hurts me to be polite to clueless tourists with their fanny packs filled with cash. "He was just trying to flatter you. That's what he does."

Dad mistakes honesty for modesty. "I'm sure you're very good. You're personable and you know the product. That's all a customer wants."

I'm not going to defend my awful sales record. "I guess so."

"Do you enjoy the work?" he asks, fingering the menu as we wait for the waitress to stop at our table.

I shrug. The job, which fell into my lap after a friend from Parson's quit, isn't about enjoyment. It's about paying the rent and having something left over for utilities and food. Even without the Jeffrey-size commission checks, ten-hour days at Stark pay considerably better than un-employment.

"You didn't mention that you had left Medici," he says, as if we chat all the time and my new job is something I failed to tell him. This is how he always talks. This is how he always plays our estrangement, like it's a topic I forgot to mention to him on the phone last night.

My dad doesn't understand this rift that separates me from him. As far as he's concerned, he has fulfilled the dic-tates of the fatherhood contract. He has held up his end—why don't I hold up mine? But he stuck to the letter of the law and ignored the spirit. He clothed me and fed me and sheltered me, but he didn't hold me or cherish me or raise me. And now it's too late. Now we're left with a rough sketch of a father-daughter relationship and nei-ther one of us has the skill to fill in the details. Love is a language you have to learn early on, otherwise you are always a stumbling, stuttering tourist with a phrasebook in your hand.

I look for the waitress, hoping she can head off this con-versation, which I don't want to have. She is nowhere in sight. "I guess I just didn't think it was very important. I hadn't been happy there for a while and had been think-ing about leaving. Getting laid off made the decision for me. I'm not sure what I want to do next but I'll figure it out," I say, hoping that will be the end of it and that we can now talk about the unusually mild summer we've been having.

Of course it's not. "I didn't realize you were laid off."

"Marcos is trying to convince investors that he runs a tight ship." I don't have to explain to Dad how unlikely a prospect this is. He already knows. Everyone in the business is keenly aware of Marcos Medici's extravagant spending habits. "It's really no big deal. I was going to leave anyway." There is a pause in the conversation and for a brief moment I wonder if I can bring up the possibility of a loan. The scene has been set by someone other than me; the timing is perfect. But even without trying I know the words won't come out. This last month has been hard and uninspired and my scaled-back vision for Tallulah Design seems more like a failure than an edited version of success, but I still can't get the words out. That's the beautiful thing about life. It lets you make the same mistakes over and over.

Dad catches the waitress's eye as she brushes past with a tray filled with sodas. She smiles and promises to be right with us. "Wanda's leaving in a few weeks," he says conversationally. "We've promoted one of the assistants to her position, which leaves us with an opening. I don't think Charlie has filled the spot yet. If you're interested."

"I'll think about it," I say evasively because the idea has already been raised and rejected—four years ago. Twenty-six days after Mom died.

"Call Charlie. He can tell you about the job. It's entry

level but assistants get to do a lot of creative, interesting work and the pay is good," he says, a trace of hope in his voice. He thinks there's an opening, a crack with enough wiggle room to woo me into the family business.

I nod and look around for the waitress, trying hard to seem casual and not frantic. This is not an opportunity. The job he's offering is exactly what I want: It's precisely the sort of thing I had promised myself I'd look for as soon as I left Medici, but I won't go after it. I can't work with him. I can't occupy the same space as him every day of my life. Twenty-six days. Mom hadn't been dead for an entire month before he took Carol dancing at the Rainbow Room.

I've been told many times by family and friends and a therapist I decided was incompetent that these twenty-six days are not an indication of how my father felt about Mom. The generally accepted spin is that she'd been sick for a long time—377 days—and Dad grieved for her then. While he put a tube into her back and drained her lungs of fluid, he mourned for his dying wife. I don't accept this. Grief isn't a race; you don't get a head start. It's not a meal you preorder before getting on an airplane. It's a storm that tears through your life, and you can judge the magnitude by the devastation it leaves behind. For me, Mom was a hurricane. For Dad, she was a downgraded tropical storm.

Maybe I'm wrong. Maybe I don't get it. Maybe Joseph West loved his wife with every fiber of his being and not with a halfhearted detachment that let him take another woman to the Rainbow Room twenty-six days after her death, but this is the shade he raised. This is the window he let me look in.

"So, Wanda's leaving?" I say, rooting around for a topic, any topic.

"Her husband took a job in San Francisco. They bought a big old Victorian house and they've asked me to do a few sketches for them. I might give it a try. I'll have to see the space first."

Dad doesn't like doing interiors. He has an affinity for bold color choices that work despite initial reservations and he is unnaturally skilled at pulling together disparate elements to make a cohesive whole, but he isn't interested in the big picture. Joseph West prefers working on one piece of the puzzle. When he first started out, before every manufacturer in the world wanted him to design something for them, he had to accept these commissions in order to put food on his family's table. But ever since his initial success with the imperial line—the Peterhoff chair, the Tsarskoe table, the Pavlovsk couch—he has stayed far away from the interiors game. He's a successful man, the sort who doesn't have to make compromises to make a living.

I'm not familiar with San Francisco and I haven't seen Wanda since my mother's funeral but I show tremendous interest in her life and times. I'd rather talk about people I barely know and streets I've never heard of than things that relate to Dad and me.

Lunch is drawn out, thanks to our waitress, who fails to improve upon acquaintance. By the time she finally gets around to taking our order and delivering food to our table, we've run out of harmless conversation about Wanda. I'm forced to ask about all the people in his office, from Charlie down to the guy who distributes the mail. It passes the time.

"How is Nicholas?" Dad asks as he lingers over coffee. The busboy has just made another round and now Dad has a full cup. I thought I was in the home stretch. I thought the bill would be signed in a few minutes and then I would be released but I've misread the situation. There are at least another fifteen minutes to go. "Are you and he still planning on joining us in the Hamptons for Labor Day? Carol is looking forward to it. She's planning a big barbecue."

"A big barbecue?" This is not the event I was pitched. "I thought it was going to be small."

"That's what I thought, too." His laugh is accompanied by a helpless shrug. "It was originally just family but every day Carol thinks of another person or two to invite. The number of guests now rivals our wedding reception. Carol really enjoys entertaining and she does it so effortlessly."

Although I'm disgusted by the way Carol operates—she always works incrementally, adding a few drops of water at a time until you are drowned completely—she has made my life easier. My presence will not be missed;

the party is too large for the absence of one daughter to be noted and remarked upon.

"I'm not sure," I say, laying the groundwork for future excuses. "I might have to work. I don't know how the system works here and I have the least seniority. I'll probably have to man the store by myself while everyone else is sunning themselves at the beach."

My excuse sounds logical, too logical, and while Dad sips his coffee, I'm forced to consider the likelihood of this happening. It's not just an excuse to worm out of awkward family gatherings; I *am* the lowest man on the totem pole.

"We'll be there the whole weekend," he says, "if you can only make it for a day or so. I think Cammie and Sammie are coming down on Thursday night. But don't worry, there's plenty of room for everyone."

I'm not worried. In a week or so I'll call his office just a few minutes before nine-thirty, which is when he usually arrives, and leave a message on his voice mail saying that I have to work the whole weekend. "I'll see what I can swing."

"Great." He looks at his watch. "You should probably be getting back. You've been away for a while."

I look across the street, where the windows of Stark are decorated with pails and shovels made out of brushed steel. I can see Jeffrey standing near the front door with a customer, a pretty woman in a floral-print dress. He's holding one of Tapiro Wirkkala's murano glass vases in his hands and his head is bobbing erratically.

I catch the waitress's eye and make the universal symbol for "check please." It's time to go back to work. Ten minutes later, she does a drive-by, dropping the check on the table while barely slowing down, but Dad is ready for her. He has his credit card already out and she has to stop, turn around and say thank-you.

When I return to work, Jeffrey is reeling the woman in. He's telling her about Stark's return policy and assuring her that she has thirty days to make up her mind. Bring it home, he's saying, leave it in the living room, see how many compliments you get, and if you can't live with the constant admiration, bring it back for a full refund. This is Jeffrey's favorite tactic. As far as he's concerned, the challenge of sales is getting merchandise into the home. Once it's there, it rarely leaves.

Ignoring Jeffrey's angry glare—and this is the true genius of Jeffrey, that he can nurse a petty grudge even while courting a huge commission—I walk over to a customer who is looking at Alessi's polished stainless-steel line. Most of these wares are reasonably priced and there's little money to be made peddling them, but I am a soft sell. I'm the sort of saleswoman who gives you space and lets you make up your mind without the coaxing and cajoling of a well-worn speech, and for this reason I often have to settle for quality over quantity. It's a small concession that saves my dignity.

2

The phone is ringing when I get home but I'm reluctant to pick it up. Hannah's plan to get cast in Adam Weller's film is actually moving forward according to schedule and there have been many calls of late sorting out the details of the Derbyshire house. Through no fault of mine, I've been cast as the estate agent. Hannah recruited me through devious and underhanded means. It happened like this:

"Let me hear your British accent," she said when she came home from the party in her stunning red dress. Her eyes were glittering with excitement and I could see the moments around her floating with possibilities. For a little while the rainstorm had stopped.

The request for a British accent seemed like a non sequitur to me but I knew it followed crooked Hannah logic. Giving in to the inevitable, I muttered a sentence about mutton and blood pudding.

She winced at my awful articulation and for a moment looked dejected and unhappy. But then she rallied. "All right, let's try it again but a little less cockney. Don't be afraid to embrace your H's."

"I was embracing my H's," I said, feeling oddly defensive.

Hannah cocked her head to the side, unconvinced. "All right, then let's stay away from H altogether. Repeat after me: The rain in Spain stays mainly on the plain."

"No. I refuse to play Eliza Doolittle to your 'Enry 'Iggins."

"Ha! You *are* dropping your H's," she said triumphantly as if a point had just been proven.

"That time was on purpose," I said.

Refusing to be sidetracked by irony, Hannah continued. "All right, now let's try something completely different. Let's widen the field. Just try to sound foreign."

"Foreign?"

"Un-American."

I opened my mouth to speak but Hannah hadn't finished listing conditions yet. "And Canada doesn't count. Actually, we're going for vaguely European. After I get off the phone with you, I want to be unsure if you're from Liechtenstein or Belgium. Got it?"

Still completely in the dark as to the purpose of this

exercise, I gave it a try. I asked the stable boy to fetch my parasol.

Hannah nodded considering. "Russian émigré. A bold choice. Not what I would have gone with but it could work. Tell me your back story."

I looked at her, baffled. "Back story?"

"Who are your people? Why did you flee? How did you wind up in New York?" she said, tossing a series of questions my way. "Keep it as close to the truth as possible. Go."

Suddenly I felt like Peggy Sawyer in a poorly run summer stock production of *Forty-Second Street*. It wasn't a pleasant experience. "I'm not making up a back story."

"Fine, I'll make it up. All you'll have to do is memorize it."

"Why?"

"Because I don't have time to write out cue cards."

"No, what's the back story for?"

Hannah closed her eyes. She was either praying for strength or reminding herself never to work with animals or children. "You're going to need something to talk about with the secretary while you're holding for the president of Universal."

Suddenly a feeling of panic swept through me. I knew where she was going. I didn't know what roads she would be taking or how much the tolls would cost, but the destination was marked on the map with a big red pin. "Hannah, why am I holding for the president of Universal?"

"Hollywood types always keep you on hold. It's a power play," she explained wisely, as if everything in the universe were known to her. "You can't take it personally. You can't take anything in this biz personally, kid. It'll tear you apart bit by bit."

I looked at Hannah. Her face was flushed, her eyes were twinkling and there was hope oozing out of every pore in her body. It wasn't my intention to crush her dreams. It wasn't my game plan to be the big bad wolf who blows her house down, but there was nothing else I could do. Some schemes didn't merit discussion. "I'm not doing it," I said firmly. To signal the end of talk time, I turned on the television and forced myself to look interested in the eleven o'clock news. Out of the corner of my eye I was watching Hannah. Her reaction wasn't what I expected. She hadn't dimmed. Her cheeks hadn't lost their color and her eyes continued to sparkle. I felt another wave of panic. Hannah wasn't done yet. There was more madcap scheming to come.

"All right," she said, stepping out of her high-heeled sandals, which she placed under the table next to her bags. She then slithered out of her dress, hung it over a chair and threw on a T-shirt and shorts for sleeping.

I narrowed my eyes suspiciously. This was just another tactic. It might not seem like madcap scheming but it was. Hannah was marshalling her forces for a surprise attack. They were getting in formation as we speak. "All right? You're cool with this?"

Hannah smiled. "Of course I'm cool with it."

I didn't know what to do with this calm acceptance. Turning on the TV had been a maneuver, a diversionary play to avoid an ugly scene. I really didn't think it would work. Hannah is like a dog with a bone. She never lets go. "I said I'm not helping you."

"I heard you." She smiled again before pulling her hair back into a ponytail and disappearing into the bathroom.

I tried to walk away. I tried to convince myself that the topic was closed, but I couldn't. There were no strings and there was no one standing behind a curtain, but somehow I was being manipulated. I followed her into the bathroom. "Why aren't you arguing with me?"

Her face was covered with soap and she had to rinse a few times before answering. "There's no need." Brushing past me, she dried her face with a towel.

"But I've just crushed your hopes and dreams," I reminded her. "I've taken my tractor and ruthlessly plowed them under like they're last year's crop. And that's okay with you? Where's the cajoling and the whining and the well-conceived argument that upon closer inspection doesn't make sense? Why aren't you throwing a tantrum or making some long-winded speech about dreams and raindrops? What's wrong?" I asked, as it suddenly occurred to me that I might have misread the signs. Flushed cheeks, bright eyes—weren't these also the symptoms of tuberculosis? I put my hand on her forehead. She was warm. "I can't be sure. You might have a temperature." I laid my other hand on my own forehead for comparison. This didn't help. I was warm, too.

Hannah waited politely as I tried to decide whether she was dying or not. "This isn't necessary," she said but she didn't move. She remained still with my palm on her forehead. "I'm not sick."

I lowered my hand. "Prove it."

"How?"

"Argue with me. Plead for my help. Tell me how this is your one chance at making it big and if you don't become a star you might as well return to Poolsville and marry Donny, your high-school sweetheart who works at the paper mill. Go on. And make it good. I'm not falling for some halfhearted effort."

Hannah laughed. "There's no need for me to tell you all that."

"Why?"

"You already know it." She took her toothbrush out of the holder and ran it quickly under water. Then she put paste on it and started brushing.

"Remind me. And I want to see tears, large fat tears the size of snowballs."

Hannah mumbled something. With the toothbrush in her mouth, she was incomprehensible.

"What?" I asked.

She spit and took a sip of water. She swooshed it around her mouth and spit again. "That's not necessary."

"Why not?"

After dabbing her lips on the towel, she put the tooth-brush back and examines her face for blackheads. She didn't find any. The light in my bathroom is weak and it makes every complexion look good. "Because you're going to agree without the song and dance."

"No, I'm not."

"Yes, you are," she said, walking out of the bathroom.

I turned off the light and followed. "No, I'm not."

"Of course you are." She retrieved the sheets from under the table and spreads them onto the couch. "You have too strong a sense of right and wrong to abandon a friend in her time of need."

"Strong sense of right and wrong," I mumbled under my breath. "What you're doing is completely unethical."

Hannah climbed into bed, laying her head against the pillow. "I know, but you're going to help me anyway."

I stared at her helplessly for a moment. I wasn't sure how I reached this place. I couldn't recall the twists and turns and the dark back alleys but here I was at the red pin. "You're awful."

She smiled sweetly and closed her eyes. "I know."

I turned off the light. "But I'm making up my own back story. I don't want to be some former ballerina who had to flee with just the clothes on her back after her hus-band and children were marked for death by the KGB."

"Whatever you say."

I opened the door to my bedroom and sought refuge. The phone rings now and I stare at it. It has to be

Heidi. It has to be Adam Weller's assistant at Sugar Snap Peas productions calling to harass me for more details. But there aren't any more. We've already covered every possible angle. She has a photo of the manor house, an Elizabethan mansion that Hannah found in a calendar of stately English homes. If someone at Sugar Snap turned it over and noticed July on the other side, Heidi hasn't mentioned it. She also has photos of the grounds, which look suspiciously like the Rambles in Central Park. I myself don't know if Derbyshire has sycamore trees, but I take comfort in the knowledge that apparently neither does Heidi. And last but not least, she has blueprints of the house. Hannah, thinking one draughty old European hovel is pretty much like another, sent over the layout for Versailles, which she found easily enough on the Web. The Sun King's palace is five times larger than the Duke of Bedford's humble abode but this discrepancy hasn't been commented on, nor has the room marked Hall of Mirrors. This is my only solace: that the good people of Sugar Snap Peas productions aren't very well traveled.

After the third ring, I pick up the phone. I say hello in my Russian émigré accent and wait. If it's someone from my real life, then I'll cough and clear my throat and pretend that the Russian émigré is just a cold. If it's Heidi, I'll cringe. This is the compromise that Hannah and I worked out. Hannah, in her psychosis, wanted me to answer the phone British Empire Reality, New York office.

"Mishka, how are you?"

It is Heidi. Nobody else in the world calls me Mishka. "I'm fine, thank you. And yourself?"

"Good. I have the contracts here," she says, getting right into it. There is no lingering small talk, no polite conversation about my life. Heidi knows nothing of the father I left behind in Moscow or the husband who drowned in the Neva.

"Yes?" I say, feeling a frisson of alarm. Hannah wrote the contract herself and sent it off before I had a chance to check for spelling errors and mistakes more egregious. I'm terrified that she took the wording from a cereal box.

"The duchess hasn't signed them yet. Gilda wants to send someone to England to scout the location but she doesn't want to move forward with this without the duchess's signature. I'm going to messenger them to you right now. We'd like them back first thing in the morning."

Gilda is Adam Weller's producer. She's tough, savvy and a former WWF wrestler. She's the sort of no-nonsense person you want ironing out the difficulties in your life. Every time Heidi mentions her name, my heart drops. Gilda's the steamroller who's going to flatten me when the duchess bomb explodes.

"I will try to get in touch with her today but she is very busy and hard to pin down," I say, as the duchess opens the apartment door. She's carrying a laundry basket filled with sheets, towels and fabric softener. "Perhaps Friday or early Monday morning."

Hearing this, Hannah gives me a thumbs-up. I'm under strict orders to delay as long as possible. Although otherwise without scruples, Hannah is reluctant to sign the contracts. She has some small inkling that promises become binding when you sign documents. Hannah is hoping to pull off this movie coup without incurring jail time.

Heidi sighs. There's nothing she can do. Duchesses will be duchesses. "All right, but we're talking first thing Monday morning at the latest. And please note that Gilda will not be pleased."

Heidi enjoys using Gilda as a cudgel, but she has no idea just how effective it is. Gilda terrifies me. In a few short weeks, she has become the embodiment of all my childhood nightmares. She's the bogeyman and the thing that goes bump in the night and the monster that hides under your bed. When this whole disaster comes crashing down—as, of course, it must—it will be on the duchess's head and on the duchess's head only. Mishka Petrovitch will disappear. She did it once before in Moscow, in the late eighties, and she'll do it again now.

"Excellent stall," Hannah says when I hang up the phone. "Monday's perfect. By then they'll be trying to get permits to shoot in Red Rocks Park. "

"Why?"

Hannah opens the oven door and takes out a fresh loaf of white bread. I never see her kneading or the yeast rising but every third day Hannah pulls a fresh loaf out of the oven like it's a rabbit out of a hat. She cuts a slice and offers it to me. "Because they say the terrain of Arizona looks like the surface of Mars," she explains.

"Thanks," I say. The bread is hot and crusty and I eat it without butter or jam. "No, I meant, why will they be shooting there, instead of England?"

"Adam loved my script and he's this close to saying screw it to the movie about the duchess and the jewel thief." She spreads peanut butter on the bread and eats the sandwich open-faced. "The studio is giving him shit about revisions—they want the characters and the language to be more modern—and Adam is getting tired of trying to hang on to his creative vision. He doesn't know it yet, of course, but I can tell. My script is mostly action and very modern, so there's not much they can object to."

"Your script?" I ask surprised. Hannah only writes treatments. She's unwilling to flesh out her ideas without the backing of a major studio.

"Yes," she says, her mouth full of peanut butter.

"When did you write a script?"

"Last week, while you were selling expensive garlic presses." She sees my eyes widen and shrugs dismissively. "Please, it's not a big deal. The general rule of thumb for a screenplay is one page per minute, which means that the screenplay for the average movie is, like, only ninety pages long. And if that weren't enough of a scam, half of each page is mostly blank space. Condense the whole thing down to one long paragraph, and we're talking twenty pages. I could bake bread in less time."

Still, it sounds like an accomplishment to me. "That's so cool," I say, sitting down on the lone kitchen stool while she cuts another slice of bread, which she offers to me. I lean over with an open hand. "What's it about?"

"A female cop who fights crime in the post-Apocalyptic future," she says. "Dresden saves the world, lots of things blow up, and a beautiful man falls in love with her. I don't see how it can fail."

I'm not surprised that this is what she went with. Hannah knows how to go out on a limb but she also knows how to play it safe. Now is not the time to pitch a sensitive art-house flick. "Dresden?"

"Dresden Quinn—*c'est moi*."

I laugh. I can't help it. Dresden Quinn is just the name I'd expect Hannah to come up with. "I like it."

"And, wait, you haven't even heard yet."

"It gets better?"

"The title: *Bombing Dresden*," she says, smiling proudly before launching into a description of the plot, which is about a cop who gets more than she bargained for when she starts investigating a ho-hum murder.

Hannah runs on for a while, detailing the exploits of a group of eco-revolutionaries who try to save the Earth from our own folly. "You see, dumping garbage on Mars was stupid. The weight threw the planet off course and it's now roaming the solar system without an orbit. Scientists are scrambling to come up with a new method for disposing of waste before the politicians get their way and start dumping on Venus."

"Ah, it's a cautionary tale."

She tilts her head to the side, considering this idea for a moment. "Not exactly a cautionary tale, but certainly a shoot-'em-out, blow-'em-up testosterone-filled action flick with a message."

The bread has made me thirsty, and I slide off my stool to get a glass from the cabinet that hangs over the sink. I take out a tumbler with a faded Pepsi decal. It's not a glass I use often but it's near the front and within reach. Thanks to the guest-host relationship, my glasses and plates and bowls are now arranged in descending size order. "You do what you can."

"I know," she says as she holds her glass out for a refill. "One of the early versions of the script explained in detail how the forty trillion disposable diapers that earthlings dump on Mars each year caused the wandering-planet problem—I even went into the science of super acrylic-acid polymers—but this slowed down the pace too much. So instead of meeting with Dresden and presenting his case, the spokesperson for HURD gets blown up by a heat-seeking missile."

"Heard?"

"Humans for the Use of Reusable Diapers," she says, clarifying for those of us who aren't familiar with twenty-fourth-century acronyms. Her plot is dense and complicated and filled with jumps that make little sense.

Whenever she painted herself into a corner, she blew up another person or thing. "Take the scene at the Coney Island Aquarium," she says, giving me an example of her writing process. "Somehow all the leaders of these various radical groups wound up in the shark tank pointing rocket launchers at one another, and I just couldn't figure out how to get anyone out alive. So I blew up the whole thing. A recently defrosted Walt Disney escapes, of course, but hideously scarred."

I'm not sure I want to know what Walt Disney has to do with twenty-fourth-century garbage, but the bread is warm and I'm feeling mellow. "Walt Disney?"

"Yes, that's the great plot twist in the end. It's all just a vast left-wing conspiracy to overthrow the democratic government on Earth and implement Disneyism, a socioeconomic system that advocates the elimination of authentic personal experience," she says, pleased with herself for following the formula so faithfully. Every great Hollywood actioner has a vast conspiracy looming over the movements of each character.

I'm not sure I should be encouraging Hannah in her endeavor to peddle empty nonsense to the American public but I do it anyway. The American public can look out for itself. "Sounds like fun. I'd go see it."

Hannah laughs. "No, you wouldn't. But I appreciate the vote of confidence."

I shrug off her thanks. This is why we have friends. This is why we keep them close and put up with their nonsense. Nobody else is going to support and encourage our madcap schemes. "And you're sure Adam is going to go with this?"

"Like I said, he's tired of wrangling with the studios over revisions. And I think my pointing out the unlimited potential for product placement cinched it. I mean, what product can't you place in the future? You can replace the sun with golden arches and nobody will complain. Meanwhile, set a movie in Victorian England and your options are what? Burberry and maybe Oxford University. I think this is a no-brainer. Adam's smart. He'll figure it out."

"Excellent," I say, amazed at the ease and success of her plan. I'm still waiting for something to go horribly wrong. I'm still one hundred percent sure that this will end in a disastrous mess that'll involve lawyers and police officers but I'm no longer tense and nervous. Whatever happens, Hannah can handle it. "And you don't have to own dumping rights on Mars to get cast?"

"Nope. That's the beauty of the new plan. In fact, I'm thinking of unloading the duchy. It's always been a burden, living up to my poor dead husband's parents' expectations of how a young duchess should behave. Mummy and Daddy Chartersmith are sticklers. Don't speak above a whisper, m'dear. Do go to the cotillion Friday next, m'dear. Don't be seen eating in public, m'dear. Do curtsy with your head bowed, m'dear. And then there's dear sweet Hilly, my husband's impoverished viscount cousin with his brood of eleven children. He's a reliable chap who won't sell off the family silver. And it's not like I need the income, being an Australian national treasure and all."

"It's for the best," I agree. "And please get rid of your estate agent while you're at it. She's starting to get on my nerves."

Hannah snaps her fingers. "Done."

I bring my glass to the sink and wash it. Ordinarily I'd leave it there for a day or two, letting other glasses and dishes pile on top and around it, but I know Hannah. She will rinse it instantly. It's nice having clean forks and plates and glasses, but the guest–host relationship is starting to oppress me. I can't stand having someone walk three steps behind me washing away my footsteps. I like leaving a trail.

"Oh, I've finally finished sorting through your piles," she says, watching me clean the glass. I'm doing it wrong— you always have to pour fresh liquid onto the sponge, even if the sponge seems soapy enough without it—but Hannah doesn't say anything. After five weeks she has learned to play the game discreetly. Now she pretends to accept my imperfections and then surreptitiously corrects them when I'm in another room. "I've made three piles. Left pile: subscription notices, bank statements, other assorted mail items and small clippings from the newspaper. Middle pile: doodles, printouts and sketches. Right pile: miscellaneous, which is to say, anything that didn't fit into the aforementioned two piles. They're in the living room."

I turn off the faucet and put the glass in the drying rack. "You didn't have to do that," I say, wiping my hands on a yellow checked dish towel. Hannah waits until I put it down before replacing it with a freshly cleaned one from her laundry basket.

"I know but this way they're organized. You might want to buy a file cabinet so that you can keep your things together. I found three years of bank statements scattered throughout the apartment. I put your canceled checks in order for you. It's amazing that you're not missing a single one, considering your odd storage method."

I want to defend myself. I want to assure her that my storage method only seems haphazard and random, but now that she's organized my mess she knows the truth. She knows I let mail and sketches and newspapers articles pile up on the kitchen counter, and when the entire space is completely covered, I stack the mess into a neat-looking pile and hide it from view. I find things are easier to deal with when I don't have to look at them. My checkbook hasn't been balanced in four years. This works for me. I've only been overdrawn three times.

Hannah has put the three piles on the couch, which means if I ever want to sit down and watch television comfortably again, I'll have to deal with them. I sigh heavily and submit gracefully to the task. As I pick up the first pile, I hear the water turn on in the kitchen. Hannah is cleaning the loaf pan that she baked the bread in. She is scrubbing the Crisco-batter residue off the bottom and rinsing crumbs off the cutting board, but she's also washing my glass. I don't have to look to know it.

I start with the bank statements, which I hate. They are dull and uninteresting and they never tell me anything I don't already know. All they do is run through my poverty line by line, like an English professor teaching "Ode on a Grecian Urn" to a bunch of college freshmen. But I don't need a slip of paper to remind me of my lack of wealth. This fact is driven home to me every time I step foot into Stark.

My first impulse is to throw everything with a Citibank logo into the trash and set fire to it, but I resist. Instead I hold on to the last twelve months' statements as a token offering to the gods of organization. But I don't look at them. I don't review amounts and check dates for accuracy or even run a cursory eye over name and address to confirm that they are mine.

It takes me almost two hours to get through the first pile. I throw away the bills and subscription-renewal forms and notices from local politicians without hesitation, but I linger over old torn-out newspaper clippings of things I'd meant to do. Here's more evidence of the alternate me, the Tallulah who not only regularly cooks healthy meals for herself but also attends lectures at the library, watches revivals at the Film Forum, goes to talks at the 92nd Y, and supports struggling productions in the East Village. She is well fed and culturally versed and emotionally fulfilled.

But that Tallulah is a figment. She's a shadowy ghost image that shows up in photos from Paris. The real Tallulah works at Stark and mourns her mother and resents her father.

Feeling sad and oddly bereft, I start on the second pile, which presents less of a challenge. It's made up of early renditions of designs I'm working on now—or rather, was working on before exhausting ten-hour days at Stark sucked the inspiration out of me—and I hold on to every single scrap of paper. To Hannah's dismay, I wrap a thick black ribbon around the pile and put it back in the kitchen, on the shelf with cookbooks that it had so recently vacated. This is the historical record. This is the marginalia that my biographer will have to sort through with painstaking precision. And even if I spend the rest of my life selling high-priced kitchen gadgets to socialites from the Upper East Side and even if I never make beautiful tables or melancholy chairs, I have to do this. I have to leave markings on the wall of my cave.

I look at the third pile and sigh heavily. I don't want to deal with it now. It's late and I'm hungry and I've made enough progress for one evening. This whole endeavor is futile anyway. The bank isn't going to stop sending me statements and my designs aren't going to stop evolving.

"I found Nestlé semisweet morsels today," Hannah says. "They were in the bottom cabinet under the pine nuts." She's standing in the doorway of the kitchen watching me. During this entire process I can feel her scrutinizing me from a few feet away. I'm an anthropological study to her: Domesticus Messimus. She doesn't understand how people like me can exist in our disorganized and disordered habitats.

I glance up. I don't know what morsels and pine nuts have to do with me but I welcome the distraction. The third pile is thick.

"If you finish that tonight, I'll make you chocolate chip cookies," she says, casting out lures.

I want to bite, but I'm cautious. I sense a trick. "Everything you need to make chocolate chip cookies is right here in this apartment?"

"Yes."

"Everything?" I ask again. My doubt is justified. This apartment rarely has the things I need.

"Well, you're out of vanilla extract," she admits reluctantly, "but you seem to have vanilla beans, so I'm sure I'll figure something out."

Because I'm sure she will, too, I agree to the deal. "But you should start making them right now. I'm gonna be done with this pile within the hour."

Now *she* is suspicious. "You're not going to just wrap a ribbon around it and put it back in the kitchen, are you?"

I'm sorely tempted to do just that, but I shake my head. "No, I'll go through it with a fine-tooth comb."

Hannah smiles, pleased with the velvet-glove delivery of her iron fist, and I'm struck again by the ridiculousness of the arrangement. This is my apartment. We should be living by my rules, but we're not. We're living by hers.

I throw myself into the third pile, tossing away catalogs and magazines and playbills and museum brochures and whole yellowed sections of the *New York Times*. I'm not a pack rat. I don't feel a compulsive need to save every item that crosses my threshold, but right now it seems like I do. There is several years accumulation stacked high and for the moment it feels as if I've never thrown away a thing in my life.

I'm more than halfway through the pile when I get to the first time-worn letter. I had forgotten about the letters, and I stare motionless at my mother's handwriting for several minutes. It's so familiar. It is so known and recognizable and so woven into my memory that it feels like a living thing. It's her breath on my cheek. It's the touch of her lips on my forehead.

Another number pops into my head. Ninety-one: the number of days after Mom's death that Dad made me clean out her closet. It was an awful rainy day in November and it took me hours and hours to sort through her things. You never know what to keep—you want to keep everything—so you come up with criteria and adhere to them strictly. Only keep cards with personal notes inside. Throw away letters that are too faded to be read. Hang on to her silk blouses because you might wear them one day. Give away her shoes because you were never the same size.

Before she died, Mom had asked me to go through her

closet with her, but I couldn't do it. It was too morbid and too sad and far too real. But it wasn't any of that for her. Her body had already absorbed the morbidity and the sadness and the reality, and all she wanted now was to know what of hers would have a second life as part of mine. She was a dying woman trying to get a brief glimpse of her epitaph and I said no.

This is my regret.

Now I'm left with things I don't understand: unsent unrequited love letters to a man named Bill Dixon, photos of a bungalow apartment in Miami, a collection of matchbooks from Parisian restaurants. These things are untranslatable. They are written in hieroglyphics and Mom is the Rosetta stone. I will always wonder what they mean. I'll always wonder why she didn't tell me about them.

The tears rise in my throat as I stare at the letters to Bill Dixon. This always happens when I hold these letters—they are like freshly peeled onions to my tear ducts—and I prefer to keep them out of sight. I don't know where they've been hiding for the last four years but it was a good place. A safe place. They have to go back.

I wrap a rubber band around the collection, careful of their delicate pages. Then I bring the packet into the kitchen. I slide the letters into the bookshelf, so they can lie against my sketches. They are notes in the margin of a completely erased text; this is where they belong.

Hannah doesn't notice me. She doesn't feel me brush

past her and she doesn't see me pushing aside the *Better Home and Garden* cookbook to make room. She is too busy watching butter soften in the microwave.

Back in the living room, I move swiftly through the rest of the pile. It's late and I'm hungry and I'm now emotionally exhausted. The last thing to be identified, categorized and dealt with is a thick white envelope that I've never seen before. I open it up and read.

"This is weird," I say softly, after a few moments examination.

Hannah is wrapped up in making cookies and doesn't hear me. I say it again, louder this time, and she leans against the archway, drying her hands on the silly frilly apron she likes to wear. She looks like a Gypsy Donna Reed. "What is?"

"I think this is a deed to property in North Carolina." I hold up a thick piece of paper with signatures on it. "To property 46F." I unfold the accompanying map and spread it out on the floor. A few hundred lots are delineated by colors and letters and numbers.

"Here it is," Hannah says, pointing to a lot in the southern end of the development that's highlighted in bright yellow. "Lakefront." She whistles softly, appreciatively. "Swank location."

Written near the edge of the map in my mother's handwriting is "Cathy Wheaton, 9:30."

"Who's Cathy Wheaton?" Hannah asks. She has seen where my eyes have wandered and followed them.

I get up and reach for the phone. "I don't know."

"Who are you calling?"

"My dad. He'll know something about this. He must," I say with too much conviction. This is wishful thinking. I want Dad to know about the property. I want him to be able to explain its meaning to me in detail. Lot 46F isn't another Bill Dixon. It isn't a small bungalow apartment in Miami's South Beach where the woman who would become my mother lived for a year. It's a known quantity. It has to be.

3

I'm idling illegally in a rental car in front of a fire hydrant when Nick steps out of his apartment building. He is carrying a gray Armani bag that he bought a few weeks ago at a sample sale in midtown. It's fashion-forward and eye-catching, and it's slung over his shoulder messenger style.

I honk to get his attention. He has the *Times* in his hand, and he skims the headlines as he descends the five steps to the sidewalk. He doesn't pause. He doesn't glance up. The sound of my honking horn doesn't penetrate his consciousness at all. When he reaches the sidewalk, he turns left to walk to the subway. I honk again, holding down the horn for so many seconds that the sound becomes uneven and trembles. Nick remains impervious. I'm not surprised. This is what New York does to you.

Even when someone is running down the street yelling your name, you rarely look up. You just assume they don't mean you—that they're trying to get the attention of another Tallulah—and calmly continue on your way. Among eight million other people, you tend to feel invisible. It's not always a bad thing.

I take off my seat belt, climb out of the car and catch up to Nick at the corner of Bleecker and Perry. I have to tap him on the shoulder to get his attention.

"Hey," he says warmly. "What are you doing over here?"

"Ambushing you," I explain.

Nick smiles. Ambush for him doesn't conjure up images of stagecoaches being intercepted and trains being robbed. It's a harmless word that he mistakes for a greeting. He looks at his watch and does a quick calculation. "I can only give you twenty minutes. I have a staff meeting at ten-thirty. Do you want to get a cup of coffee or is this one of those times when you need a second opinion? What is it? A dress you like or a gift for someone? You still haven't bought your dad a wedding present, have you?"

This is indeed the truth but it's so far away from the point that it doesn't bear thinking about. "What I have in mind is a little more time consuming," I say, tugging on his sleeve. We're now walking in the direction of the car.

"Then why don't we do this after work?" he suggests. "I have some notes I wanted to organize for the meeting."

"I wouldn't worry about organizing notes for the meeting."

Nick looks at me fondly. He's thinking of my disorganized life and the way I face future events unprepared. "Of course you wouldn't."

"No," I say, overlooking the condescension, "I meant *you* shouldn't worry about organizing notes for *your* meeting."

Mildly amused by my antics, he asks why he shouldn't worry about notes for his meeting. The literal meaning of ambush has yet to catch up with him.

"Because you're not going to it," I explain.

"Of course I'm going. I called it."

I shrug. "No, you're not. You're taking the day off."

Nick stops walking. He roots himself to the sidewalk in front of his apartment and looks at me with the first stirrings of annoyance. But that's okay. We are now a few feet away from the rental car. "Lou, I know you hate working at Stark but playing hooky for a day isn't the solution. You can't run away from your problems." He lays a hand on my shoulder. This is Nick struggling to be sympathetic. He has notes to organize and a meeting to preside over but he still wants to be there for me. Just not now. "Let's get together for dinner tonight—my treat—and talk about it."

I laugh. He is so earnest and sweet and so completely wrong. "I'm not running away from my problems and we're not playing hooky for a day. We're taking the rest of the week off." I walk to the car and open the door. "Hop in. We have miles to go before we sleep."

A light dawns in Nick's eyes. It's not understanding. He still has no idea what's going on, but he finally realizes that this is something new. This is not run-of-the-mill Tallulah neurosis. Run-of-the-mill Tallulah neurosis doesn't invest in a rental car. "What's going on?"

"Road trip."

"Road trip?" Dripping from his lips, the words sound almost foreign.

"Road trip: you, me and Interstate 95 laid out before us like a patient etherized on a table."

Nick shoves his hands into his pockets. He is tempted. The open road is very seductive. It's freedom and fresh air and sunshine glinting off your Wayfarers. "Lou, I can't go looking for America right now. I have to get to work."

There is regret in his voice, sad, poignant regret that he can't hide. I feed it. "Carpe diem, Nick," I say, stealing more words from dead poets.

Carpe diem is a phrase that other people use, and Nick examines me carefully. Now he sees it: the giddiness, the happiness, the jump-out-of-your-skin excitement. He relaxes enough to smile. "Since when does Tallulah West seize the day?"

"I'm a landowner," I announce proudly. The sentence sounds so sweet to my ears that I have to fight the impulse to say it again. "Do you know what that means?"

Nick thinks he knows the answer, but nothing today has

gone as expected, so he answers cautiously. "You own land?"

"I own land."

"You own land." It comes out as a statement but it is really a question: Since when do you own land?

"I own land. I'm a landowner."

He leans against the car door. He's not ready to hop in yet, but he's several steps closer. "That's excellent, Lou. Where?"

"North Carolina, just thirteen miles east of Asheville. I'm a Southerner, Nick, a landowning Southerner."

Laughing, he congratulates me on my new pedigree. "What are you going to do with it?"

"Stand on the edge of my land and be master of all I survey."

"And then?"

I shrug. "I don't know. Meet the other squires in the neighborhood. Maybe plant turnips and rotate them every three years."

"I'm really happy for you, Lou," he says, squinting against the sunlight that's dancing between the leaves of a tree.

"Then come with me. Run your toes through my grass. Dig your heels into my dirt. Take a deep breath of my fresh Southern air."

"God, I'd love to. But work is very busy right now."

Work is always busy for Nick and his sense of responsibility runs deep, but I'm confident I can root it out. Everything can be dug up and removed. "Call in sick.

You'll only be out three days. The world won't end in three days."

"We have a project due in a few weeks. My staff—"

"Fuck your staff."

These are harsh words and Nick stares at me with bug eyes. "What?"

"I said fuck your staff. They're a bunch of ungrateful self-centered whiners who don't appreciate what a great boss you are. So what if they have to do a little bit of work in your absence? Fuck them."

Nick is silent as he considers my argument. With unusual delicacy, I have understated the case. Nick's staff hates him. They dislike him with the fierce resentment that you save for a dictator or an evil stepmother and no matter what he does, what offerings he concedes or what concessions he offers, they treat him like shit. It's the great irony of his life that the diplomat's son can't broker peace among six squabbling underlings.

But it's not his fault. The men and women who work for Nick are contentious and irrational and fanatically attached to the belief that they should be the boss and that they should have the large corner office and that they should be allowed to take three-hour lunches. Even though they are working at one of the last dot-coms standing, they have an awful sense of entitlement. They are medical miracles, but they don't understand their condition. They're people living with artificial hearts who blame their doctor because they can't climb Kilimanjaro.

Any other boss would have given them their walking papers long ago. But not Nick. He has too much invested in the notion that you can pluck a chicken without ruffling feathers. As a baby, he suckled on the milk of conciliation and was swaddled in tact. His father taught him to worship at the altar of diplomacy, and just because his faith is flawed, he cannot renounce it. The more he's tested, the tighter he clings.

I look at him now leaning against the passenger side door of the rented red Toyota. He is wondering what this trip means. He doesn't know if agreeing to go is a cessation of hostilities or an admission of defeat. It's neither, of course. It's just a road trip to see a plot of land in North Carolina. You can imbue an experience with greater meaning but you can't change what it is. Symbolism only surrounds an object; it doesn't touch it.

"Come on, Nick," I say after a moment. It's too beautiful a day to stand out in the sun and brood about things you can't change. "I'm going to North Carolina whether you come or not. Please don't make me do this alone." I'm not begging yet, but my voice has taken on a distinct wheedling note and I'm about to start listing things that I've done for him. I don't want to resort to quid pro quo arguments, but I will if I have to. "Please."

He tilts his head as if he's still trying to decide, but the decision is made. I know it is. He's smiling broadly. "Who gets radio control?"

"All Nick radio—all you, all the time."

He pushes against the door and stands up straight. "All right, let me throw a few things into a bag and call the office."

I yell yippee and do a brief victory dance that is uncoordinated and sloppy and ostentatious enough to grab the attention of a passing elderly neighbor. She points her cane at me as she whispers something to her companion, and although I should feel self-conscious, I don't care. I have few worries this morning and so much energy that I could practically run down to Asheville on foot.

I link my arm through Nick's and walk with him up the stairs. "Have I mentioned that I'm a landowner?" I say. "I own land. I'm now like the great impoverished nobility that dot the European countryside: land rich and cash poor. I'll probably have to marry off my daughter to the evil industrialist whose land borders mine on the south to get my farm out of arrears."

4

We are approaching the Thomas A. Edison rest stop on the New Jersey Turnpike when Nick shows interest in my plan.

"How long do you think it'll take us to get there?" he asks as I pull into the parking lot. Although I know absolutely nothing about the migration patterns of the Americanus Travelerus, I'm surprised by the number of cars in the lot. We have to settle for a spot off to the side.

I turn off the car, open the door and step out onto Jersey tarmac. Even that feels good. "I have no idea."

"Well, how many miles is it?"

I shrug. "It depends."

Nick nods. This makes sense. "What are our options?"

"I'll let you know as soon as I take a look at a map. That's why we're here: to buy a map and some Goldfish."

He holds the door open for me. "Goldfish?"

"You know, those small Pepperidge Farm crackers in the shape of fish," I explain, making a beeline for the gift shop. "And feel free to pick up whatever else you want. We're not stopping for lunch until we're halfway there."

"Where's that?"

I take off my sunglasses. "Like I said, I'll let you know as soon as I take a look at a map." I pass a Chee•tos display and take two bags—regular and cheesy cheese flavor. I hand them to him. "Here, why don't you be in charge of perishables. I'm going to go find a tent and a flashlight."

Nick follows me. "A tent?"

I add a box of Oreos to his pile and nod. "A tent. I think they should be over there by the lanterns."

"We're camping?"

"I'm a landowner, Nick."

"Yes, I got that part."

"I own land."

"Yep, I'm pretty sure I got that part, too."

I stop in front of a rack of potato chips and consider my options. I settle on plain chips. I don't like cottage-style. "The point of this trip it to be with my land. That's why we're camping. We're going to lie on my soil. We're going to sleep under my stars. We're going to be protected by a canopy of my trees. We're going to be eaten alive by my mosquitoes."

Nick laughs and suggests that we pick up some bug repellent while we're here. He doesn't quite understand any of this but he's perfectly happy to go along with the program. "You're very possessive all of a sudden."

I shrug. "I'm a landowner," I say, as if this explains everything. I know it doesn't. I know that it explains absolutely nothing at all but it's the only answer I have. I'm a landowner. I own land.

Nick wanders off to find a basket for all the perishables, and I look for tents among the basic survival gear. There are first-aid kits and road atlases and pocketknives but no tents. I grab a map and meet Nick by the cash register. He's reaching into his wallet to pay for the provisions but I head him off. I jump in front of him and stick my credit card under the saleswoman's nose. She takes it with an annoyed glance in my direction.

"This entire adventure is on me," I say as I scribble my signature on the sales receipt. "My property, my expense."

Because it goes against Nick's grain to accept a free ride, I expect an argument. I expect a heated dispute in which he insists on paying his own way, but he agrees easily and offers to carry the shopping bags. I hand them to him and open the door. The stale air of New Jersey hits us smack in the face. It's beautiful.

When we get to the car, I unlock the doors and toss Nick the keys. While he adjusts the mirrors and plays with the seat, I unfold the map of the United States. It's large and cumbersome and missing the sort of detail we'll need to find Twin Lakes, North Carolina, but it's a start.

"All right," I say, running a finger from Manhattan to Asheville, "we want to go south."

Nick doesn't respond. He's trying to find an acceptable radio station among the country and oldies choices that dominate the dial. The car has a CD player and we both brought a wide selection of discs, but it's too soon to abandon the public airwaves. We're only thirty-seven minutes outside of New York.

"What'd you tell Stark?" Nick asks after he settles briefly on a rock station playing a grunge tune he likes. As soon as the song finishes, he'll start fiddling again. This is his way. This is why every car trip we take is a battle for radio dominance.

I fold up the map the way I think it's supposed to go and stick it in the glove compartment. The road to Asheville is simple and straightforward and doesn't vary until miles after Richmond. "I imagine the same thing you told your people."

He smiles slyly, and for a moment he looks dark and mysterious. "That you're having your appendix removed?"

"God, no. I went for something a little more tame— E. coli poisoning."

"A wise choice," he says, nodding with approval. "Depending on the severity of the case, you can be out for a week or just a day."

"Not like appendicitis, which requires a hospital stay and leaves a scar." I take off my shoes, cross my legs and turn to face him. "What were you thinking?"

"That it had to be convincing or I'll never hear the end of it. They'll stand by the door to my office—because that's what they do now, they make sure I'm within earshot—and complain about how the boss man gets to call in sick whenever he wants but when they do it they need a note from the doctor."

"Do they need a note from the doctor?"

"It's company policy to get notes if they're out sick for more than five consecutive days, but I'd never enforce it."

"They really talk about you right in front of your door?"

"Yep, they've streamlined the gossip process. This way I don't have to hear how much they hate me through the grapevine. If only they could turn that eye for efficiency to the job, we might be able to stay in business a little longer."

Every six months Nick has to meet with the music television network he works with and remind them why they need a Web site. He's forced to defend a value-added endeavor to bottom line executives.

A Madonna song comes on and Nick takes another frustrating trip around the dial. I'd rather listen to news than the gobbledygook of passing stations.

"You should just fire the whole stinking lot of them," I say. It's something I think often but usually keep to myself. Nick knows how I feel.

"It's very complicated," he says evasively. "You're not management, so you don't know what it's like. You can't just fire the people you hate."

"No, I'm not management but I'm a—"

"I know, you're a landowner."

"Actually, I was going to say employee but this is also true. I am a landowner."

Nick laughs and changes the subject. He's never comfortable talking about office stuff. "Speaking of this land, where did it come from? You haven't mentioned how you became a landowner."

"Mom left it to me. Apparently I've been a landowner for four years," I say, launching into an explanation of how I found the envelope and concluding with the conversation I had last night with my dad. "He says he told me what it was at the time but he must have given it to me, like, three days after she died. My memory of that first week is sketchy. Actually, all I remember is that her coffin was brown and shiny."

"Why'd your mom buy land in North Carolina?"

That is the logical follow-up question. Mom wasn't a real estate speculator and she had no interest in property values. "About six years ago, she and Dad had been visiting a client of his in Asheville when she saw the property and instantly fell in love. Mom always wanted a house on a quiet spot by a lake," I say, remembering how she never got the hang of the Hamptons. There were always too many people hovering in their Manolo Blahniks. "Actually, now that I think about it, I have a vague memory of her telling me something about property in North Carolina. But then she got sick and the lake house got lost in the shuffle."

Nick nods slowly as he plays with the radio dial. "What do you want to do with it?"

I shrug, suddenly feeling melancholy and alone. No matter how many years pass, you always want your mother. It doesn't grow less keen. It doesn't grow less frequent. The only thing that changes is your ability to deal with it. "Own it," I say. "Revel in the unholy act of possession. As a New York City dweller who lives in a box—and don't get me wrong, I *love* my box—I find the thought of having a piece of earth that is mine and mine alone to be extremely appealing. Maybe I'll start an artist colony or build a log cabin with timber I cut down myself. I don't know. Anything is possible now. I own land."

The car in front of us slows down and Nick puts on his blinker to change lanes. Traffic is flowing nicely and we are already at exit 12. Just a dozen more until we hit Delaware.

"Snack time," I announce, reaching into the back seat for the bag of goodies. "All right, what do you want for breakfast? We've got Goldfish, Chee•tos, potato chips or Oreos. I'm going to start with the Oreos, move on to the Chee•tos and finish with a nice side of chips."

"What, no Goldfish?"

"I'm saving them for lunch."

"I thought we were stopping for lunch at the halfway point."

"We are. But I'll be hungry way before that."

"And where is that?"

"Where is what?"

"The lunch at the halfway point."

"I don't know."

"You said you'd tell me as soon as you got the map."

"I forgot to look."

"Well, look now."

"Fine," I say, reaching for the glove compartment, "but meanwhile keep your eyes peeled for a Wal-Mart or a Target."

"Why?" His fingers are around the dial again, and brief snatches of music and talk assault me from the speakers.

"We still don't have a tent. We can't go camping without a tent. And here"—I reach into his Armani messenger bag and pull out the first jewel case I touch—"put this in. I can't stand listening to you listen to the radio."

5

We stop in Dinwiddie, Virginia, for lunch. The restaurant Nick picks is a truck stop called the Sandman. It's a roadside diner that sells greasy French fries, oil-soaked onion rings and hamburgers so rare they drip with juice. This is not the fare I requested. It's not the fried green tomatoes and hush puppies and grits that we Southerners always eat, but it's good food and it's filling and it leaves me with a contented smile on my face. I give Nick a thumbs-up and don't complain when he flips compulsively through Dinwiddie's radio stations. Even with one of his favorite CDs in the player, he has to take a random sampling of what the town has to offer.

We are back on the road for almost an hour before I spot a Wal-Mart off I-85. The building is wide and flat and ugly. It's a squat structure that sits on a vast concrete plain like a large rock in the desert and offers up insults to the sun. This is what happens when you put function before form. These cinder-block bunkers and steel-corrugated boxes are what you get when you don't strike a balance between usefulness, practicality and beauty. But this store is not a statement or an architectural achievement. It's just a place to buy tents and pressboard furniture, and I can accept that. My eyes don't have to meet beauty everywhere they turn. They don't always have to be amazed and humbled by the simple perfection of other people's ideas.

As we walk in, Nick snags a shopping cart. He has had several hours now to digest my plan and he's written a shopping list of his own made up of things other than Goldfish and tents.

"We need toilet paper," he says, strolling briskly down the book aisle. Here are paper goods but not the ones he's looking for. "Or I should say, you need toilet paper. Being a man, I've pretty much got that one covered."

Nick is smiling smugly. There are few times when he's able to claim biological superiority and I let this one slide. "Fine, but don't pee in the corner like you're marking your territory."

"All right, how about I pee in the corner like I'm peeing in the corner?"

We walk by bright red tomatoes and fresh ears of sweet corn and Golden delicious apples looking golden and delicious. This is a Super Wal–Mart and we have wandered into the section that makes it super.

Nick sees me eyeing the corn and hands me a plastic bag. "Here, go get a few ears. And pick up some bell peppers and portobello mushrooms while you're at it. I'll find hot dogs, buns and relish."

I take the bag but stare at him, confused. He's pulling together a barbecue, that much is obvious, but I don't know how. "You understand that it's a completely empty lot? There aren't going to be barbecue pits and other campers there."

He hands me his list. "Item number four."

Of course his list is numbered. "Hibachi grill."

"Item number five."

"Charcoal."

He holds out his palm and I return the sheet of paper. "Now, without further questioning of the grand plan, would you like mustard on your hot dogs?"

I nod and watch him walk off with the shopping cart.

Although the produce section is crowded with shoppers and their small children, it's easy to navigate around them. The area is large and airy and there's enough space for small vehicles to zip by. I enjoy the novelty. My Gristedes on West Fourth is a nightmare of claustrophobic aisles and bruised, dented fruit. Frustrated and annoyed customers squeeze by you with inadequate plastic baskets hanging from their arms.

I pick an assortment of vegetables and run Nick to

ground in the toy aisle. He is standing in front of the board games with an expression of deep consternation on his face. When he sees me, he smiles. He almost seems relieved. "Pick one: Monopoly or Scrabble."

"Scrabble."

He throws it into the cart and wheels away. Next stop: sleeping bags.

Almost an hour later, we meander over to the checkout lines. In our shopping cart we have much more than a tent and a flashlight. We have enough provisions to last us forty days in the desert.

Nick piles some of our stuff onto the counter. The man at the cash registers runs the tent and the sleeping bags through and gives me the total.

"Oh, wait, there's more," I say, pointing to the cart, which is still full. I try to unload the Hibachi but Nick has suddenly become possessive.

"Uh-uh. Camping is your adventure. Barbecuing is mine. Here"—he hands me the flashlight; this is his concession—"you can pay for that."

The flashlight is made of thin pink plastic and barely costs five dollars. I take it and add it to my bill as a matter of principle, but I'm far from appeased. I make a mental note of Nick's total.

"I'm going to pay you back," I say as we roll the cart to the car. "Maybe not today, maybe not tomorrow but someday and then for the rest of your life."

Nick laughs, unconcerned by my threat. "Don't knock

yourself out trying to stick singles into the back pocket of my jeans. It's not worth it."

As we approach the car, I pop the trunk. It floats open. "This shouldn't cost you anything. You're my guest."

"Guest shmest. I'm a man. We're going camping. My inner caveman demands that I stand over an open fire with charred tongs in my hand. I grill, therefore I am. You shouldn't have to subsidize my biological imperatives." He whips out a camera and holds it up. "Now say cheese."

Behold Homo Campicus with camera. I don't pose. I don't say cheese. I simply throw both sleeping bags into the trunk of the car with a disgruntled look in his general direction. Nick snaps a photo—an action shot.

"I should at least pay for the camera," I grumble, once again behind the wheel. "It's my trip you're documenting."

But he ignores me. He's flipping through the Twin Lakes housing brochure, enthralled by the sample houses that can be easily assembled on the property. He holds up the colonial. "I think my grandmother has this one."

There is nothing remarkable about the colonial. It's a house. It's where people live. "The first thing I'd do is knock out that side wall and add a sun porch. Then I'd raise the roof about twenty feet and make a cathedral ceiling. Oh, and I'd put in a skylight, one of those Richard Meier porthole things."

"Excellent," he said, with a nod of his head. Then he flips the page: the immortal split level. "And this one?"

"Expand the kitchen by twenty square feet, put in textured aluminum laminate cabinets and polished concrete counters, add a reflecting pool and replace the bay windows in the dining room with uninterrupted floor-to-ceiling glass. I'd also install a glass dome on top of the garage and turn it into a library."

Nick shows me the next one. It's like we're running through flashcards, only of midcentury American track homes instead of multiplication times tables.

I glance quickly at the ranch and try to think of ways to modernize it. "Tear the whole thing down and build Mies van der Rohe's Barcelona Pavilion, only with a kitchen and one and a half baths."

He laughs and turns the page. When I finish remodeling each and every house, he returns to the first page. He starts at the beginning and has a go at them himself. This passes the time nicely and it so thoroughly engrosses Nick that he forgets to play with the radio for more than an hour.

6

It's twilight when we reach the Twin Lakes development. Nick stops the car and insists that I get out for a picture with the Welcome To sign, but I'm momentarily disconcerted. I've been arguing so vehemently against the political viability of Disneyism that I don't realize we're there.

"What?"

"Get out and stand by the sign." He's already on the side of the road lining up his shot. "This is for posterity, so make it good. Try to look like a landowner."

There are petunias and impatiens around the base of the sign and I carefully avoid crushing them. "I embody landownerness," I say, squinting at the setting sun. "It's not something I have to work at."

After the photo shoot, we return to the car and enter

Twin Lakes. I let Nick drive because I want to be unencumbered. I want to be free to look left and right and behind. There are butterflies in my stomach and I'm suddenly anxious. I close the air-conditioning vent because I'm shivering from nerves.

Twin Lakes is a winding development, and we twist and turn on Bald Eagle Lane for several miles before finding Robin Drive. The streets are quiet and shaded. Most of the houses are set back from the road and all you see are streetlights, mailboxes and driveways.

Nick stops the car. He turns to me and takes my hand. "Ready?'

I take a deep calming breath. There's no reason for me to be nervous. There's no reason for my heart to be jumping at this accelerated pace, but it is. This is just land. This is just a small plot of earth that Mom owned for a few years.

She never lived here. She never built a home here. She never planted turnips or parsnips in this fertile soil and watched them grow. She just stood here on the edge of a quiet lake and felt at home.

I squeeze his hand and let go. "Ready."

Nick presses gently on the gas and we creep around the curve. You can't miss lot 46F. It's the only plot of land completely covered with trees and underbrush and flowering dandelions. I get out of the car and walk into the forest, my forest, sheltered by wide flat leaves that sway in the wind. Shards of light from the setting sun filter through the canopy, falling warmly on my arms and bathing the coppice in an emerald glow. This is what my mother left me: a green wood.

I find a small clearing a good distance from the road and call to Nick, who is standing by the car. "Here," I shout loudly, my voice traveling up to the treetops and perhaps to the neighbors, "we're making camp here."

Then I run back to the car and give him a hug. He has a sleeping bag in each hand, and he has to drop them both in order to catch me. Nick wraps his arms around me and holds me close, and for a moment I'm ridiculously happy he's here. I could have done this on my own. I could have driven down to North Carolina in a red rental car all by myself, but it's so much better this way.

"Thanks," I say, feeling grateful and moved and closer to Nick than I ever have before.

He shrugs it off with a smile. "Hey, thank you for getting me out of a very boring meeting." Then he picks up the sleeping bag and walks toward to the campsite. "Did you see the lake?"

"Not yet." I take the tent out of the trunk and a gallon of water. "Let's set up camp before it gets dark and then go exploring. And I think we should move the car off the road. I noticed as we drove in that nobody has their car on the street."

The tent is round and nylon and easily erected once you figure out how to put the poles together and where exactly they go. I hammer in the stakes while Nick shoots pictures and laments the lack of a video camera.

When the tent is up and stable, I reach for the camera. "Here, let me document the barbecuing."

Nick takes the Hibachi out of the box, puts it on the blue plastic folding table he picked up at Wal-Mart and holds the bag of briquettes in his arms. He's posing for the before shot. This is how he sets up the grill, arranging a composition and stopping every few minutes for me to immortalize it.

When he's done, he suggests that we look at the lake before lighting the fire. I agree. It's almost completely dark now.

Tallulahland is dense but small and the lake is only a few dozen yards away. We reach the muddy bank and look out onto the water. The lake is large and calm and dotted with decks and speedboats. Across the way, I can see kids diving off a wooden raft anchored several feet from shore. Their laughter is distant and dim and can barely be heard above chirping birds. From this vantage point, I can see easily into the backyard of my neighbor to the east. Someone has hung red paper lanterns around their deck like Christmas garland.

I breathe deeply and calmly and sit quietly with Nick on the bank until the light is gone and then negotiate a path back to camp. Because we are camping in the middle of a development, it isn't completely dark. There is light from the street and light from the neighbor's back porch and light from cars that pass every five minutes or so. I sit down at the table to watch Nick's inner caveman work and to take photographs whenever the spirit moves me.

The chair, covered with plastic strips, is uncomfortable and wobbly on the uneven ground, but I don't mind. I'm feeling a rare sort of happiness that is anaerobic and self-sustaining and perpetually in motion.

The fire crackles and charcoal smoke wafts my way. Nick shouts with satisfaction. "Yes! I knew if I just kept adding lighter fluid, sooner or later a fire would take hold—and voilà!"

"Does that mean dinner is soon?" I ask, reaching for the bag of potato chips. Our last meal was hours and hours ago.

"It's imminent. Just as soon as this fire heats up, we're ready to go. But I'll take a chip in the meantime."

While the charcoals heat up, Nick takes a beer from the cooler and sits down next to me. He listens to the sound of distant cars and crickets for a moment. "Do you think the neighbors know we're here?"

I shrug. I hadn't thought about anyone but the two of us in a while. We are in the middle of suburbia but it feels isolated and rural and far from the madding crowd. "I don't know. I imagine we must make a picture with our tent and our blue Wal-Mart furniture."

"I feel like we're on a movie set," Nick says, taking a sip of beer, "and any second now the stage manager is going to shut off the lights and tell us to go home. It's the details. They're so precise they feel fake."

"But they can't send us home," I say. "I own this land."

"That's right. You're a landowner."

"I'm a landowner," I repeat softly.

Nick puts down his beer and gets out of his seat. "The coals are probably hot enough by now. Do you want to peel the corn or wash the vegetables?"

"I'll do the corn."

"Excellent." He hands me the bag.

Nick and I don't often cook together but we know each other's rhythm and how to keep out of the way. Dinner is perfect. The hot dogs are burnt and the corn takes so long to cook that we have it for dessert but these things are inconsequential. An hour later we are throwing water onto the coals and patting ourselves on the back.

When dinner is cleared, we play Scrabble by the light of the lantern, drink beer and make up stories about the neighbors. Nick soundly trounces me in the first game, but I call for a rematch and manage to put down a seven-letter word.

"Herbist?" he asks, as I lay down the tiles.

I look up. "One who studies herbs."

"That's an herbalist," he says.

"Prove it."

But he can't. He failed to pick up a dictionary at Wal-Mart.

"In that case," I say, in the indignant silence that follows, "that's eleven points, plus a double word score, plus my fifty-point bonus." I do the quick calculation in my head. "That's seventy-two points total." I lean over to read the score by the light of the lantern. "Does that put me in the lead?"

Nick doesn't answer. He's still staring at me with outrage. Then he leans forward, brushes a strand of hair out of my eyes and presses his lips against mine. He presses his lips against mine and opens his mouth and kisses me.

This is crazy. This is absolutely insane and impossible and completely without precedent. I pull away and examine him with suspicion. "What are you doing?"

But this isn't some tactic to win the game. This isn't some ploy to throw off my concentration. Nick is grinning at me foolishly. "I'm not sure. You figure it happens early or not at all."

"Yes," I say, because that's exactly how I figure it happens. You don't do this. You don't find yourself in a green wood suddenly lusting after friends.

"But that's completely wrong," he announces, not at all concerned by the topsy-turvy nature of his thoughts or his actions. "It's thoroughly and completely wrong because here we are. I had an inkling this morning when you shanghaied me on the way to work—why else would I ditch an important meeting to go traipsing across country with you—but it was nothing compared with this thing that's been snowballing inside me all day."

I stare at his intense eyes and his foolish endearing grin, fighting this breathless feeling. This is Nick. This is familiar, reliable Nick who wants me to have a healthy relationship with my father and do something useful with my life. But it isn't. Not really. The man before me is beautiful and seductive and not quite a stranger. I've always known that Nick has a magnetic allure that draws women—the dark hair, the cerulean blue eyes, the uncertain grin. I've caught glimpses of it out of the corner of my eye in crowded Soho bars, but he's never aimed it at me before. He's never turned his tazer onto "full charm" and pointed it in my direction. "Why now? Why at all?"

"After years of my having to push you forward, you're pulling me along. It's novel." He kisses me again, longer and deeper and with his intentions clear. "It's irresistible."

I'm finding him hard to resist myself but I know this change is temporary. I know it's just a short-term phenomenon. I'm a falling comet and he's a stargazer who doesn't realize that something like this happens only once every seventy-six years. "It will go away," I assure him. "I'm still an inert object."

"No"—he's so close now his breath is on my cheek—"you're not."

I want to close my eyes and block him out, but I can't. I can't do anything but stare at him with a pounding heart. "Yes, I am."

"No, you're not." He pulls me toward him and looks me deeply in the eyes. "You're a landowner."

There are several logical arguments that can be made in response to this, but they are useless right now. We can debate and argue and quibble over the details until the fire has gone out, but in the end he's correct. I am a landowner. I am a landowner who makes bad choices and does stupid things and wastes weeks and sometimes months in relationships with the wrong people. I have a history of this. I have a well-documented past that supports this sort of behavior, which is why it's no surprise that despite misgivings and doubts and qualms that will not be squashed, I follow him into the tent.

"I forgot to light the mosquito coils," Nick says. He's trying to sit up and correct the oversight, but I won't let him. I'm not ready yet for him to move. I'm too comfortable. My head is resting on his warm chest and I can hear a steady, reassuring *thump thump.* This is what I miss—the sound of a heart beating beneath my ear.

"Please, I forgot to brush my teeth and wash my face and I'm pretty sure I brought some zit cream with me, which I forgot to dot on my face," I say, running through a litany of things that hadn't been done thanks to the seismic shift in our relationship.

Nick laughs and stops squirming. He throws his arm over his head, sighs deeply and pulls me closer. Outside, the wind blows gently and the shadow leaf patterns on the roof wave and flutter. The full moon is bright and has turned the dull gray of the tent a shimmery silver shade. I stare at it, wondering why I'm not wondering what I've done.

"When was the last time you went camping?" I ask to distract myself. I don't want to think about this. I don't want to analyze and dissect my sudden fearlessness. It's a new experience that I don't want to end. Not yet. Not now while I'm listening to Nick's heart beat steadily beneath my ear.

"Two years ago," he says. "My brother and I went up to Acadia National Park in Maine. We took a boat to some beautiful island miles from civilization and hiked for three days. I think it was fun, but to be honest all I remember are the mosquito bites. The left side of my face, from temple to chin, was covered with them, and not since chicken pox in third grade have I felt such an insane need to itch. God, how I wanted to scratch my face off."

"Is that when you discovered mosquito coils?"

"Oh, no. We used mosquito coils. The Townsend men never travel into the wild without mosquito coils."

"Then why do you bother lighting them?"

He shrugs. "It's like lighting a votive in church. It throws a pretty light and there's always the off chance that some god is listening. What about you?"

"Oh, I don't believe in the mosquito gods."

"No, I mean, when was the last time you went camping?"

This should be weird. This conversation should be

awkward and stilted and dotted with painful silence, but it's not. It's normal and comfortable and precisely the kind we would be having if things hadn't shifted seismically. Even if our clothes hadn't been scattered throughout the tent, in a haze of passion, we'd be lying in the dark talking about the last time we went camping.

"EuroDisney, six years ago," I say, recalling the experience clearly. It had been an awful misadventure, the sort that keeps you out of tents for the rest of your life. "My friend Anna, who was a whiz at saving a pound and stretching a pound, had coupons for the campground at EuroDisney. Pay for one night, get the second night free. So we took the bus from London to Bournemouth, picked up her car at her parents' house and drove to Disney via Ostend and Brussels. It was April and still cold and no matter what we did, we couldn't get warm. So we shivered and shook for the first night—I had her dad's old army sleeping bag but it made no difference. It must have dropped into the thirties that night—and then spent the second night in the laundry room on the campground. The heat was nice and so was the shelter from the wind but around four in the morning we started to feel like prisoners of war. The lights were glaringly bright and they pump country music into the room twenty-four hours a day. Isn't that what we did to Noriega?"

Nick laughs. "And that proves my point."

I'm disconcerted by this. There are no points in the

tent, only imperfect memories and leaf shadows on the ceiling and conversations that should be awkward but aren't. "What?"

"Disneyism: controlled artificial experience. People will embrace it."

My neck is stiff and I move my head to the hollow of his shoulder. "How so?"

"Being a real POW sucks," he says reasonably.

"That's not the point."

"Okay, but if we can replace all the bad in the world with painless imitations, people won't care when we replace the good. Desensitivity—it's the wave of the future."

"What's this we?" I ask, yawning loudly. "You speak as if you're their candidate for president."

"Oh, I'm not a believer. I'm all for the wide range of human experience. I just think people will embrace it."

"Give it up," I say, closing my eyes.

And he does. Twenty minutes later.

7

In the morning I am stiff. My right arm is numb from the weight of my body and my shoulders are achy. I stretch gently and slide out of the sleeping bag, careful not to wake Nick, who is sleeping soundly. It's warm in the tent. The air is thick and oven-baked and the back of my neck is covered with droplets of sweat. Despite the blanket of trees overhead, the sun is stealing through. It is dropping onto the tent and making patterns on the roof.

I throw on boxer shorts and a gray T-shirt and look at Nick. He is lying on his back. His arms are folded over his chest like a mummy's and his breathing is evenly spaced and regular. He seems as dear and familiar as always, and I wait for a wave of regret to wash over me. But it doesn't. I'm completely without remorse and I leave him there undisturbed. As soon as I unzip the tent, fresh cool air rushes in.

Outside, I slip on my mules, pick up the unlined pad we used for score keeping the night before and wander to the lake. It's early. The day has scarcely begun and nobody is awake except me and the ducks and a few green beetles skimming the edge of the water. In a little while I will want coffee and a bathroom with walls and running water but right now I'm content. Right now it's enough to sit on the bank and watch ducks float by in the morning sun. I like the peace and the tranquillity and the way everything has stopped for a moment. This is the still point of the turning world; you can't fall off here. There are no edges to slip over. There are no steep cliffs to tumble down. It is all gentle slope.

I could stay. I could chop wood, fish in the lake, grow vegetables, build an outhouse with rudimentary flushing, and stay forever in this small forest a dozen miles outside of Asheville, North Carolina.

The thought makes me smile. Tallulah West living deliberately, fronting only the essentials of life, and learning what the woods have to teach.

Next door, a woman in a fluffy white bathrobe steps out onto her red-lanterned deck with a steaming cup of coffee, reminding me just how much I like the inessentials. She sees me relaxing by her lake in my T-shirt and boxer shorts and waves. After I return the friendly gesture, she slides back inside the house, perhaps to call the police and report a trespasser.

Even the prospect of being hauled down to the police station for questioning doesn't disturb my serenity. Here in this green wood I'm far removed from worry. The random malice of Marcos Medici doesn't exist. Jeffrey's aggressive sales style is a figment of my imagination. Carol is only an unconfirmed rumor. These are albatrosses and without them anything is possible. For the first time in five weeks, ideas are flowing freely and I make rough sketches as they occur to me. Designs that I had given up on suddenly seem rife with potential. This is worth holding on to. Any place that can make you feel alive is worth clinging to with both hands.

I close my eyes and see the land without Walden-size expectations littering the yard—a cozy wooden shack with a refrigerator and thick yellow insulation and a claw-foot porcelain tub that sometimes gets clogged.

There are arguments for why this won't work. There are reasons for why moving here is an insane decision, but I can't hear them. They're hoarse cries in a stadium full of cheering fans and their voices are drowned out. Why shouldn't I do this? Why shouldn't I sit by a quiet lake and draw all day?

The peace runs so deep it reminds me of the shaded meadow where Mom is buried. Dad and I were with her on the midsummer afternoon she picked it out. Neither one of us wanted to go but Mom was insistent and resolute and determined to be practical. Something about choosing a grave site gave her a sense of power. It was a meager thing—a torch against a pack of wolves—but it felt good. She seemed almost like her old self as she told the cemetery salesman that she wanted the cheapest plot. He tried talking her out of it. He showed her pictures of their more expensive, pastoral locations, but Mom was having none of it. She was adamant. She was strong. She was alive.

"All right," the man said with a sigh, handing over a map of the cemetery with our new family plot circled in red. "But please take a look at it before you sign any papers."

Mom agreed but she was only humoring him. She couldn't imagine how it would matter to a dead woman where she was buried. But then she got to the plot. Then she saw the train tracks and the dead trees and the weeds that were as high as her knees and started to laugh. It was a thick laugh, a forceful laugh, a well-woman laugh and tears started welling up in my eyes. I looked over at my father and knew he was thinking the same thing: Maybe, oh, God, just maybe, she was finally getting better.

"It doesn't matter but it does matter," she said in between bouts of laughter. "I don't want to be buried here."

Dad and I started laughing, too—from relief, from nerves, from genuine amusement. The Wests were never a real family. We were always a rickety kitchen table that was missing a leg. But on that day we got it right and I was so happy I could barely breathe.

That intense happiness wouldn't last but I didn't know it yet. Nor did I know that Mom was almost dead or that my father was about to abandon me. But this is how it works—the earth is always bathed in gold just seconds before the sun disappears.

I'm wondering how you relocate your whole life when I notice my neighbor. She is now wearing a pink dress and walking toward me at a rapid clip. I stand up.

"Hi, I'm Mrs. Lydia Costello. I live at 1421, next door," she says, as if I haven't just watched her entire approach. "Are you the owner of this property?"

"Yes, I am," I say, unsure of how to proceed. Should I offer my hand? Should I introduce myself? Her response is swift and precludes further action on my part.

"Thank gawd! My husband and I were terrified that they had started renting out this property as a campground." Then, afraid that she might have given me an idea, she says, "Not that turning your land into a private campground is legal. County Ordinance 546 prohibits it. You can look that up in the sheriff's office if you don't believe me."

There is something about her manner that convinces me that if Ordinance 546 doesn't already exist, it will by the end of the day.

"Are you and your husband moving here?" she asks, looking over my shoulder.

Husband? I follow her gaze. "Oh, you mean Nick. He's just a friend," I say while an unexpected blush overtakes my cheeks. I'm not embarrassed about last night. I'm not ashamed about what happened between me and Nick, but her manner makes me uncomfortable. There's something about her shuttered gaze and her pursed lips and her jumping squirrel nose that drives the truth home: Last night with Nick doesn't exist. Not really. Not in the world where people work and pay bills and stand stoically still while their doctor tells them the bad news. Last night is a bubble. It's a wonderful, special, floating bubble that drifts gently above our heads and is seconds away from popping. But it's not Lydia Costello's fault. She's just the first sharp point to cross my path.

"Of course. It's so confusing. I saw just the one tent, you see, and drew the obvious conclusion."

I'm feeling defensive. I'm feeling judged and found wanting but I fight the urge to protest. It's none of her business. "To answer your question, I don't know what I'm going to do. At the moment, I'm just checking out the property," I explain, although I'm already several steps ahead. Now the cabin has a sun-dappled garden and friendly duck visitors.

"Checking out the property? Hmm. Well, I hope you don't make a practice of camping like this. There is no ordinance per se against camping on your own property, at least, not that I know of, but we do have very strident public decency laws and this is a family neighborhood. I trust you've made arrangements to deal with the…" Her lips tighten into a thin line as she tests and rejects words. "Shall we say *inconveniences* of the human body in a decent and civic-minded manner."

I'm tempted to play dumb. I'm tempted to tilt my head to the side and ask what inconveniences of the human body, but I take the high road. "Of course."

She doesn't believe me. I can tell from the way she bats her eyelashes and presses her lips, but she doesn't call me a liar. She restrains herself and wishes me a good day. "And you will call on me, Miss…"

"West, Tallulah West," I say, holding out my hand.

Either fearful of all human contact or mindful of those inconveniences just discussed, she waves her hand briefly near mine; we air-shake. "Do feel free to call on me for anything, Miss West. I always have a cup of sugar for a neighbor."

I thank her for her thoughtful offer, which seems either out of character or out of place—or perhaps both. She assures me that her generosity is nothing and returns to her house, pausing a few times to look quickly over her shoulder as if not quite sure that I'm real. After the third brief, embarrassed glance, I wave to prove my corporeality. I watch her scurry up the stairs to her deck.

When she is gone, I return to camp. Nick is sitting next to the tent with a cup of coffee reading the newspaper. This is the wilds of suburban North Carolina but he looks like he's sitting in a café on Bleecker Street and my heart beats faster at the sight.

"Where'd you get that?" I ask, eyeing the steaming paper cup with curiosity and suspicion and a heaping dollop of envy. The origins of the French roast are unclear and I can envision only two scenarios: The coffee came to him or he went to the coffee. But there is no evidence of a roving breakfast cart like the sort you see in the city and Nick is still undressed. He's lounging in a blue plastic chair in green boxer shorts with the *New York Times* on the ground to his left. His legs are crossed, in deference, no doubt, to Twin Lakes' strident public decency laws.

Nick looks up and shakes his head sadly. He's disappointed in me and perhaps my whole generation. Kids today. "From the coffeepot on the fire. You know, the rule in my house is the first one awake puts coffee on."

Ignoring his rules, which amount to little more than him doing what he wants when he wants—he is the only one in his house—I approach the stainless-steel coffeepot cautiously. It looks hot.

I'm about to lay my hand on its black handle when Nick sputters loudly. "For God's sake, Lou, use the potholder. Do you *want* to be a burn victim?"

Burn victim is not part of my plan, and I look around for the potholder, which is not in plain sight and whose existence is not the sort of assumption I would make. After a protracted search, I find it hiding under the bag of ground coffee beans below eye level. Although Nick is as silent as a church mouse, I know he is laughing at me. Ostensibly immersed in the Science section, he's watching me root around in the wilderness like I know what I'm doing and marveling at how I have no resources whatsoever. I have resources, of course. I have New York resources. I can bring a bridesmaid dress in for a final fitting at nine-thirty on a Thursday night and have the tailored product in my hands more than twenty-four hours before the big event on Saturday. It's not coffee brewing on burning coals, but it's another sort of survival skill. And I can learn others.

I pour coffee into a cup without pain or incident and sit in the other chair. Twin Lakes is waking up. Cars are driving by and I can see my neighbor on the other side loading her children into a beige minivan.

"So, what's on the docket for the day?" Nick asks. He lays the paper on his knees, leans forward and takes my hand. And I let him. This adventure is almost over, but it won't end badly. It won't wind up in a bout of tears or disgust with neither one of us knowing where to take shelter. This is different. My moving away is a loophole. It's not me dumping him. It's not him dumping me.

"Breakfast at a greasy spoon, then the sights of Asheville," I say.

"Excellent. I've never been to North Carolina before and was hoping to do a little sight-seeing. There must be an art museum and some historical society devoted to the culture of the Blue Ridge Mountains." He finishes his coffee and puts the cup on the ground on top of the

Metro section. A soft breeze blows the corners of the newspaper, knocking over the cup. It rolls under Nick's chair.

"Are we in the Blue Ridge Mountains? See? I know nothing about the area. How can I move here if I know absolutely nothing?" I say this casually, as if it isn't very important, but I know I'm dropping a bomb. I know I'm rolling down my window and tossing a Molotov cocktail into a busy city street.

"Move here?" he asks, stiffening his back. Then he lets my hand fall and looks down at the paper in his lap.

"Yes, move here," I say again, growing even more comfortable with the idea. And it's not a bad idea. Relocating to peaceful Twin Lakes is the right thing to do. It doesn't frighten me. It doesn't make me want to crawl under the covers and hide.

Nick continues to stare at the Science section with intense fascination. "U.S. Panel Backs Risky Effort to Save Grand Canyon Fish" is more interesting than me, but I don't care. I go forward with my presentation like a PowerPoint executive at the annual shareholders' convention. "Welcome to Tallulahland," I say, gesturing to the green wooded expanse that would soon be home. "I see a small log cabin by the lake. Nothing fancy, just a few rooms and studio made out of timber from my own land."

Another gentle breeze blows across the property, rattling the leaves and the newspaper and stirring Nick. He looks up. "You do know I'm not a lumberjack, don't you?" he says easily. "I can watch you chop down trees and document it with a camera—or even a camcorder if someone wants to buy me one—but I can't actually jack lumber." He's smiling pleasantly and squinting at the early-morning sun. He has the relaxed air of a carefree vacationer, but he can't fool me. I'm too familiar with his Townsend training to be hoodwinked by an adopted pose. Nick is relieved. Even now as he gazes up at me with mildly amused eyes, he's heaving a sigh of relief. He knows the truth as well as I: Despite last night's madness, we are still not each other's solution.

"What happened to your inner caveman?" I ask, glancing toward the heated coals that are crackling quietly. It's easier to look here than at Nick. Ending it now is the only thing to do, but it suddenly feels wrong. New relationships are small green sprigs. They're tiny shoots of life peeping out of the soil and they deserve better than to be smothered before you know what's growing: a flower or a weed.

"Making fire, hunting woolly mammoth, clubbing women on the head—that's the caveman code," he says, continuing in that unconcerned way of his. "There's no mention of chopping down trees."

"I didn't realize the code was so limited," I say. Then I suggest that we get dressed to end the conversation.

"Excellent idea," he says, popping out of his seat and walking to the tent. I'm undoing the zipper when the same thought strikes us both. Do we really want to be in the tent together?

"Um…ah, you know what? I meant to finish my coffee first." Nick steps away and stands by the fire. His movements are awkward and jerky and not part of his usual routine. I'm used to insouciance, not this strange uneasiness with its fits of starts and stops.

"I'm starving," I call from the tent, determined to act normally despite the extraordinary circumstances. "Also, I could use a bathroom. It's harder to find a secluded little spot in the middle of all this bright dazzling daylight."

8

When we return to base camp, it's almost seven o'clock. I'm wearing a thick cotton Hanes T-shirt that falls almost to my knees. It has a picture of a smiling Tommy the Tank Engine on it and says Great Smoky Mountains Railroad in big red letters. In my backpack is a sun visor decorated with a color drawing of Asheville's main street for Hannah. Nick resisted the lure of souvenirs, even a vase made by a local potter that I know his mother would love. The only things he spent his money on were food, admissions and a cup of coffee at the Asheville Botanical Gardens.

As soon as we get near the tent, I pull off the T-shirt. It's hanging off my frame like a heavy wool blanket and offers none of the comfort or freedom of a Gap baby T-shirt. It was an impulse buy. Not at all like Hannah's visor, which I debated and deliberated over for more than ten minutes.

"I think perhaps we should have dinner," Nick says, putting the grocery bags down on the table next to the grill, "and then consider going back into town for a drink. I saw a bar on Haywood that looked quaint and fun—if that sounds like something you'd like to do."

The day has been stilted and long. It's been stressful and weird, but we've managed to get through it without a painful discussion or useless emotion dripping through. This was effortless for Nick but hard for me—I am haunted by his look of relief. "Yes, I'd like to go into town. That's a very good idea. Thank you for suggesting it," I say, no more inclined than he to hang out by the scene of the crime.

Although this is an usual speech for me, Nick doesn't bat an eye. He nods and turns away to work on the fire. This is what we've been reduced to: treating each other with the cold hyperpoliteness of congressional members. Would the esteemed gentleman from Greenwich Village please pass the salt?

As I reach for a bottle of water, I notice a woman with a chocolate cake approaching the tent. She's vaguely familiar, and after a second I realize that I've seen her before. This morning she was packing her children into a beige minivan.

"Hi," she says, cheery and friendly in her khaki pleated shorts and pristine Reebok walking shoes. "I wanted to welcome you to the neighborhood, so here I am with the proverbial cake."

Because there is no Formica counter to lay the plate on, she holds it awkwardly for a moment before handing it to me. I'm instantly assaulted by the scent of Betty Crocker chocolate frosting. It's heavenly.

"This is so lovely of you," I say, genuinely taken aback by the niceness of the deed. "You really shouldn't have bothered yourself on my behalf."

"What bother?" she asks as if she truly doesn't know the meaning of the word. "You're going to live next door; we should know each other. In a year when you're collecting the newspaper from our stoop because John and I brought the kids to visit his parents in Raleigh for the weekend, is it going to be a bother? Of course not. It'll be neighborly."

I like her enlightened self-interest. I like the fact that her agenda is unfurled and waving proudly in the wind. It'll be ages before I have the white-picket fence, but I'm a good investment. I will pick up her mail for her when they're away and keep a spare key in my garage. "Nevertheless, this is a very kind gesture. I'm Tallulah West and this is my friend Nick Townsend."

"Lovely to meet you, Tallulah. And you, Nick. I'm Elyse Yankou. Me and my brood live in the house right there." She points to her house, a colonial that looks just like the picture of the model in the pamphlet. She even has the same curtains as the house in the photo. "We've been wondering who owned this land. It's always been a great mystery. Did you just buy it?"

"Actually, I inherited it from my mom."

Elyse is instantly contrite. "I'm sorry, dear. I shouldn't have brought it up. I'm too nosy. John is always saying so."

"It's all right. She died a few years ago."

"Well, that's just awful. She must have been very young. I see from your car that you're from New York." Her contrition is short-lived.

"Yes. We're from Manhattan."

"Ah, so you're city folk, used to the bright lights and fast pace. There's nothing for you kids to do around here."

That's part of the appeal but Elyse Yankou doesn't know that. "I don't think—"

"Do you have family in the area?" she asks.

"No, but that's not—"

She nods slowly. "City folk with no attachments. You don't want to live down here, do you? Don't worry. I have a solution."

"Solution?"

"Yes, John and I have always loved this property. We are good people who cherish the things we love. We'll give you ten thousand dollars for it. It's a fair price and you'd be—"

"Aha!"

The scream is high-pitched and squealish and it doesn't emanate from any of us. It comes from the tent, which is now bobbing erratically from the exertion of an angry woman trying to open the zipper. I look on in horror as Lydia Costello emerges from inside. Her eyes are glowing fiercely with anger as she whacks her neighbor with a red-and-white-checked dish towel.

"I knew it! I knew it! I knew it!" she shrieks in a tone of voice so high it's almost out of the range of human hearing. "When I saw you frosting that cake, I just knew it. You conniving bitch. You're not getting your grubby dishpan hands on my land."

"Your land?" Elyse Yankou throws back her head and laughs but she's not amused. "Your land. That's a good one. *This*"—her voice is now a sneer—"is my land. I saw it first: four days, twenty-two hours, thirteen minutes and fifty-five seconds first. Don't you *ever* forget it."

A vein pops out of Lydia's forehead. It's purple and thick and you can almost see the blood pounding through it. "I've taken care of it."

Elyse snorts in disgust and takes a step closer to Lydia, despite the dangers of a fitfully flinging dish towel. They are now nose to nose, like combative baseball player to umpire. "Taking peaches from the trees for your awful peach cobbler doesn't count."

Lydia flinches as if she's been struck with an open palm. She throws back her shoulder and with very calm and carefully enunciated words, she says, "My peach cobbler is not awful."

At a loss for what to do, I look to Nick, but he is useless. He's so entertained by this unexpected turn of events that he's doubled over with his arms clutched around his stomach. So much for his fine upbringing. So much for the diplomatic corps and their ethos of tact and conciliation. The first real crisis of his career and Mr. Diplomat's Son almost splits himself in half with hysterical laughter.

As my neighbors continue to hurl unending streams of insults at each other, I take Nick by the arm and pull him a few feet away. At the moment he's incapable of conversation and I wait patiently as the laughter rises and falls in his chest. Then I punch him in the arm.

"What the hell is going on?" I ask, keeping a wary eye on the two women, both of whom are now shouting at the top of their lungs. Although I can't see them, I know other neighbors are about. They're peeking out of their windows and slowing down their cars as they drive by.

Nick pulls himself together long enough to answer. "They both seem to want your land."

"I got that much. What do I do?"

His moment of clarity has passed and I have to wait for another one. He's like a drunk teetering on the brink of unconsciousness. "Find out how much."

This is not the suggestion I'm expecting. "What?"

He observes the play of emotions on my face—shock, dismay, interest—and abruptly stops laughing. He has to take several deep breaths to calm himself down but he manages to bring the relentless flow of guffaws to an end. "Appease them. Let them put in their bids. Then tell them you'll think about it and send them home. You don't have to take any of it seriously, but it won't hurt to listen."

Although there is something inherently painful now about the two women, I realize this is true and approach them warily. In order to get their attention I have to interrupt two tirades: one about a dog who shits on everyone's lawn and one about a window that someone's son broke with a baseball. These are old wounds. These are ancient insults that have been fed and watered and nourished for many growing seasons.

"All right, if you want to discuss buying my property, we can discuss buying my property but you're both going to have to calm down," I say in a normal speaking voice. I refuse to talk over them or shriek like a fishwife, so I rattle off a few nonsense sentences in this reasonable tone. My tactic works. Lydia and Elyse are like babies crying at the top of their lungs, and they settle down because of some nascent instinct to hear what the adult in the room is saying.

"If you both can behave yourselves, we will discuss the property in a rational manner," I continue. "If you can't, if you both start shouting and screaming again, I'm going to march across the street and offer the property to the neighbor with the pretty portico."

This threat works. The two women make eye contact and almost imperceptibly nod their heads in agreement. They can do this. They can work together if they have to in order to keep the coveted plot out of the hands of the woman across the street. Whatever this unrepresented third party has done, her trespasses equal more than a broken window and an untrained dog.

I start with Elyse because she brought me a chocolate cake and didn't treat me with pinched-lip suspicion. Apparently it is true. You can catch more flies with honey than with vinegar. "All right, Ms. Yankou, what's your offer?" I don't want to do this. I don't want to listen to them haggling over my wooded retreat like it's a chicken in a souk. I won't sell this place. I can't. Ideas flow freely here and Mom feels near. She feels remarkably near.

Elyse scrunches up her nose as she does quick calculations in her head. This isn't what she'd expected. This isn't what was supposed to happen. She only came by to drop off a cake. It was just a harmless errand. "Ten thousand."

Lydia is better prepared. She doesn't have to think. "Twenty thousand."

Elyse closes her eyes and runs through the figures a second time. Slowly she says, "Thirty thousand."

Lydia: "Forty thousand."

Elyse's fingers curl and she seems ready to choke her neighbor, but she reins herself in. She regains control of her emotions, factors in the kids' college funds and tries again. "Forty-five tho—"

"Fifty thousand."

Elyse turns away. She'd rather study the tent than look

at Lydia Costello, possessor of unlimited funds, destroyer of dreams. As much as she wants this land, as much as she wants to deprive her neighbor of it, she can't keep doing this. She can't keep increasing her bid in increments of ten thousand or even five thousand dollars. The Yankous don't have that sort of money, and lot 46F isn't worth a second mortgage on her home.

While Elyse Yankou tortures herself about things beyond her grasp, I think about things within reach. I have no idea how much this land is worth. There is some supply-and-demand formula, some calculation that divides the number of properties in the area surrounding Asheville by the number of people who want to own them, but that doesn't interest me. I'm measuring the value of the property in real terms: in studio space, in computers, in prototypes, in trade-show fees, in business cards and letterhead and envelopes that say Tallulah Designs. This wasn't my intention. This isn't where I planned to go. But suddenly I am here, at the edge of a precipice.

After she collects herself, Elyse turns around. She shifts her eyes from the gray nylon tent to the beet-red face of her arch nemesis. Something is different. Something has changed, and if you look closely you can see it in every line of her body. She is no longer defeated. "Fifty-five thousand."

Lydia doesn't look closely. "Sixty thousand," she says with a smirk. She knows she's going to get the property. She knows that her pockets are deep enough and wide enough and plenty enough. As far as she's concerned, it's only a matter of when and how much.

"Sixty-five thousand," Elyse says without her customary hesitation. The money isn't real to her anymore. She's playing with Monopoly dollars.

I look at Nick. He sees what's happening and he gives me a thumbs-up. For him there is no choice. This cliff might be steep but it's navigable. There are footholds and ledges and ropes to hold on to. You don't have to fall.

I want to close my eyes and hide but I force them to remain open. I force them to look at the tall trees and the wide-leaf plants and the soft yellow flowers no higher than my ankles. This is mine. I'm a landowner. I own land.

Lydia offers seventy thousand.

Elyse offers seventy-five.

Nick smiles widely. He sees it all coming together. The giddiness, Carol, the aborted attempt to ask Dad for a loan, the long checkout line at Wal-Mart, the inheritance discovered four years later—it was all gaining momentum and coming here. This was always the final destination. But I lack Nick's confidence. I lack his clear-sighted conviction in the way things are supposed to turn out. Nothing is clear to me.

"Eighty thousand," Lydia says, even more confidently. She knows the end is near. The Yankous can't afford this. They can barely send their children to summer camp.

"Eighty-five."

Two paths diverged in a green wood.

"Ninety thousand dollars."

"All right!" I holler, because I can't take anymore, because this pressure in my chest is more than I can bear, because something this unexpected and lucky and so beautifully insane will never happen again in my lifetime. Mom's death took things from me. It stole her warm comforting hand and her wonderful consoling voice and her sweet familiar scent and left me with my father. It left me completely alone with a man I barely knew, a man with whom I had only two things in common: a love for my mother and a love for design. He took the former from me; I took the latter from him.

But I'm the baby and I threw myself out with the bathwater.

"Yes!" says the crazy Mrs. Costello, making a fist and punching the air. "It's mine, all mine. I get to build a guest house and plant a garden and put in a swimming pool. Can't quite play with the big boys, can you, Elyse?" She is all victory. She's all triumph and glowing conquest, and she's rubbing it in her neighbor's nose. But she doesn't know the truth. She doesn't have the smallest inkling that she could have gotten the property for almost half.

Although I feel a tinge of guilt, I refuse to give into it. I am only a bystander here. This isn't my feud. I didn't set it in motion. It wasn't my dog and it wasn't my baseball.

"I'll just go write you a check," Lydia says, after she high-fives the air a few times. "See that, Elyse, I can write a check for ninety thousand dollars. I just have to fetch my checkbook and a pen. I don't have to be underhanded like you. Oh, I knew what you were about the minute I saw that cake. You didn't stand a chance once I entered the picture. Ten thousand dollars? In your dreams, honey. In your dreams!" She walks off talking to herself and cackling.

Elyse isn't bothered by her neighbor's gloating and reveling. She has her own victory to savor. "You don't have to thank me, you don't have to give me ten percent," she says. "Virtue is its own reward. But," she grabs the plate from my hands, "I will take my chocolate cake back." Then she stomps off through the underbrush with a big smile on her face. She's picking her moment. She's trying to decide when to tell Lydia she's been had.

I turn to Nick, stunned. "Oh, my God."

He seems equally nonplussed. "I know."

I sit down. I have to. My legs are no longer capable of sustaining my weight. "Oh, my fucking God."

"I know."

Taking deep breaths, I consider the situation. "Well, this changes everything."

"I know."

"We can't eat here."

"All right."

"I need to go into town and have a drink."

"A stiff drink wouldn't be inappropriate right now."

"And then we'll find the most expensive restaurant in town and have dinner."

"Sounds great."

"My treat. We'll make business plans. You can help me come up with a logo. I'll save the receipt and write it off. My first business expense." For some reason, this makes me cry. For some inexplicable reason, tears gather in my eyes and roll slowly down my cheeks.

We are still sitting there gathering our wits when Lydia Costello returns. She brings a large bald-headed man with her. "Here's your check. I told you I was good for it. Now you sign this." Bending her knees, she comes down to my level and hands me a sheet of paper. "This is a contract I hastily drew up on my computer. It states that you promise to send me the deed to the property as soon as the check clears. Is that understood?"

My brain understands little now but this seems simple enough. I sign my name twice.

"Very good. Mr. Lewis here is a notary public and he's going to notarize the document. It's legally binding. Go back on our agreement and I'll drag you through the U.S. court system. You." She points to Nick. "You witness, too. The more people who sign, the more people I can subpoena."

He jumps to her command. We all do and within minutes I'm holding a check in my hand for ninety thousand dollars. I'm not quite sure what to do with it. Nick takes it from my boneless fingers and puts it away. He folds it into a small rectangle and sticks it into my wallet. Then he sits with me for a while.

I have lost my peace. My stomach is quivering with the mad fluttering wings of one thousand exotic birds and I can't stop the blood from pounding in my ears. Everything now is racing: heart, thoughts, nerves, ideas, adrenaline, terror. In a little while I will pull myself together. I will stand up and go into town for dinner and return to New York City and rent studio space and build prototypes and make Tallulah Designs something my mother would have been proud of. I will do all of that in a little while. But for now I can only sit here and wait for the world to stop spinning.

The Babylon Line

1

Hannah wakes up early on the morning of the International Contemporary Design Fair. She's too excited to sleep, and by the time my alarm goes off at six-thirty, she has already showered, eaten and arranged everything in neat piles and is sitting on the couch with her jacket on. When she sees me trudging slowly past her on my way to the bathroom, she wants to hurry me along. She wants to apply pressure to my back and push with all her strength but she resists the urge. Instead she stares at me with her baleful glance until I disappear behind a closed door; then she rearranges her neat piles, putting all the press folders together and moving the brochures to a bigger box.

I am washing the soap out of my hair when she knocks on the door. I tell her to come in.

"It's six forty-five now," she says, little beads of sweat forming at her temples. In the winter, heat pours out of radiators I can't control, making my apartment unbearably hot if the windows aren't open. Hannah hasn't considered this yet. She's too anxious. She's too ready to leave to think of making her stay more comfortable. "In a minute it will be six forty-six." She closes the door and returns to the couch.

This is Hannah's debut. She didn't design the furniture or gamble her future on a risky proposition that might send her hurtling down a dark abyss, but this is still her show. Tallulahland Designs is her baby. It was she who woke at three in the morning to give it a bottle. It was she who cradled it in her arms for hours until it fell asleep.

The truth is a little less Hannah-centric—I myself did a fair number of late-night feedings—but her sense of reality is not completely skewed. Tallulahland is a two-person operation. We were both at the Jacob Javits Center last night until one in the morning setting up the booth.

Once out of the shower, I dry my hair quickly and get dressed. It's seven-nineteen when I'm ready to go.

"In one minute it will be seven-twenty," Hannah says as she picks up a box of brochures. "In two minutes it will seven twenty-one."

I take the box filled with business cards, fabric swatches and press releases. "And your point is…?"

She opens the front door with one hand and catches it

with her hip before it slams shut. "Time is passing. Actually, it's speeding by so quickly we might as well stay here, since it's going to be time for bed in a second anyway."

There is no reasonable response to this, so I don't make one. I just put the box down outside my apartment and lock the door. Hannah runs down the stairs with her arms full. When I get to the rented SUV, she's impatiently tapping her foot and holding up her watch. "In a minute it will be seven twenty-four."

I don't panic. As far as I can tell, time is progressing at a normal rate.

We put our stuff in the back and climb into the car. Hannah wants to get behind the wheel but I don't let her, and she contents herself with a little passenger-seat driving. There isn't a car on Sixth Avenue that she doesn't want to pass.

Even with her snide comments about my driving, I'm glad she's here. Hannah has helped. Despite the almost constant distraction of *Bombing Dresden* rewrites—Adam wants more Walt Disney, Adam wants more sex, Adam wants more Jupiter—she has devoted herself tirelessly. Her enthusiasm and her attention to detail and her compulsive need to take over any project she's involved with have worked to my advantage. I could have done this myself—I could have built Tallulahland on my own—but it was nice having her there to hand me the wood planks as I lay down the floor.

I pull into a lot near the convention center and take

several deep breaths before getting out of the car. I'm trying to calm down. I'm trying to convince myself that today isn't very important in the scheme of things, but I'm too smart to distract myself with the big picture. I'm too clever to be talked down from this high ledge. This show is make-or-break. It's do-or-die. You only get one chance to light a spark, and if editors look away and buyers breeze by, then this is the end of the Tallulahland Express. Exits are to the left; please watch your step while deboarding.

Hannah waits patiently as I screw my courage to a stick. She doesn't tell me what time it is now. She doesn't tell me what time it will be in one minute. Stage fright is something she understands. It's very common where she comes from.

The Javits Center is large and impersonal and swallows you whole. As soon as we step inside I feel like Jonah in the belly of a whale. I'm devoured by a mass of people rushing to their booths, all with the same purpose as me, and I can only wait until they spit me out.

Impatient again, Hannah takes my arm and drags me behind her, energized by the rushing masses. Large groups of people are her lifeblood. No matter how they are arranged—in a crowd, in a mob, in a throng—they are an audience. They're hands waiting to clap.

I follow Hannah to the booth. I trail after her because I'm not really sure where it is. The International Contemporary Design Fair is a kaleidoscope of sliding images, and I can't focus on any one thing. When I look around me, I don't see chairs and computer desks and sleek night-stands with built-in lights, only bright swirls and swatches of color. When Hannah looks, she sees markers. Turn right at the art deco kitchen. Turn left at the three hanging stainless-steel lamps.

"It's seven fifty-six," Hannah says when we reach our aisle. I know we're close because things are starting to look familiar. In a second, we'll pass the Carlo Moretti vases. They'll be on our left. "In one minute it will be seven fifty-seven. In two minutes it will be seven fifty-eight."

I sigh heavily. If Hannah is going to toll each minute like a church bell, it's going to be a very long day. "Yes, yes, I know. In three minutes, it'll be seven fifty-nine. In four minutes it'll be eight. Time is passing, Hannah. You've made your point. I get it."

Hannah doesn't agree. Her point might have been made but it hasn't been chewed and digested. "Time is *racing,* as evidenced by the fact that it'll be eight o'clock in *three* minutes. The doors open at eight, Lou, and we aren't even there yet."

No, we're not standing on Tallulahland soil yet, but the banner that marks our territory is in sight. It's only a few feet away.

"Calm down. This isn't Loehmann's on the day after Christmas," I say. "There isn't a rabid mob of shoppers with their bodies pressed up against the doors waiting for them to open."

Hannah, impervious to reason, increases her speed. She

quickly covers the distance to the booth with a swift walk-run that she usually saves for crossing streets against the light. But I don't rush. I want to savor the sight. Tallulahland: a postage stamp sandwiched between Alessi and Baccarat Crystal. We are shoulder to shoulder with giants, like some tiny European nation-state at the turn of the nineteenth century. We're sparsely populated and brimming with color and trying hard not to shudder from nerves.

Meet the locals:

The Freeport: 3D clocks measuring six inches in diameter. Their black hands are molded to curved numberless faces as if struggling to hold on. The Freeport comes solid or banded with color.

The Merrick: wool felt throw pillows. They come in six designs, two sizes and an infinite variety of color combinations.

The Bellmore: nested marquetry tables with op-art designs. Each pattern is made out of colored strips cut so smoothly that the table's surface looks as if it were fashioned from one fascinating sheet of plastic laminate.

The Wantagh: modernized-aluminum wall lights. Silver-colored rods in alternating lengths burst out of the center like rays of starlight.

The Seaford: duo-tone ultrasuede couches that convert easily into twin beds for overnight guests. They're swathed in wide fields of dark blue and accented with dark blue pillows.

This is the Babylon line—my debut collection devoted to simplicity of color and form. It's not everything I wanted to do—some designs had to be cut because of time and money—but it's everything I wanted it to be. Four years hunched over a desk adding up Marcos's receipts suddenly seems worth it.

Hannah lays her box down on one of the nested tables and then throws herself dramatically onto the Seaford daybed. I'm not surprised. The couch screams drama at the top of its lungs and Hannah hears and obeys. Minutes are racing by, but she lingers here, with her head against the cushions and her arms spread wide like the wings of an eagle. Hannah loves the couch. She considers it her finest achievement, and even though she knows how impossible it is, she wants me to give it to her. She wants me to say, "Here, Hannah, because you love it so much and because you've worked so hard." But I can't. The couch is one-eighteenth of my inheritance.

Hannah looks so comfortable it makes me smile. "Feel free to lounge there all day looking just that content. You're a great advertisement," I say, putting my box in the corner with the other extraneous printed materials. I had no idea how many brochures and press kits to put together—every conceivable number seemed way too high—so I let Hannah decide. This was a mistake. She made up four hundred brochures, a large unwieldy number that implies the conquering of a great many kingdoms. But it is the other way around. We're the ones who'll be vanquished.

"Please," she said scornfully when I protested, "I'm being conservative out of deference to your frayed nerves. I really think we'll need at least twice that."

Looking now at the brochures and press kits stacked in the corner of the booth, I'm embarrassed by her optimism. I'm mortified by her confidence in me, which seems overblown and grotesque and completely out of touch with reality. I put five of each on the marquetry table in two neat piles and hide the boxes under bubble wrap as if they're some awful dirty secret I never want to come to light. Then I sit down at a rickety old bridge chair and watch people breeze by my booth. This is what I'll do today. This is how I'll pass ten hours.

"It's eight oh three," Hannah says.

I close my eyes. I can't take much more of her calling out the time like some medieval town crier.

"Hey, don't make that face at me," she says. "I'm just pointing out that it's only three minutes after eight. Nobody is here. You can't be a failure yet."

"I didn't say I was a failure."

She waves a hand dismissively. "You don't have to say it. I can always tell what you're thinking, Lou. You're like a comic strip. The thought bubbles practically burst over your head."

"If that were true, then you'd know that I wasn't sitting here thinking I was a failure," I say waspishly. I don't like the idea of being an open newspaper. "You would know, rather, that I was sitting here thinking about how the truth of my failureness will slowly sink in as the hours of the day crawl by."

"God, Lou, you have to lighten up," she says, walking over to me. Some pep talks have to be given face-to-face. They can't all be hurled across seven feet of open space. She sits down in the other worn bridge chair and lays a hand on my shoulder. This is supposed to be comforting. "You have no idea how any of this is going to turn out. Unless—" She cocks her head and examines me. "Do you have a crystal ball you never told me about? Second sight? The ability to read tea leaves? Do psychic abilities run in your family?"

She wants me to smile but I don't. I answer with a straight face. "No."

"Did you ask a Ouija board? Consult the Eight Ball? Have someone read your palm? Oh, I know. You have a time machine, don't you? You've already traveled to the end of the week and seen how this turns out. Tell me, do I get the couch or does some rich man in a white stretch limo and alligator boots buy it?"

I shake my head. I refuse to be teased or cajoled out of my funk. Complete and total personal failure is no joking matter. "I just know. I have very good instincts about these things."

Hannah laughs. "Honey, your instincts are shit. If they were any good you would have quit your job and made beautiful couches years ago. You have more talent in your little finger than most of the people here combined, and you've wasted four years of your life fighting it and re-pressing it," she says as the two small stacks I'd made ear-lier catch her eye. Not bothering to hide her disgust, she reaches for the boxes, brushes away the bubble wrap im-patiently, and extracts two heaping piles of brochures. "This is a very big day for me," she adds, arranging the bundles neatly, "and I'd appreciate it if you'd stop ruining it with your gloomy expression."

I have some defensive comment to make but I don't get the chance. A woman from the Alessi booth next door sticks her head over the low partition and asks if she can borrow our hammer. This is like Goliath asking David for a slingshot.

Although we spent most of the previous day pound-ing nails into two-by-fours, I'm not sure where the hammer is. While I'm looking for it, the woman ex-amines the throw pillows. She seems particularly in-trigued by the Bubble Band design, a collection of varying-size circles that cut across the center of the pil-low.

"I love these." She runs her hand over a large one, feel-ing the smoothness of the fabric. "Did you do these your-self?"

I nod.

"They're very good. Actually, I've been thinking about getting new pillows. I'd like to order one," she announces, looking at me as if this were no big deal, as if I sold throw pillows every day of my life.

"Really?" I ask, almost confused by this turn of events. I've been so consumed by fear and nerves I've forgotten that I'm here to sell things. This is a business proposition. This is not a social experiment to see how much dread my body can absorb. "You want to buy one? Like, now?" This sentiment slips out unintentionally. It's a thought bubble that isn't supposed to pop in public.

"You're right," she says, taking the hammer from me. "I should get back to work. Our booth is still only half done. But I'll drop by later." She grabs a brochure and waves and then carries on with her life as if she hasn't just changed mine.

After she's gone, I sit down with a pleased, foolish grin on my face. I'm in business. Me, with my vellum printouts and my prototypes and my squares of wool felt cut out by Hannah—I'm in business. One pillow sold. Here it is: the dollar you frame and hang on the wall behind the cash register.

A few minutes later, when I'm sure Hannah's not looking, I reach into the box of brochures and take another bunch out. Then I add it to the pile.

2

Nick drops by at three. I'm so busy explaining how the tables are made to an assistant editor at *I.D.* magazine that I don't hear my cell phone ringing. I don't hear Hannah pick it up and agree to meet Nick in the lobby with a pass to get him in for free. Admittance to the show is expensive and there's no reason for friends of mine to pay border fees in order to pass into Tallulahland.

As soon as he enters my aisle, Nick sees me earnestly explaining how the laser-cutting process works and raises his hand in greeting. I wave back and try to concentrate on the editor but for a split second my mind wanders. For a fleeting moment, it's back in a green forest and Nick is looking relieved.

Life since Asheville has been a whirlwind. It has been

a roller coaster of things to do and things to finish that left me little time to have dinner with friends or hang out with Nick. The conversation we might have had—what happened, why did it happen, what do we do now—never took place. Instead it was tossed overboard. It was thrown into the let's-forget-about-it sea and allowed to drift to the bottom like sunken treasure. A fresh layer of silt has already settled over it.

"Hey," he says, kissing me on the cheek as soon as the magazine editor is gone, "the booth looks fantastic."

I stare at him in his business-casual clothes and his falling-into-the-eyes hair and his easy, nothing-gets-to-me manner and marvel at how familiar he seems. This is Nick. Friends have sex and conversations get waterlogged and drowned, but Nick remains the same. He's a mountain indifferent to rain or snow. This is generations of breeding at work. This is the stiff upper lip that brought the Crimean War to an end. But I'm not like him. I'm not a Townsend with a ramrod-straight spine. I can't go onstage day after day and be flawless. I flub lines and drop cues and miss so many marks that I'm never sure where I'm supposed to stand. But Nick ignores this. He goes blithely on with his speeches as if I'm as perfect as he.

"Thanks," I say after one of these moments.

"I hear it's going really well."

Of course he has. Hannah can't keep good reviews to herself. She's a liquid crystal display that's updated hourly.

"It's going fine," I say cautiously. The response so far

has been good—more than two dozen editors have taken press kits—but I refuse to have my head turned. Success is a complicated, unreliable formula. It's a some-assembly-required Christmas present that doesn't work when you put in the batteries. Even though you've put joint A into slot B like the diagram says, there you are—on the shag carpet with torn wrapping paper, a thousand little plastic pieces and a broken heart.

"Just fine?" he asks, grinning with amusement. This is exactly the sort of wary response he expects from me. Tallulah West never makes an unqualified statement. "So New York 1 didn't come by and film a segment on your tables?"

I smile. "No, they filmed a segment on my tables all right. I babbled about laser-cutting for five minutes before they cut me off."

"Well, then, maybe *fine* isn't the most appropriate word for the situation."

"Check back with me after they *air* the segment," I say. "Then I'll reevaluate my choice of adjectives."

"And the two tables you sold?" he asks. "When do they count?"

"The tables haven't been sold, they've only been ordered," I explain, watching a tall thin woman in a fur stole slow her pace and examine the daybed. There's a glint of interest in her eye. I worked at Stark long enough to recognize it. "Do you mind waiting here a second? There's a woman ogling my couch and all of a sudden I feel a compulsive need to peddle my wares."

Nick urges me to be true to my inner retailer and wanders over to the Alessi booth to be true to his inner consumer.

I consider the woman for a few moments, wondering if I'm really going to do this. Am I really going to go up to her and ask if she needs help? For hours now buyers and design experts have been coming into my booth and looking at my stuff, but for some reason I still feel like a hawker accosting people on street corners with fake Rolex watches.

While I dither from a distance, the woman sits on the couch. She lowers herself gently onto the cushion and tests its firmness. Here is a sign: Obviously she would appreciate an offer of assistance. Why else would she be testing the firmness. I walk toward her. But then I stop. Another thought occurs to me: She probably wants to determine the quality of a cushion in peace. She could be me in the dressing room at Benetton trying to brush off a pushy saleswoman who keeps offering to fetch a different size or color or style.

The woman catches my eye and smiles. I return the gesture as if nothing is wrong, but I feel as though she has caught me peeping through the priesthole in her bedroom.

"Good afternoon," I say, the heat rising in my cheeks. "Is there something I can help you with?"

"This couch is very beautiful. I love the way it feels under my hand."

I blush again, with pleasure this time. "Thank you."

"Is it yours?"

"Yes, I'm Tallulah West." I hold out my hand and she takes it even though she's still sitting down. She doesn't give me her name. She doesn't have to. It's written on her trade-show pass: Emma Robinson.

"I like your designs." She gestures to the Bellmore tables a few feet away. "Especially those. They're very distinctive, aren't they? Even though I saw something rather similar earlier, these stand out."

Although nobody notices, my heart trembles and pauses. At the words *something similar,* the blood stops pumping through my veins for a few painful nanoseconds and I struggle to appear normal. I know we are all products of the same culture. I know we're all Elizabethan playwrights reading *Plutarch's Lives,* but it's still shocking. It's still your worst nightmare pulling into your driveway.

"Really? Something similar?" I'm trying to sound as though I'm asking about the weather or a topic equally unimportant but I don't know if I succeed. I'm too close to the situation to judge objectively. I'm too inside my head to get out of it. "Do you recall where?"

Emma Robinson adjusts her fur stole and apologizes for not being able to remember which aisle. "It was somewhere over there." She gestures in one direction with her hand, but this doesn't help. Our proximity to the room's eastern wall means that she has indicated all but three or four rows. "If I had taken a card I would have been able to tell you but it simply wasn't worth the effort. I'm sorry, dear."

I shrug. I'm trying to convince her and myself that it doesn't matter. "That's all right." I want to offer her my card but I don't. Instead I torture myself by waiting to see if I'm worth the effort. "Is there anything you'd like to know about the couch?"

She considers the question for a moment. She gets to her feet and circles the duo-tone daybed. "It's an intriguing piece. How long is it?"

This is the sort of question someone asks when they're imagining your design in their living room: Will it fit along the back wall or will it have to go against the window? In response, I hand her a brochure, which has all the dimensions. It also has my contact info. So much for discipline. "It's designed to accommodate a full-grown male adult. When you take these away"—I remove the light blue row of cushions—"you have a sleeping area equivalent to a twin mattress. And it's very comfortable."

Nodding thoughtfully, she takes the brochure. "Thank you. I'm sure I'll be in touch. Good luck with the show."

I offer my own thank-you and watch her walk away. I might never get a fish to bite. I might never get to reel in a customer but at least my bait isn't floating in the water completely ignored. At the end of the week I can say that I had a few nibbles.

"That was good," Hannah says, sucking on a Blow Pop that the booth on the other side of Alessi is handing out.

Bribes—we didn't think of that. "You're still too tense in the shoulders and your delivery is off but your lines are almost perfect. You know when to hold 'em and you know when to fold 'em." When I open my mouth to make a comment she raises her hand to forestall me. "I know. You didn't pay for the deluxe package but I'm throwing in a critique for free. It's just a little something extra I do for all my partners."

We're not partners. When I returned from Asheville frantic and flush with cash and notions of business success, Hannah tried to get in on the ground floor as an investor. I never quite grasped the fine intricacies of her plan, which sought to subsidize her lack of personal wealth with the personal wealth of others, but the broad strokes sounded like a pyramid scheme. In the end, she settled for most favored employee status. But I don't bother reminding her of that now. This is all part of her plan to get the couch. It won't work, of course. I'm reasonably sure she knows that.

When Nick returns from his travels, he has a Coke in one hand and a canvas tote filled with fliers and brochures in the other. He hands me the bag. "I thought you might want to check out the competition. But don't worry. You've got the best stuff here and your booth is by far the brightest and most eye-catching. I should know—I've been around and my eye has scarcely been caught. Although, in the interest of full disclosure, I will admit that I stopped at the beginning of this aisle to watch a woman painting rugs, but it was more the novelty of the live demonstration than the work itself. I don't think rugs should be painted. Hooked and weaved, sure, but not painted."

I appreciate Nick's encouragement but I don't let it go to my head. The trade show is huge and he's only been gone for ten minutes. His eyes haven't seen much. "Thanks," I say, taking a few brochures out of the bag and flipping through them. Although most are like mine—color copies on cheap white paper—a few are thick and glossy and filled with color photos. "I haven't had a chance to walk around yet. Things here are too hectic."

He takes a sip of Coke and looks around. "Have you seen Marcos?"

Although I haven't seen Marcos yet, I know he's here. I sent his check to the ICDF more than six months ago. This is the place where he plans to unveil his new line. I'll drop by his booth to say hello later in the week, but I'm hoping to see him sooner. I'm hoping that he'll stumble across Tallulahland and do a double-take. I want him to whip off his glasses and clean the lenses and examine my booth as if he can't quite believe his eyes. I want him to run his hands over my op-art tables and test the firmness of my ultrasuede daybed and wonder why he ever fired me. I want remorse. I want regret and a pang of disappointment. You don't let Wests go without a backward glance.

These thoughts run through my head but I don't share them with Nick. I only shake my head and say no. "No, I haven't seen Marcos yet."

Nick knows me well. He knows there's more to the story than this abrupt negative, but he doesn't push. He only nods understandingly and jumps to the next question. This is the new balance we've struck. This is the latest solution we've thrown together at the last minute. It lets us live with the mortification.

"And your father?" he asks, forging ahead. He will accept all the short answers I give him without balking.

"My father?"

"Yeah, isn't this something he'd come to?"

My father hasn't come to the International Contemporary Design Fair in years. It was one of the things that factored into my decision. It was one of the reasons I was able to jump into the Tallulahland pool with both feet. "No, he always goes to Italy in early January. His designers might come and report back to him that I was here but I don't mind. By the time he returns at the end of the month it'll be too late."

Nick is thrown off by this. He's examining the Coke can with unusual intensity and trying to appear as if he doesn't have something to tell me. But he does have something. He wouldn't look like a little boy with his hand in the cookie jar otherwise.

I sigh deeply and prepare for the worst. "What?"

"I sent your father a postcard."

But I'm not prepared. I've underestimated the harm Nick could do. "Excuse me?"

"Actually, you sent your father one of your postcards."

This is worse. This is much worse than the things I imagined in my head. "I sent my father a postcard?"

"With a little personal note: Hope to see you there."

I'm horrified. I'm a small child looking at the shredded remnants of her beloved blankie and trying not to scream. "Hope to see you there? I told my father that I *hoped* to see him?"

"And you put an exclamation point on the end, like you really meant it."

I don't know what to say, so I sit down on my five-thousand-dollar couch and stare at Nick helplessly. I don't bother to hurl threats or accusations at him. It's late and vitriol is useless and I'm too scared of what will happen next. I'm too afraid of my postcard, with its swirling designs and sad little plea, begging for attention on the side table by the front door. It won't get any. It will just sit there and be quietly smothered by furniture catalogs and supermarket circulars and packs of coupons bundled together in blue envelopes. This is what will happen. And there it'll finally be: uncontestable proof that I don't matter. Not really. Not in the way a daughter should.

Nick sits next to me and pats my back gently in a show of support, but he doesn't apologize. He doesn't grovel or beg my forgiveness or hang his head in disgrace. "He was going to find out anyway," he says reasonably.

Of course he was going to find out, but from someone else—an employee or a friend or a client whom he hasn't seen in years. Not from his daughter, not from a colorful postcard with a desperate, cheery "hope to see you" scribbled on the back.

When I don't respond, Nick, with his bottle-fed obstacles-are-what-you-see-when-you-take-your-eyes-off-the-goal optimism, persists. "You never know. He might surprise you."

I stare at Nick wearily. There are no surprises, only unexpected, unpleasant disclosures strung together on a rope.

Nick reads my expression. He sees my gloomy countenance and my defeated slouch and my persistent refusal to concede any silver lining and gets angry. Even the bridge-building sons of diplomats have boiling points. "Damn it, Lou, you don't know what he'll do. You think you do. You think you have all of us figured out, but you don't have a clue." Nick's eyes are blazing and he's fighting the urge to shake some sense into me. I can tell by the way he clenches his fists. If we weren't in a public place, my teeth would be rattling by now.

I look around the booth. Hannah is talking to a woman with thick black glasses. She has the brochure open and is pointing out the different designs of the nested tables. The woman is interested. She's asking questions and listening intently to the answers.

Nick is right. I don't know—you never *know*—but after twenty-nine years, you can make accurate guesses.

After a lifetime of disappointments, you can throw your dart at the target without even looking and hit the bull's-eye.

"I should probably get back to work," I say, determined to put an end to this conversation. It can take us nowhere good. "Hannah says I need to circulate more."

Nick doesn't want to leave it here—he has more spleen to vent and more anger to spew—and he stares at me for several long moments. Just when I think he's going to push the issue, he shakes his head. Even though he's the one who's completely out of line, he seems disappointed with me. "Yeah, I should probably get back to work, too." He turns to leave, then stops and looks at me. "What are you doing tomorrow night?"

"Nothing in particular. Probably going home and crashing. Why?"

"I told Hannah I'd take you guys out to celebrate," he says. The note he strikes is upbeat and cheerful, but it's just a pose. It's a just facade he assumes to hide his frustration. Silence is the diplomat's worse enemy. Nothing can be resolved if nothing is said. "I'll make a reservation at Le Deux Gamins. We'll eat and drink and talk about how wrong it is to paint rugs," he adds, trying to be careless.

This isn't how I work. This isn't how I operate. I'm not a well-oiled Ferrari that changes gears in a blink of an eye, but I manage a weak smile. Tomorrow night is a distant shore. It's so far away, I can barely distinguish its outline. "Sure, that sounds good."

Nick gives me a go-get-'em-slugger hug. Then he taps Hannah on the shoulder, says good-bye and leaves Tallulahland. I stare after him because I know he's going to turn around. He's going to walk a few feet, stop and twist his head in this direction to make sure I'm still standing despite everything I've been through in the last five minutes. This is what he does—he always takes a second to make sure the people he cares about are all right. And I am someone he cares about. I know that. But it's not enough anymore. Since the Tallulahland earthquake, the thoughtless camaraderie of very good friends no longer fits. It's a favorite suede jacket that's too tight in the shoulders.

"Lou," Hannah says, approaching with the dark-rimmed glasses woman at her elbow. "This is Martina Byrd, the style editor for *Elle Décor.* She has some questions about your tables that I can't answer. I was trying to tell her some specifics about the laser-cutting technique but halfway through I realized that I didn't know what I was talking about. I'm just here to brighten the place up. Tallulah's the go-to person if you want to know anything but color and price." Hannah smiles self-deprecatingly. This is her sales technique. This is her shtick for courting customers. I'm the window dressing. Tallulah's the window.

While Hannah wanders off to chat up a very good-looking man in a charcoal-gray scarf—from her body language it's hard to tell if she's trying to interest him in the wall light or herself—I answer the style editor's questions about laser cutting, careful not to rattle on endlessly like I had that morning for New York 1's cameras. I'm grateful for her interest and extremely excited at the prospect of *Elle Décor* doing a write-up on my work but I can't help glancing around distractedly. I can't help looking for my father's face in the passing crowd. This, I realize with creeping despair, is how I'm going to pass all my minutes until the last one of the show. As the truth of this sinks in, the faint outline of tomorrow night grows impossibly fainter.

3

At seven-thirty the next morning I lock the door to my apartment, shuffle down five flights of stairs with Hannah at my heels and step outside into the frigid air. It's a very cold morning, and even though the SUV is parked less than a block away, it feels far. We miss the light at Tenth Street and wait and shiver as deliverymen zip by in their heated trucks. We are crossing the street when Hannah suddenly stops short and grabs my arm.

"Don't panic!" she says, her fingers closing tightly around my flesh.

It wasn't my intention to panic—the street is quiet and there are only a few of us walking against the wind with our heads down—but her command flusters me. Her tight grip makes my heart jump in fear and I look around

Bleecker Street, expecting to see a mugger or a stamped-ing elephant bearing down on us. There's nothing there. The only threat here is the wind-chill factor.

Hannah pulls me across the street. "Just stay calm and everything will be all right."

"Damn it, Hannah," I say, alarm growing as I try to pull free of her grasp. She won't let me. "What's wrong?"

Hannah shushes me. "See that woman over there?"

I follow her finger. She's pointing to a woman across the street in a wool toggle jacket. There's nothing par-ticularly remarkable about her. Her coat is green and her hair is covered with a plaid fleece hat. "Yeah."

"That's Gilda."

Now I stop short. Now I panic. "Gilda?" I whisper, sur-reptitiously looking again. This time I notice how tall the woman is and how thick her shoulders are underneath the jacket and how easily she could crush me. She's not quite a stampeding elephant but the effect is the same.

"Don't worry. I've got it all under control." Hannah's as-surances are hardly comforting. Her idea of control is to take the brakes off a bicycle and send it hurtling down an icy hill.

Gilda reaches into her pocket, takes out a scrap of paper and then looks at the buildings she's passing. The scrap of paper has an address written on it. My address. "You have what under control? I thought this was all over. Aren't they making your sci-fi epic?"

"No, we're back to the duchess and the jewel thief, but

don't worry. I have a plan." With that she raises her arm and shouts Gilda's name.

"What are you doing? Are you crazy?" I want to run and hide but there are no foxholes on Bleecker Street. There are no trenches or tall trees for taking cover.

Hearing her name, Gilda turns around. She waves at Hannah, crosses the street and walks toward us. Her steps are wide and eat up the pavement.

"Stay calm and everything will be all right," Hannah says soothingly, as she tilts her head and considers me carefully. I know that look. She's concocting my back story. "Just remember: You're Tallulah West. You're a designer from the East Coast who has just started her own business. Your mother is dead and you have unresolved issues with your father. We met in college, during my pre-duchess days." Her voice is low, her words quick. "You needed help and since I'm cooling my heels in the colonies, I offered my services. You support my acting career but know nothing about—" She breaks off her recitation in order to greet Gilda, who is now only a few inches away. "Gilda darling." She extends her hand like a king to a courtier; it's unclear as to whether she expects Gilda to kiss it or shake it. "How lovely to see you again. It's been simply ages. What are you doing here this brisk morning? Perhaps a breakfast meeting at one of our cozy cafés on Bleecker Street? Do let me recommend the most charming little place on Christopher. It's only a few feet away. Simply turn right at the corner and—"

Hannah's imperious manner and her long vowels don't give Gilda pause. She's used to them and doesn't mind cutting them off. "Actually, I was coming to see you, your grace."

I turn my head abruptly to stare at Hannah. I can't believe her unmitigated gall. I can't believe her impudence extends as far as telling another human being to call her "your grace."

"How lovely, Gilda," her grace says. "I do wish we could sit down and have a tête-à-tête but I'm already engaged for the day. Tallulah West," she waves her hand in my general direction; I fight the urge to curtsy, "meet Gilda Brace."

I hold out my hand and utter a one-syllable greeting. I'm afraid if I say too much I'll sound like a Russian émigré.

"Nice to meet you," Gilda says, barely sparing me a glance. She's a woman with a purpose and she doesn't have time to spare for bit players who don't have stately English manor houses. "Your grace, I have the contracts—"

"Tallulah is a very well-known New York designer," Hannah says. "Perhaps you've heard of her?"

When Gilda says no and tries to bring up the subject of the contracts again, the duchess interrupts with a catalog of my accomplishments. She rattles off a list of credentials so impressive that I'm terrified she's going to instruct the producer to call me "your grace" as well.

"How nice for you," Gilda snaps at me, as if it's my fault

she's just lost five minutes of her life to meaningless brag-gadocio. It's not. I'm a victim here, too. "Turning to busi-ness, your grace, I have the contracts with me. I'd like you to sign them."

"But my estate agent—"

"Is impossible to work with," she states emphatically.

I take offense at this. Madam Petrovitch has been noth-ing but accommodating and obliging. But rather than protest, I bow my head and bite back a smirk.

"Really? I have always found her a pleasure to work with," Hannah says, her eyes wide at the criticism. Then she launches into a long-winded speech about her estate agent's finer points. But Hannah's not really defending me. She's not really standing up for an absent colleague. This is her character: a woman who's always straying too far in the wrong direction.

Gilda lets her ramble for a minute, then interrupts. "Getting back to the contracts, I have them right here." She slips them easily out of her briefcase and hands them to Hannah. "Let me get you a pen."

Hannah takes the contract and flips through it, remi-niscing about the last time she signed something whilst standing out in the cold—February two years ago, Pen-nine Alps on the border of Switzerland and Italy, dear Uncle Reggie's birthday card.

Although ostensibly immersed in the story, I'm en-thralled by the expression on Gilda's face. She's dying to interrupt. She's dying to tell the duchess to just sign the fucking papers but she's not sure you can say the word *fuck* to nobility without getting your head chopped off. Then she straightens her shoulders and takes a deep breath. Screw it, she's thinking. This is America.

"Sign the contract," she says forcefully, putting a pen in Hannah's hand. "This has already taken up too much of my time."

Hannah knows when she's pushed something as far as it will go. She knows when it's time to stop talking and just sign the fucking papers. And I watch, wondering how this will play out. Hannah isn't a duchess. She isn't the owner of an Elizabethan mansion surrounded by rolling green parkland. She isn't the beloved national treasure of the Australian people. The reality of her existence is a little less sublime. The truth of her situation is considerably more absurd and it will all be revealed sooner or later. Her deception will be uncovered and the curtain will drop and Hannah will return to D.C. just as she left it—in the fourth row of a Peter Pan bus. That is, of course, if they can't throw you in jail for impersonating British aristocracy.

Gilda watches Hannah sign the contracts with hungry eyes. She has the look of a wolf who hasn't eaten in a month and almost licks her chops when the duchess returns them to her.

"There," Hannah says, as if oblivious to the pulsing undercurrent, "I hope that helps."

"Thank you, your grace," Gilda say, feeling charitable.

Now that she has the signed contracts in her grasp, she can afford to drop an honorific or two. "Well, don't let me keep you. I know you have a busy day planned. I'll be in touch later this week to discuss our scouting schedule. I assume you'll want to be there when the film crew arrives to take preliminary shots."

Hannah waves her hand dismissively. "Not at all. I trust you implicitly not to ruin the damask curtains and the Louis the Fourteenth tallboy. You will contact my estate agent for anything further, won't you?"

Gilda yes-duchesses and waves good-bye. There is a bounce in her step that wasn't there before. The poor woman. She has no idea what she's gotten herself into. After she disappears around the corner, I look at Hannah. She's smiling broadly. There's no sign of fear or repentance on her face.

"We should get going," she says, back to normal. Her chin is no longer tipped forward and her syllables are short and to the point. "It's already seven-fifty. We're going to be late as it is. Maybe I should drive."

Hannah is psycho. There's no way I'm letting her operate heavy machinery. "We need to talk about this," I say, torn between getting to the Javits Center and standing right there on the corner of Bleecker and Tenth until I know everything.

"I think it went well," she says, blinking her eyelids at me several time. She has the innocent thing down pat. She has it perfected and playing nightly on her CD player.

"Don't you?" Hannah's not conflicted. She has no doubt about what to do or where to go and continues up Tenth in the direction of the car. I follow.

"What well? You signed the contract. You are now legally bound to come up with a British ancestral home with a Hall of Mirrors and sycamore trees." The car is a few feet away and I press a button to unlock the doors. "Do you realize how impossible that is?"

She opens the door and climbs in. "Lou, I was right there signing the papers, so I don't need you to break down the scene for me."

She was there but she wasn't paying attention. "You're going to jail."

Hannah laughs. She's not disturbed by the prospect of hard time. "I'm not going to jail."

I turn on the engine. Cold air comes pouring out of the vents. "You are going to San Quentin with con artists and drug dealers and men who strangle their wives while they're sleeping. I'm not visiting every week. I'll come on holidays and your birthday but that's it."

"I'm not going to San Quentin. Tweaking your identity and signing papers under an assumed name are not jailable offenses. Besides, I have a plan." She turns up the fan on the heater even though the car hasn't heated up yet. I close my vent.

"You have a plan?" I put the car in Drive and check the street for traffic. The coast is clear.

"Yes, I do. So there's nothing to worry about."

"Tell me your plan." I want to hear it and be horrified now, not later when I'm looking over shoulders for my father.

"It's not in the telling stage."

I pull away from the curb. "Not in the telling stage?" This sounds like a stall to me. This sounds like something you say when you don't have a plan.

"It's gawky and awkward and in that painful formative stage when you don't want pictures taken. I'll tell you the plan when it matures."

I sigh. This is code. This is text that needs to be deciphered and translated. "You don't have a plan, do you?" I ask.

"I have a plan. It's a half plan. I promise I'll tell you as soon as I've figured out all the niggling details."

"And it won't involve me. Promise that it won't involve me." Although I never want to be cast in one of Hannah's schemes, right now is a particularly bad moment. I have my own disasters to think about it.

Hannah smiles. It's a secret self-satisfied smile that chills me to the bone, but she promises to keep me out of it.

I make a right turn onto Hudson and drive without commenting. Hannah will do what she wants. Despite the promises she makes, she'll do what's best for Hannah. The heat has finally started to work and I open my vent to let the hot air defrost my fingers. After a few minutes of silence, I ask her what happened to *Bombing Dresden*. I can't help myself. I'm curious.

She's staring at the passing buildings. "Hmm?"

"Everything was set for a futuristic crime drama. What derailed it?"

"Timothy Weymouth liked the original script," she says, glancing at me. "He's attached."

"What?"

"He's going to play the thief."

"Who's Timothy Weymouth?" I ask, feeling tremendous animosity toward him. Who is he to attach himself to anything?

As I turn right onto the West Side Highway, Hannah shoots off a list of Timothy Weymouth's acting credits. Although I can't remember ever seeing any of his work, I have a clear visual: dark hair, chin dimple, broad shoulders, brooding eyes, star of the WB's *Dracula Files,* TV-heartthrob seeking matinee-idol status.

"Adam's very excited," Hannah says, after she finishes critiquing Weymouth's turn as Hank Tinley (dry and peevish) in *Northanger High,* the recent teen adaptation of the Jane Austen classic. "He sent the script to Weymouth's agent almost a year ago and when he didn't hear back he just assumed there was no interest. But Weymouth himself called last week to say that he's definitely attached."

"Will this help or hinder your ultimate success?" I ask as the Javits Center comes into sight. It's black and monstrous and unaffected by the cold. "Is this a fly in the Hannah ointment?"

She shrugs, playing with the temperature control. The hot air pouring out of the vents isn't hot enough for her. "It's not ideal but I can work with it." She smiles again and tells me to stop worrying. "Really, Lou, I have everything under control."

"Your plan?" I am skeptical. My voice is bathed in doubt.

"My plan. It's a good one. Trust me."

Trusting Hannah is a difficult thing. It requires strength and patience and a willingness to believe that the world turns on her skewed axis. It doesn't, of course. People are not toy soldiers on a battlefield to fall in line with her schemes. She isn't General Wellington and the employees of Sugar Snap Peas aren't the third battalion. But I don't say anything. I just pull into the parking lot and think about my father and wonder when the world's going to end.

4

Hannah disappears around noon. I think she's making a quick trek to the hot dog vendor along the north wall but she never comes back. She takes her bag and her cell phone and leaves me alone with magazine editors and television producers and manic store owners who lavish compliments on your work while avoiding your eyes. Although I'm able to handle the attention without Hannah's help, I'm surprised how lonely I feel without her at my elbow. I know this is my gig. I know owner-designer is a character I created and I'm happy to go onstage every night to play her, but it feels different without a supporting cast.

Nick drops by around five. This isn't what we arranged. He's supposed to meet Hannah and me at the restaurant in a couple of hours, but he's had a long day of petty complaints and short tempers and homemade cupcakes distributed to everyone but him. He's spent endless hours dodging angry looks and poisoned darts and now he wants to see a friendly face. He wants to see me and Tallulahland and these works that took me almost thirty years to create. He wants to be reminded that some stories end happily.

"I'm not a happy ending," I say, sitting next to him on the couch. The crowd is still thick and I keep my eye trained on the passing traffic. I don't expect much—I don't expect anything—but some habits are compulsive. Some habits are so uncontrollable that they break you instead of the other way around. "There's too much wrong with my life for anyone to call it happy."

But Nick isn't listening. My inveterate pessimism has no effect on him and he continues to stare at me as if I'm a shining example. "I should fire them," he says, revealing the depth of his misery. Nick never says the F word. "I should line them up in a row like Caesar and knock off every tenth man."

I'm in complete agreement, only I wouldn't stop there. I'd get rid of the whole rotten barrel, run an ad in Sunday's *Times* and start fresh. New year. New you. "Excellent idea. Make an example of one. But who would you choose?"

"That's the million-dollar question, isn't it?" he says thoughtfully. Nick doesn't rush to judgment. He doesn't make hasty decisions, and I watch as a pensive look spreads across his face. In his mind he's running through a check-list: attitude, performance, creativity, promptness. He's de-vising a formula. He's adding up small acts of cruelty and dividing by productivity.

While he deliberates, I hawk throw pillows to a man browsing harmlessly in Tallulahland.

"They're one hundred percent wool," I say, approach-ing hesitantly and glancing quickly at his name tag. My comment is a non sequitur. It has nothing to do with any-thing else in the world but I have to start somewhere.

The man—short with rounded shoulders and thick hands—nods and examines the seams. He doesn't appear to mind my intrusive presence. "Is it durable wool?"

I say yes and mention the standards tests that the fab-ric passed. It's not glamorous picking textiles but it's easy when you know what to look for.

"And the design? It won't peel off in a couple of weeks?"

The strips of wool are secured to the pillow with super industrial-strength glue. Hannah and I have spent whole mornings trying to pull them off. This is Tallulahland quality control. It's not very technologically advanced but it's conclusive. "Definitely," I say. "Throw your worst at them. They'll hold up. And they can be dry cleaned."

He takes my offhand sales pitch as an invitation to mis-chief and tries to tear off the design, placing the pillow between his legs and pulling hard at the strips of wool. They don't budge. They stay firmly affixed to the pillow as I knew they would. Then Mr. Peterson fluffs the pillow and it assumes its original shape.

"I'll take twenty," he says abruptly as he puts down the pillow. "Six of the large and fourteen of the small."

"Okay," I say calmly. I'm playing this scene cool and collected and a little bit indifferent but I'm really ecstatic. I'm really fighting the urge to jump up and down with joy. This is beyond my wildest imaginings. At my most optimistic I figured I'd sell ten over a lifetime.

"I'll need them right away," he adds patting his pockets. He's looking for something. After a moment, he stops, withdraws his wallet and takes out a business card.

I stare at it greedily as he fingers the small white piece of paper. His name, Michael Peterson, isn't familiar. I don't know who he is or where my pillows will wind up—on a shelf in a home-design store in the Berkshires or in the windows of Neiman Marcus—but he's my favorite customer. Even if he buys these twenty pillows and disappears from my life, he'll always be my favorite customer in the world. Twenty pillows! God bless him and the horse he rode in on.

"That won't be a problem," I assure him quickly, although I really have no idea if this is true or not. Only ten pillows exist, and they're all here on display. "When do you need delivery?"

He extends his arm as if to hand me the business card but just as my itchy, greedy fingers are about to make contact, he steps back. He pulls the card away, takes out a pen and begins scribbling on the blank side. I watch helplessly as he jots down a name and a telephone number. These words I can read clearly. It's the other side that remains elusive. "We'll need them by the end of next week," he says.

The end of next week is incalculable to me. In my excited, flustered, just-sold-twenty-pillows state, I can't figure out how many days away it is or how many pillows I can make in that time. My mind has stopped working. It's a foreman on a construction site taking lunch, and all I can do is smile at Mr. Peterson and make promises I can't keep.

"Very good." He picks up one of my brochures and sticks it in his pocket. His business card disappears. "My assistant will get in touch with you by the end of the week to discuss the details. I look very forward to getting them," he says. "They're exactly what we've been looking for."

"Thank you. That's very lovely to hear."

With a nod, Mr. Peterson leaves. Without saying another word, my favorite customer takes his business card and walks out of Tallulahland. I stare after him. But all is not lost. A split second later he stops and turns, digging in his pocket. "I almost forgot to give you my card."

I take the card and watch him leave, even though I'm dying to read it. I don't want to look too eager and it's only when he's out of sight that I look down. Michael Peterson, Set Designer, Dirty Laundry Productions.

"Well, come on. What does it say?" Nick is trying to

read over my shoulder, but he can't. I'm holding the card at the wrong angle. "Don't keep me in suspense."

"He's a set designer for a production company." I can feel the excitement growing but I fight it. I fight it with everything in me and I wish once again that Hannah were here. She'd know Dirty Laundry Productions. She'd be able to rattle off a list of everything they've done in the last ten years.

"What's it say on the back?"

I shrug and hand it to him. "It's just the name and number of his assistant."

Nick turns it over and whistles dramatically. "All together now," he says. This statement is as cryptic as his whistle. They both explain nothing.

"What?"

"All together now. He wrote the name of the show he works for on the back. *All Together Now.* Michael Peterson is the set designer."

Grabbing the card back, I stare at it. There it is: *All Together Now.* "Holy shit."

"Your pillows are going to be featured on a sitcom. How cool is that?"

"Not featured," I say. "They're pillows, not character actors."

This reasoning doesn't deflate Nick. He's still puffed up and excited. "What's *All Together Now* about?"

"Six adults who do nothing," I answer. I've seen the show. Sometimes it's funny. Sometimes it's not.

"That's right. And where do they do nothing?"

I know this is a leading question but I can't see where it's going. "In a coffee shop?"

"Yes, but *where* in the coffee shop?"

Then I get it. Like the sky after a summer shower, it's suddenly clear. "On the couch! They sit and do nothing on the couch."

"On the couch with *your* pillows," he says, a hint of awe in his voice. Nick believes this is success. Nick is convinced that my future is set and secured and waiting for me to walk up to it. He's looking at me, this shining example of entrepreneurship and freedom and brass-ring ethos, and thinking highest-rated sitcom ever, ten million eighteen- to thirty-four-year-old viewers, endless loop of syndication. He's convinced his grandchildren will see my pillows on Nick at Night and order a dozen.

But I'm not the way and the light. A guest spot on *All Together Now* isn't success. It's a flash of lightning and a loud clap of thunder that lingers for only a second. It's a pretty show with good special effects, but it will self-destruct. Tallulahland won't flourish; it probably won't even be a postage-stamp-size spec twelve months from now. I know hope is essential to the human spirit. I know it springs eternal but I refuse to give in to it. I refuse to let its talons grip my heart. Hope is a cruel practical joke. It's that awful thing that keeps you bailing water even though your ship is at the bottom of the sea.

The last time I was hopeful was the week Mom died. It was the week her swelling had gone down and her dialysis went well and her appetite returned and she slept through the night. It was the week I kissed her on the cheek and climbed onto the Long Island Rail Road, believing for the first time since they removed both cancer-ridden kidneys that she was going to be all right. It was the week I held Mom's swollen hand in the emergency room, uncertain if she was unconscious or watching me with steady maternal eyes. It was the week I ran down a white air-conditioned hallway yelling to my father: Now. The nurse says we have to decide now. It was the week I told a man whom I'd never seen before and whom I'll never see again and whose face has dissolved from my memory like cotton candy on a child's tongue, Do not resuscitate.

My mind has wandered off for a moment. It has traveled far from the noisy crowded convention hall but Nick pretends not to notice. He waits until my eyes focus on him and then asks where Hannah is.

"I don't know. She ran off hours ago," I say, before updating him on the duchess's travails. "I'm not sure but I think she's working on her plan. At least I hope so. I wasn't convinced this morning that she even has one. I keep expecting the Gildamonster to march in here with a cadre of officers and haul her away in chains."

Nick takes the blow well. He laments the loss of thousands of potential Disneyism converts and moves on. "Weymouth is decent as Dracula. The scene where he realizes he can only quarterback in the night football games is powerful."

Although I don't know the specifics of what he's talking about, I get the general gist. "You actually watch *The Dracula Files*?"

"It's an excellent television show," he says defensively. "It's the classic struggle between good and evil."

I roll my eyes. "It's about a vampire who travels from 1800s Transylvania to modern-day Ohio in a time machine."

"Hey, there was a disturbance in the space-time continuum."

The show is winding down for the day and the woman from Alessi, my very first customer, waves as she walks by with her coat over her arm. Another day done and still no Dad.

Tallulahland is disheveled from the usual wear and tear I inflict on any space I inhabit—the newspaper is a black-and-white heap in the corner and a take-out container is under the bridge chair where I left it after lunch. The booth is messier without Hannah trailing behind me with her cleanliness neurosis and her garbage bag. "Whatever. The show's still ridiculous. 'Not every bloodsucking vamp is on the cheerleading squad,'" I say quoting the show's print ad, which you see all over on buses and subway platforms. "What's up with that? Not a little misogynistic, don't you think? And the plot makes no sense—he's a vampire but he never eats his classmates? What's the point?" My stack of brochures has dwindled into a few scattered sheets and I refresh the supply from the box, which is now less than half-full. It's possible, I concede in light of how quickly the stock is depleting, that four hundred isn't quite the gargantuan number I thought it was.

"He's just a confused teenager in a strange place trying to get a grasp on who he is. Isn't that what high school is all about?"

I snort derisively and start tossing newspaper into the white plastic bag my lunch came in. Although the day was busy and gave me little time to browse the papers, I've somehow accumulated all three: the *Times,* the *Post* and the *Daily News.*

Nick continues to outline the show's genius as he helps straighten up. He fluffs pillows and Swiffers tables and tries to convince me that *Dracula Files* is the best show on television. His mood is lighter than before and he laughs easily as he relates ridiculous plot twists. He only stops when he gets to the Dustbuster. Its cord is entwined and knotted and requires all his attention to untangle. From several feet away, I watch. From several feet away, my heart contracts at his confounded expression and knitted eyebrows, and I admit the truth: This pinch I feel whenever

I look at him these days is not ego. It's not self-esteem curling into a ball. It is regret.

"There," he says with a satisfied sigh as he unties the last knot. He stretches the cord to its full length and looks at me. His eyes are sparkling and he's grinning eagerly, but rather than toss compliments, I turn away. I don't want to get caught staring.

This awful moment is just another missed cue and Nick pays it no attention. He plugs in the Dustbuster and vacuums the booth.

In a little while we're done. Tallulahland is small and requires little in the way of maintenance. My neighbor to the left, Baccarat, is not as insouciant about its space. Every night a cleaning crew comes. I see them with their vacuum cleaners and their industrial-size Windex and their willingness to scour every surface twice.

We're in the cab a half hour later when I tell Nick to ix-nay the eymouth-way. "Hannah thinks he's a crappy actor and won't appreciate your lavishing compliments on his head."

"I think I said he was decent." He laughs but he knows it's true. Hannah blows things out of proportion. She takes meager compliments and inflates them until they are balloons about to explode.

Hannah is not at the restaurant when we arrive, but we sit down anyway. We order wine and talk and wait for her to saunter in on her own schedule. The restaurant is crowded and small, and Nick is sitting so close to me that I can almost feel his breath on my cheek, but I don't panic. I hold on to my composure and remember my lines and accept that some steps cannot be retraced. That look of relief was a drawbridge. It was a forty-foot wooden plank suspended over a muddy moat and it has been lifted.

When Hannah arrives an hour later, she's exuberant. Her color is high and her spirit lively and she quickly assures us that everything is proceeding nicely. But she won't give details. She keeps the particulars of her plan to herself and orders a glass of red wine. While she waits for it to arrive, she smiles knowingly and evades questions about her day by asking me about mine. This is Hannah being mysterious. This is her hoarding confidential information that she's not ready to divulge yet. It doesn't happen often.

Although it's against the spirit of secret-keeping, Hannah lets us take guesses. We are given three chances each, but neither Nick nor I pays any attention to the rules and we spend the next forty-five minutes coming up with outlandish plots to extricate the duchess from her binding land agreement. But Hannah says no—no to the horde of locusts that ravaged the manor house and destroyed the lands, no to the thirteenth-century ghost who haunts the mansion and hates film crews, no to the disturbance in the space-time continuum that uproots the home and sends it soaring four hundred years into the future where peace-loving Martians mistake it for a god.

Dinner is fun. It's relaxing and absorbing and it takes my mind off everything for a few hours. By the time we step outside into the still cold air to walk home to the apartment, I've forgotten about her plan and my father and Nick's look of relief.

5

In the morning I'm bleary-eyed and hungover from too much cheap red wine and I roll out of bed craving greasy home fries and bacon. I have neither of these in my kitchen—at least as far as I know—and I trundle to the fridge to stand indecisively in front of the open door.

The phone rings and Hannah gets it. Even though she's in the bathroom she answers it, which makes me realize the phone is in there, too.

The doors here are thin and I can here her clearly.

"She's in seclusion," Hannah says.

I'm eyeing a fresh loaf of bread and trying to decide how I feel about buttered toast when the phone rings again.

"No, I'm sorry. She's in seclusion."

Then it happens again: pause, ringing phone, talk of seclusion.

It's only after the third time that I take an interest. This is what a hangover does to me. This is what it makes me feel: indifferent to the events going on around me and dull-witted. The synapses aren't firing.

I take out bread and butter and shut the door. Then I pause for a moment of thought before calling Hannah's name.

"Yes," she says through the door.

"I'm not in seclusion, am I?"

"Not as far as I know."

I'm relieved to hear it. Although the answer seemed obvious enough—I can recall no events of the night before that would make me run and hide—I'm relieved to have it confirmed by an outsider. I cut two slices of bread and stick them in the toaster. The phone rings twice more while my bread is toasting. I'm retrieving a knife from the silverware drawer when another thought occurs to me.

"Hannah," I call again.

"What?"

"Are you in seclusion?"

"Yes," she says, before the blow-dryer makes further conversation impossible.

I take my buttered toast to the living room—as pristine as ever; even in seclusion, Hannah has taken the trouble to fold everything neatly and put it in the corner—and sit on the couch. I turn on the TV and flip through channels, trying to find something interesting. But there is nothing interesting today. I'm too hungover for interviews with self-help gurus and reports on how to find the best airfare bargains. I stare at the television and eat my toast and wonder when my head will stop pounding.

Hannah opens the bathroom door ten minutes later.

"Can you get me some ibuprofen?" I ask, leaning my head against the back of the couch and closing my eyes. The morning newscast is running through the weather: sunny and cold with wind chills in the single digits. Take your scarves. "They're in the medicine chest behind the mirror."

A few seconds later Hannah tells me to put out my hand. I obey.

"The phone has stopped ringing," I say, gathering my strength. In a little while I'll be able to get up and walk to the sink. In a little while I'll be able to fill a glass with water and swallow these two tablets.

"I took it off the hook."

"Oh."

"You don't seem well," she says. Hannah is alert this morning. Her synapses are firing just fine.

"I'm hungover."

"It must have been that fifth glass of wine. I had four and feel fine." Her voice is very chipper for someone in seclusion.

Sighing deeply, I close my hand around the ibuprofen. I want to know why she's in seclusion but I won't be able to deal with the answer until I'm feeling better. I sit up and open my eyes. Hannah is there. Hannah is there with rounded cheeks and two never-before-seen chins.

It takes me a second to realize something is wrong with Hannah. My eyes are puffy and thick from a dissolute night spent drinking in a tavern, and my befuddled brain accepts the one-to-one correlation: swollen eyes, swollen images. But my science is faulty. Eyes don't do things like this. Hannah does.

I shut my eyes. It hurts to look at her. It hurts to stare at her strange bloated face, not because she's suddenly grotesque but because I know the explanation will be long and complex and completely insane. This has to be the plan. Somehow these extra pounds of flesh hanging from her cheekbones are going to save her from the Gildamonster.

"I know you're probably thinking—"

I raise my hand. "No."

"But I want to tell you—"

Again I insist that she stop talking. This time she complies and waits silently as I drag myself off the couch and walk to the sink. There, I fill a glass with water, swallow the two pills and take several deep breaths. Even though the medicine has barely entered my bloodstream, I feel better. Help is on the way.

I pour a glass of orange juice—the toast has calmed my

stomach and made the thought of nutrients bearable again—and stand in the entranceway. I lean against the arch that separates the kitchen from the living room and consider Hannah. She's scarcely recognizable. With her feathered wig and her metallic blue eye shadow and her chubby cheeks, she's someone else: Hannahcus Secludicus.

"All right, I'm ready," I say, submitting to the inevitable. There's no way to avoid this. There's no trick door in the middle of my living room to escape through. "In a hundred words or less tell me what's going on."

"I've outed myself," she says with a broad grin. "There, that was three."

The point of the word limit is precision; it isn't an excuse for her to be more cryptic. "You've outed yourself?"

"I've outed myself. It's all over." She looks at her watch. Although it's not yet seven o'clock, minutes are passing. "Shouldn't you hop into the shower?"

Hop into the shower? "What do you mean, 'outed yourself'?"

"I told the truth. The myth of the Duchess of Nottingham is thoroughly debunked," she explains.

This should make me feel better but it doesn't. I know there's more. I know there's a tremendous amount she hasn't told me yet. She has gone to a lot of trouble to change her appearance, and as I stare at her I'm struck with an awful, terrible, sinking feeling that she really did out herself. "Who are you?"

Hannah knows what I mean. She doesn't even bother to pretend that she doesn't. "Geri Webster."

"Geri Webster?"

"I'm an actress from Rockville, Maryland," she says, launching into her back story with something like relish. "I have two siblings: an older brother, who's a dentist and a spare-time gourmet and an older sister—she teaches kindergarten and is married to a very dull civil engineer. I have one niece. I went to school in D.C., at American University, where I discovered a love of acting. I started as a Spanish major but switched to drama in the second semester of my freshman year. I spent my junior year abroad in London, studying with the Royal Shakespeare Company. I once came within two feet of Judi Dench but she was called away before I could introduce myself. I'm a huge fan of Fellini and Dorothy Arzner, my favorite meal is chicken parmigiana, and I hope one day to direct."

I'm fascinated. Against my will and better judgment, I'm rapt by the way these invented facts slide easily off her tongue. Madam Petrovitch's life never laid itself out so clearly. The details crowded in my head, each one clamoring by the door to get out before it was forgotten. "How do you know Hannah?"

"We were in a production of *The Children's Hour* together at the American Century Theater. She played Rosalie and I played Mary," she says. I remember the show. Hannah's character was a neurotic jealous child who told lies to get attention. "That was three years ago, about the same time when the duchess was allegedly in Australia winning hearts and national acclaim."

"I see. And I suppose you have the program to prove it?"

"Of course," she says with a satisfied smile. It's nice to be understood. It's nice to have friends who know where you're going before you get there. "Actually, I have all her programs. I've been seething with jealousy for years, ever since Hannah stole the part of Ophelia from me in a Georgetown production of *Hamlet*. That should have been me onstage in front of three hundred people each night. I was the one sleeping with the director."

"And how do you account for your name not being in *The Children's Hour* program?" A horrible thought occurs to me. "There isn't an unsuspecting Geri Webster out there, is there?"

Hannah waves the idea dismissively aside. She doesn't invent real people. "I broke my leg and had to drop out of the production. It was a skiing accident over the holidays. I was never very graceful."

I nod. This is only half the story. Geri Webster and her seething jealousy are the ammunition—they still need a delivery method. They still need a gun or a cannon or a missile launcher to be shot out of. "Who'd you tell?" I ask, knowing that it's futile to hope that she simply called up Sugar Snap Peas Production and told them. Hannah paints in colors brighter than that. Subdued grays and sedate browns are not in her palette.

"That's the best part," she says, brushing past me to get the newspaper that's lying on the kitchen counter. She hands it to me.

I take it but I don't open it. I don't even look at the cover. I just stare at her with amazement. This I can't believe. Hannah and her false duchessdom are not news.

"Go on," she urges, "open it. Page six."

The first thing I see when I turn to the page is Hannah's headshot. Here is Hannah, looking pensive and contemplative, on Page Six of *The New York Post*. Just then my cell phone rings. It's a distraction I don't need right now, but the phone is within my grasp, so I pick it up.

"Get the *Post,* turn to page six and call me back," Nick says. He sounds well-rested and eager and as if all his synapses are firing, too. I'm the only hungover person in New York City.

"I'm looking at it now."

"Tell Geri I think she's an evil genius."

"How'd you figure it out?"

"I know the work of a master when I see it. I've gotta go but tell Hannah I want to hear all the details later."

I put down the phone. "Nick says hi." I don't pass along his gushing and his admiration. Hannah doesn't need the outside validation—she's pretty pleased with herself as it is—and he'll just tell her himself the next time he sees her. Instead I read the blurb. I read about an up-and-coming New York-based director and the small-town actress who deceived him.

★ ★ ★

The Duchess of D.C.: Hollywood, a town that prides itself on peddling fairy tales to the American people, bought some magic seeds last month when it cast Hannah Silver, an actress from a tiny town outside of the capital, to play a duchess opposite *The Dracula Files'* Timothy Weymouth in an upcoming World Studio production, believing—wrongly, it was revealed yesterday—that she herself was the widowed Duchess of Nottingham. "She had all of us fooled," says on-the-rise director Adam Weller, who went to high school with the not-so noble. "Her accent and mannerisms were in perfect keeping with that of an American who had married into the aristocracy and lived among them for five years." Other longtime friends are not surprised. "Hannah has always manipulated the truth to get what she wants," says former costar Geri Webster, who revealed the truth to us yesterday in this Page Six exclusive. "She's ruthless and very intelligent—two traits that combine to make her a brilliant actress." Ms. Silver is chastened but unrepentant: "To break into this business you need an edge, something that you and you alone bring to the table. Being the Duchess of Nottingham gave me that edge," she said yesterday over the phone. So what's next for this artificial aristo? "I'm looking into several projects right now," she says from her home in New York City, "but I haven't found anything I can really sink my teeth into yet. I'm in the market." Hear that, Hollywood? Caveat emptor.

I read the article twice before putting it down. My head still hurts but the throbbing has lessened.

"Well?" asks Hannah excitedly. She's waiting for my pronouncement. She's waiting for me to give her an unequivocal thumbs-up like Nick did. And it's hard not to. She is a master and an evil genius and the sort of person who can extricate herself from any and all situations. But I don't. Instead I just say that anything that gets the Gilda-monster off my back is a good thing.

"A good thing?" she asks, almost appalled by the understatement. "Tallulah honey, I'm a bona fide scandal. This is the best thing that's ever happened to me. *Entertainment Weekly*'s doing an article on me. *Entertainment Tonight* and *Access Hollywood* are trying desperately to set up interviews. *Hollywood Squares* wants me to be a square—middle left. This is so perfect."

Because it does seem as though she's arranged things perfectly, I nod and wonder if I should congratulate her. "So why hasn't Geri Webster walked off into the sunset yet?"

"First she has to have breakfast with a writer from *EW* who wants to get background info about Hannah-me from Geri-me. Can you believe it? I'm being researched. That's why Hannah-me is in seclusion at the moment—well, that and the fact that I want to play it coy for a while.

If I'm inaccessible, I won't seem like the conscienceless media whore that I am." She looks at her watch again. It's now after seven. "Shouldn't you be getting into the shower?"

I'm suddenly suspicious of her. She's smiling up at me with concern, as if her only care in the world is that I get to the convention on time, but Hannah has many cares and few are focused on anyone but herself. "Why are you so anxious for me to shower?" I ask warily. I wouldn't put it past her to hold a press conference in the living room while I'm washing my hair.

Hannah considers her answer carefully and decides to fess up. She knows she might be able to mislead Cindy Adams and the Gildamonster and all of the *New York Post* readership, but not me. Not when my headache's receding and my synapses are starting to fire. "I need the car," she says. "I was hoping to drop you off early and then take it to my meeting with the *EW* guy."

"Why do you need the car for your *EW* meeting?"

"Because Geri's a soccer mom now from Westchester who takes her SUV into the city all the time to buy antiques at the flea markets in Chelsea," she explains. "I need the car to keep it real."

There are many reasons to say no—her name isn't on the insurance, she's never driven in New York City, the car is obviously a rental with its Enterprise decal, she's completely psycho—but I don't list any of them. I simply tell her to take Metro North and finally finish that

Oprah book she's been reading for months. Then I hop into the shower. When I get out, Hannah is on the telephone with her parents. She's telling them not to worry about the *Post* story detailing her recent exploits. "It's such a tiny little piece," she's saying in a comforting tone. "AP probably won't even notice it." Pause. "No, I don't think you should tell Grandmom. It's unlikely that she'll hear anything about it."

This is a out-and-out lie and I roll my eyes as I walk through the living room. The minute she hangs up with her folks, Hannah is going to call the AP. She's going to ring up the Associated Press and Reuters and any other news organization she can think of to make sure that they not only notice the tiny little piece but pick it up as well. If she has her way, every grandmother in America will have heard something about it by the end of the day. This is Hannah being a scandal—it doesn't count if you don't scandalize everyone.

I duck into my bedroom to get dressed while she pitches herself to the several broadcast news networks in the city. Her voice is disguised by a thick Midwestern accent. Meet Cathy Roedale, Hannah's publicist from Chicago.

"No," I say, walking into the kitchen to stick another slide of bread in the toaster. Now that my hangover's gone, I'm hungry. "I don't want to hear about the farm she grew up on or the scholarship to Northwestern she didn't get or the awful job she had as the publicist for

Steppenwolf Theater Company. Keep your newest creation far away from me."

Hannah pouts but agrees to stop harassing me with back stories. "Fine, but if anyone asks you about me or Geri or Cathy, please tell them that you have no comment. If you're not going to familiarize yourself with the details of the story, then I want you to stay clear of it. Only I control spin, got it?"

The way Hannah does things makes me speechless. It makes me stand at a safe distance and marvel silently. "I *have* no comment," I assure her.

But Hannah thinks I'm practicing. She thinks I'm running lines. "Good, but a little less emphasis on the 'have' next time. Say it like this: I have *no* comment."

Sighing deeply, I take the keys from the hook, grab my cell off the counter, throw my jacket over my arm and walk out of the apartment. Breakfast is burning in the toaster and Hannah is calling after me with instructions for how to deal with her scandal but I don't care. I have to leave. I have to get away from Hannah and her madness and all the loud messy noise surrounding both. This isn't how I thought the morning would go. This isn't what I expected when I lifted my bleary head off my pillow less than an hour ago, but this is life with Hannah and there's only so much you can take before you start bashing your head against walls.

6

Without Hannah to follow, I get lost on the way to Tal-lulahland. I'm not paying careful attention and miss the turn at the three red leather chairs. I wind up on the other side of the room, near the hot dog vendor and a man who makes furniture out of yogurt containers. Although I'm fascinated by an end table with an alternating Yoplait-Dannon pattern, I don't linger. I've spent too much time idling in traffic on the West Side Highway to do a little personal shopping. Instead I identify the east wall and start walking toward it. This is how I inadvertently stumble onto Marcos's booth. This is how I unexpectedly find myself standing in front of high-gloss tables with colorful designs pieced together with thin strips of cut plastic laminate.

At first I think it's my eyes again. I think it's my hangover that's making me see swirling colors and wild moving stripes and spinning circles. But this isn't a trick of light. This isn't an optical illusion. This is the Bellmore, far from Tallulahland.

I take a step closer and run a hand over one of the tables—Morph in blue. Marcos hasn't gotten it right. His edges are rough—he didn't use a laser to cut out the pieces—and his surface has the uneven look and feel of a mosaic. The smooth-as-glass, cut-from-one-cloth aesthetic is drowned in a sea of bumps, bulges and ridges. Marcos has taken my carefully annotated blueprints and created an abomination in his own image. This table with its stitched-together seams is Frankenstein's monster.

"It's a lovely piece, isn't it?"

I look up to see a dark-haired woman smiling with cloying friendliness. She has mistaken the look of revulsion on my face for interest. I stare at her for a moment, surprised by her presence. The horror and rage and painful fury that whirls around violently in my stomach like a tornado trapped in a glass bottle has overtaken me so thoroughly that I think I'm alone. I think I'm the only person here this morning at the Jacob Javits Center—it's just me and these Frankenstein tables and an awful, blinding hatred of Marcos.

When I fail to reply, the woman says, "I can see from your reaction that you're very taken with it. It's an impressive work and, I believe, one of Marcos Medici's finest.

It's part of our innovative new line that we are debuting here at the show. The nested tables come in a variety of patterns and colors...."

There are so many invectives and curses screaming in my head like terrified children in a haunted house that I can't hear her; there is so much vitriol and wrath running through my veins that I can only stare at her with seething eyes. There is a devil in me and the woman recognizes it. She mutters "okay" snidely as if I'm an unbalanced person who must be humored from a safe distance and slowly backs away.

I don't know who she is. I don't know when she was hired and where she came from but right now she's the object of my hate. She's the only associate of Marcos Medici here to dodge my venom.

"Hi," I say, following her to the corner of the booth, where she scurried, "you don't know me but I designed those tables. I fucking designed those tables, so don't you ever fucking tell me that it's Marcos's finest work, that little rat bastard!"

The woman looks around. We're not alone. We're in a convention hall filled with people. Nothing will happen to her here. This psycho woman can't hurt her with all these trade-show exhibitionists walking around. "Please leave now," she says bravely. "I don't want any trouble."

I step back. I don't want any trouble, either, and I don't want to terrorize a frightened little woman whom I've never seen before. I want to terrorize Marcos. I want to pound on his chest and pull out his hair from the roots and make him cry. How dare he do this to me. How dare he lie, cheat and steal. How dare he turn me into a violent ball of anger and energy that has nowhere to go. I look around for an outlet. The tables. The tables are mine. I walk over to them. There are three sets here, making six in total. I pull them into a semicircle with me in the center and try to move all six at once. Individually the tables are light but together they make a heavy, bulky mass.

The dark-haired woman looks on with her cell phone in her hand. She doesn't know if she should call the police or just scream for help.

"Tallulah, what are you doing?" a voice asks. I turn around. It's Abby. She's here to help with the booth but she's staring at me with wide-eyed wonder. This isn't what she expected to see when she came to work today. She never thought her former co-worker would be red from the exertion of trying to drag six tables across the floor of the Javits Center. Well, neither did I.

"Tallulah?" echoes the dark-haired woman. "This is the Tallulah who left the files in a disorganized mess?" She makes this statement with a hint of dawning comprehension in her voice. Where she comes from, people who can't file well have tenuous connections with reality.

I resent the implication—my connection with reality is stronger than most people's and my filing system makes perfect organized sense—but I can only fight on one front at a time, so I ignore her dig. "I'm taking my tables," I say, breathing heavily.

Abby stands in front of me as if to block my progress but it's unnecessary. There hasn't been anything resembling progress yet. There are too many tables. "I don't understand. What do you mean your tables?" she asks. Abby knows I'm not crazy. She knows I'm not the sort to jump off the deep end unless given a very hard push.

"These are my tables, Abby," I say, striving to appear calm. People only take you seriously when you aren't spitting fire. They only listen to you when you aren't raging madly like a horse with a burr in its saddle. "I designed them. When I worked as Marcos's assistant, I drew up designs for furniture on the computer in my spare time. These tables are a few of those designs. Marcos stole them right off my computer."

As I explain this to Abby, I'm struck by my own stupidity. To leave my designs there unguarded, to fail to consider the depths of Marcos's lack of conscience, to underestimate the originality of my own work—these are my mistakes. These are my blunders and slipups that I'll carry with me for the rest of my career. I know perfectly well that there's no getting out of this. There's no getting away from these copies and pale imitations that'll follow me around like newborn ducklings. I can yell and scream and pound on Marcos's chest all I want but I'm powerless to make him come clean. He has no reason to. I'm just the person who sat at the desk by the door answering phones and balancing his checkbook. Nobody will believe that Marcos took from me. Nobody will believe that I didn't take from him. And the few who give me the benefit of the doubt will simply pat me on the head and talk about influences, as if it were the knee of Marcos's genius that I learned at. The idea is so ridiculous and frustrating it makes me want to cry. I'm Tallulah West. I'm the daughter of the legendary Joseph West. That is the quality of knee I learned at, not some trash-can-making hack's.

Abby walks to my side and tells me to shove over a bit.

"What are you doing?" I ask with narrowed eyes. I'm suspicious of anyone who works with Marcos.

She wraps her hand around one leg. "Helping you move the tables."

"You believe me?"

"Please. I knew something was up the minute he gave me the sketches and told me to work up 2D models. They're more interesting than anything he's ever done before," she says, before calling to the hovering dark-haired woman in the corner. "Iris, we need help over here. If we each take two tables we should have them out of here in no time." She turns to me. "Where are they going? Straight to the police station or to a Dumpster in the back?"

Although Iris warily leaves her safe haven, she doesn't push. She hovers closer and enjoys the better view, but she doesn't add her elbow grease to the effort. But that's all right. I know what Abby is doing. She's taking the wind out of my sails. She's demonstrating the uselessness of my plan and waiting for me to accept the truth. That she believes my story is beside the point. The tables aren't going anywhere. They have no place to go.

I sigh heavily and lean my body against one of the tables. Now that the tornado has passed through me, I'm fighting tears. I'm battling a torrent of emotion with everything inside me. I don't want to break down in front of Abby or this dark-haired woman who's already convinced that I'm the lunatic fringe, but I can't straighten my shoulders and leave. Not yet. This moment is too full of humiliation and horror for me to walk away.

I close my eyes tightly so that no tears can fall. It's painful and demoralizing to realize that people will think that *I* stole from Marcos. It's deadening to the spirit to know that they'll believe this twisted and perverse interpretation of events. I don't have an ego, but this disaster touches something deep inside of me. It gnaws at the bone of who I am and stirs a sense of self that's been tucked away for years in a heart-shaped locket. I am my creations. I am these beautiful colors and these swirling patterns and these smooth laser-cut puzzle pieces, and I deserve better than to be Marcos's cut corner. But that's what will happen. Marcos will sell the design of the Bellmore to some mass-producer of living room schlock who'll trade quality for quantity to insure wide profit margins. In my mind I can already see thousands of Frankensteins running around Kmart like unruly children.

"I'm sorry, Lou," Abby says sincerely. "I can't imagine what you're going through but if there's anything I can do to help…."

Because there's nothing she can do, this is a safe offer to make. It puts her on the side of the angels while risking nothing. "Thanks," I say, suddenly aware of the crowded aisle and the swarm of people passing by. "I should probably be getting back to my booth."

"Your booth?"

"Yes, I've started my own company. We're on the other side of the room next to Alessi." I take deep calming breaths and stand up. I don't need to lean against the table anymore. I'm strong enough on my own. "You should drop by and see what the tables are supposed to look like." There's more than a trace of bitterness in my voice. It's not supposed to be like this. My version isn't supposed to be the cheap museum gift shop print. It's supposed to be the signed original.

"Oh, Lou, I had no idea." She takes my hand and squeezes it. "I knew you were upset about the tables but it never occurred to me that you actually made them and brought them to the show. I wonder if Marcos knows about this yet. I'm sure he assumed you'd disappear into the woodwork after he fired you." She pauses for a moment, thinking, no doubt, about the hole I should have crawled into. "What a diabolical revenge," she says slowly.

There's a curious light in her eye. The depth of my disgrace is good news to her. It means that Marcos will be brought face-to-face with his own iniquity. But this doesn't help me. These are demons that he will fight in the privacy of his room.

I tell Abby I'll see her later and she waves good-bye, but she's no longer listening. In her head, she's already watching the playback: Marcos shocked to see me, Marcos frantically searching his mind for some explanation that doesn't implicate him in any wrongdoing, Marcos raising hell because a mere receptionist dared to copy his brilliant designs and pass them off as her own. All Abby has to do is come up with an innocent way to get Marcos to my booth. All she has to do is move a few pawns around the chessboard. Then she can stand back and watch the fireworks.

I walk back to my booth, hoping Abby will not get her way. I want to confront Marcos about his thievery. More than anything else in the world, I want to stand nose to nose with the lying, cheating son of a bitch and defy him to take credit for my work, but I won't do it in front of Abby and the staff of Alessi and trade show customers who happen to be passing the booth at the time. Marcos is slippery and well-known, and with an audience at his heels, he'll quickly turn the whole thing around. Within seconds he'll be enacting an improvised little pantomime in which I'm the evil villain who ties innocent maidens to the train tracks.

No matter where the showdown takes place—in a crowded room or a ghost town with tumbleweed blowing past—there will be no vindication for Tallulahland. There'll be no apologies, no sorrys, no I-shouldn't-have-done-thats, no I-won't-ever-do-that-agains. I live in an unjust world. This is what I've learned in emergency rooms and convention halls and at the knee of my father.

I sit down in a bridge chair and stare at the couch, wondering what to do next. There is a deep well of sadness inside me, an awful sense of futility that I cannot overcome, but I know this isn't heartbreak. This isn't sorrow that wraps its fingers round your neck and presses slowly and watches you struggle for breath. This is just a puddle of grief that pools in your stomach. It will go away. The drains are clear and the sun is shining and after a while it'll dry up.

Although I want to wallow in self-pity, I have to be Tallulah West. I have to woo shop owners and court editors and convince producers of home-decorating shows that my ultrasuede daybeds and my comfy throw pillows and my previously-innovative-and-genius-but-now-pilfered-and-demeaned op-art tables are the next wave.

The day drags. Aside from a single telephone call from Nick to gush again about Hannah's brilliance, I'm left alone to deal with life. I'd hoped that Hannah or Geri would stop by after lunch to help out and keep company but this proves fruitless. Hannah is off being a scandal.

It's almost five o'clock when Abby succeeds with her

plan. While I add more brochures to the pile on the table, she saunters up the aisle with Marcos at her side. Although she's still more than twenty feet away, I can see the gleam in her eye. It's a triumphant twinkle that sends my heart racing. I don't want to do this. My knees feel weak and I have to lean on the shaky bridge table for support. I really, really don't want to do this. I'm awful at confrontation. I can't lodge complaints in a civilized manner or outline grievances in list form. I can only repress and ignore and walk away when things get ugly. This is why I spent four years working as a personal assistant to a garbage pail designer. This is why I'm a superhero only when nobody is looking.

Abby catches my eye and waves discreetly. She thinks we're in this together. She thinks this is a great prank that we've perpetrated on the unsuspecting Marcos.

I turn my head sharply and look away. I'll take whatever Abby or Marcos or the mosquito gods throw at me but I won't welcome it with open arms.

Seconds tick by. My muscles are so tight they feel as though they'll snap from the tension. Any moment now my pounding heart will break through my chest and beat all over the table. Unable to bear the suspense, I tilt my head to the left and glance out of the corners of my eyes. Marcos is talking to the woman who paints carpets. He's intrigued by the idea and is asking questions about the process. Abby is jittering impatiently at his elbow. She knows he'll cross the remaining ten feet sooner or later.

She knows in her gut that this moment is inevitable, but the wait is still killing her. With her tapping fingers and her darting eyes, she's a terrible stage manager. By now the houselights were supposed to be down and the actors onstage.

When he's had his fill of rug painting—that is, when he knows enough to re-create the effect in his own studio under his own logo—Marcos walks to the next booth. He doesn't linger at Baccarat. Instead he charts a course to Alessi and follows it right past my booth.

Abby freezes. She hasn't anticipated this twist and she's doesn't know how to respond. The playback in her head is slowing and stopping and burning up from the heat of the projector. But then she reacts. Then her nimble fingers rescue the film.

"Oh, look, Marcos. It's Tallulah. What a coincidence," she says, enunciating each syllable clearly. She's overacting but Marcos doesn't notice.

He turns to me with a friendly smile. For a moment he seems genuinely happy to see me, but then he remembers. He remembers how he fired me and how he stole my designs and how those very designs are here in the convention hall. Whoops.

"Lou," he says, stepping forward and then stepping back. My tension eases. He's more nervous than I. "This is a wonderful surprise. How're you doing?" His eyes haven't taken in everything yet. They haven't grazed the Tallulahland sign or touched on the tables.

"Good. I was very good," I say. "You see, I set up my own business, drew up my own designs and made prototypes."

Marcos nods. He's happy for me.

"And then I came to the show and things were going very well. Lots of interest from magazines, a short interview for New York 1—I even sold twenty pillows to the producer of *All Together Now*," I say, the anger growing with each accomplishment. Things *had* been going very well. Despite the melodrama I created, life had been pretty darn good twenty-four hours ago. "But then this morning I wandered across your booth and saw my tables. Yes, that's right, Marcos, my tables—you know, the ones I designed while I was your piddling assistant fetching and carrying for you? Well, I saw my tables in your booth and things sorta went south from there. Isn't that funny? How just knowing that someone ripped you off really brings you down?"

Marcos's eyes dart around the booth. Finally he sees them. He doesn't blanche or pale or flinch. He doesn't show any reaction at all.

"Take a good look at them, Marcos," I say, my voice a grating false chipper that can't hide the rage or resentment or the ugly stream of bile that's rising in my throat. "See how smooth the surface is? Notice how it doesn't look like the wall tiles in the bathroom of some Greek peasant? That's what craftsmanship will get you. And these lines. Amazing how I've managed to arrange the strips perfectly. This is the way the table's supposed to look. I know it's alien to you, seeing something done right without cutting any corners or taking shortcuts. Go on, take a good close look because I don't want you to forget it, Marcos."

Marcos takes a step forward and rests a hand on my shoulder. "That's wonderful, Lou. I always knew you'd do something great if given the opportunity, which I did, of course, when I let you go for financial reasons. But obviously the pressure to create exciting and innovative work is too much for you. If not, why would you have borrowed my design?" I'm about to protest but Marcos continues smoothly. He's calm now and no longer nervous. I've put him on the defensive, which is where all his rhetorical skill lies. Offense is a strange and difficult maneuver that's practiced by football teams and armies, but defense is familiar ground. It's a walk through a park on a sunny day with birds singing lovely melodies overhead. "And I do think *borrowed* is the right word. I don't doubt that you got overwhelmed as the show grew nearer and panicked. However, stealing is not acceptable and I'll have to send out a press release denouncing you first thing tomorrow. You're very young, my dear, and made a terrible mistake. Still, there's a useful lesson to be learned."

Marcos as wise elder is unbearable. Marcos as high-minded instructor is worse than anything I expected and it almost cuts me in half. In the pit of my stomach I can feel the tornado stirring again. I can feel the clouds gathering and the winds picking up and I have to ball my hands into fists to keep myself from scratching his arrogant eyes out. I'd rather be publicly scolded than endure his condescending swagger. I'd rather be held up and humiliated in front of a thousand people than listen to this hack and thief imply that I could learn anything from him.

I take deep breaths and struggle to hold on to my temper, but it's impossible with him looking at me with that superior expression. Marcos thinks he's outmaneuvered me. He thinks he's handled the situation nicely and that I'll go gently now into the good night, but he's wrong. There's too much pain whirling inside me for sensible action—I've been cautious my whole life and look where it's brought me. I open my mouth to scream and hurl invectives and to curse generations of Medicis, but I'm stopped by the sound of my father's voice.

"Tallulah," he says from behind me.

There's a loud rushing in my ears and then a deep silence. My feet are firmly rooted to the spot, but I feel as if I'm in free fall. I feel like I'm plunging and dropping and disappearing from view. So this is what the edge of the world looks like.

From a painful distance, I can see the light of understanding dawn on Marcos's face. He's never before noticed the resemblance—the same dark green eyes, the same dimpled chin, the same steady stare that's disconcerting and a little bit distressing. He's never before put two and two together and come up with West. But that's all right. It doesn't matter what he's noticed in the past. All that matters is what he notices now.

Before I can turn around and say hi to my dad, Marcos steps forward with an outstretched hand and an obsequious manner. "Mr. West," he says, almost tugging his forelock, "what a great pleasure."

Dad knows Marcos by reputation and sight but they've never met. Ever since I started working for him, Dad has nurtured a profound dislike of the plastics man that transcends his run-of-the-mill scorn for artists he doesn't respect. Still, he steps forward and accepts Marcos's hand with grace. Beside him Carol is smiling. She is tan and wrinkly and the freckles on her face are out in record numbers.

While Dad and Marcos exchange pleasantries, Abby looks on with eyes as wide as saucers. This development—this unscheduled guest appearance by a superstar—is better than anything she could imagine. The highlight reel in her head clicks away as it records the new drama.

Although the initial seismic shock has passed, I still can't believe what is happening. I still can't believe that the scene in front of my eyes is real. This is my father's final betrayal: to show up now.

When Marcos is finished complimenting Dad on his newest collection, he jumps right into it. He's not the sort to linger when there's destruction to be done. "Mr. West," he start somberly, "I'm very sorry to have to be the one to tell you this, but your daughter has copied designs of mine and is trying to pass them off as her own." He says this with his head bowed as if embarrassed and disappointed. From his bag of tricks, he's pulled out the pose of a high school principal informing on a teen who was caught smoking in the girl's bathroom. "But don't be too hard on her. She's young and she has many lessons to learn, this one included. Starting a business is tough work. She wouldn't be the first person to break under the pressure."

Marcos's pleading for leniency on my behalf is unbearable. For the first time in my life, I want to run and hide. I want to go into seclusion like Hannah and shut my door and never ever open it again. The world outside is too harsh; the glare that reflects off the glint in Marcos's eye is blinding. I don't say anything to defend myself. I will not be charged with protesting too much.

My father says nothing. He's incapable of speech. These charges have been laid at my door but he's absorbing them as if they were made against him. This is his ego at work. My success and failures are only reflections on him.

Marcos judges the moment and decides retreat is tactical. He has thrown his grenade and now it's time to run in the opposite direction. "Well, I'll leave you alone with your father now. Lou," he says, placing a hand on my shoulder to show that there are no hard feelings, "you'll be fine. You have talent, my dear. Just believe in yourself."

He turns to leave; Abby follows. Before she goes, she gives me a parting smile, as if to thank me for the great show.

"Well," says Carol as soon as Marcos and Abby disappear from sight. She's the only one brave enough or foolish enough to break the silence. "I can't say that I'm shocked, Lou. You've been doing nothing but filling out and sending invoices for years and then you suddenly decide to start your own design firm—that in itself was fishy. I would've never said anything to your father about it, but I had some small inkling that something like this was going on. This must be very humiliating for you, but as your boss said, it's a lesson. If this experience has taught you anything, then it isn't a waste. Of course, we didn't have to come back from Italy early for it. But your father was insistent. Now I wish I could have been more convincing in order to spare him this."

One strong gust of wind and Tallulahland topples. This is my fault—I taunted the mosquito gods, I tried to build something, I nurtured the tiny sliver of hope in my heart that wouldn't be stamped out.

Carol's words are the nail in the coffin but I don't care. This isn't about her spite and her meanness and her clawing ambition. This isn't about anything anymore but a beautiful ruin and I stare at my father, waiting for him to throw dirt on the grave. My shoulders are back and my spine is straight and I'm determined not to crumble. Even though this suddenly feels like heartbreak, I will not disintegrate. I will not fall to pieces or try to explain my-self or beg for understanding. I will just stand here with my shoulders back and my spine straight and absorb everything.

Dad makes a rude noise. It's the sound of disbelief and impatience. "Carol, don't be ridiculous. Tallulah didn't steal anything from that man."

I'm delusional. I'm a drowning woman about to pass out from lack of oxygen and this is that sense of peace you always hear about. Dad isn't really saying these words. I know he's not. We're in a theater that has been rigged by a ventriloquist who's forming the sentences for him.

"She didn't?" Carol asks, her voice full of challenge. She, too, knows the truth—that this Joseph West is only a blank-eyed dummy.

"Of course not. If that man felt it necessary to spread lies it must be because he stole designs from Tallulah." He looks me in the eye. "Is that what happened?"

"Yes," I say, the tension in my back and shoulders loos-ening. But I'm still afraid to let down my guard. I'm still afraid that this is all a trick of poorly firing synapses.

Carol narrows her eyes suspiciously. She feels like she's being sold the Brooklyn Bridge. "How can you be cer-tain?"

"I know my daughter's work," he says matter-of-factly. "That couch over there is a variation on her senior proj-ect. Those pillows have her mother's stitching on the

side. The designs on these tables are op-art. Lou has always been fascinated with Bridget Riley's early work.
That starburst light fixture on the wall is made of mod-
ernized aluminum, which is exactly the material I would
have used. And besides," he says, as if almost an after-
thought, "Wests don't steal. We don't have to."

For the first time since my mom died, I don't feel like
an orphan. This is what parents do: They take your side
and they have faith in you.

I'm trying to regain my composure when Carol says
she's sorry. I'm trying desperately to seem self-possessed
and not on the verge of emotional collapse when Carol
assures me that she regrets the misunderstanding. She's distant and insincere and the only thing she regrets is that
the charges leveled against me are false, but this doesn't
matter. Her apology gives me a moment to pull myself together. I take deep breaths and count to ten and wonder
what to do next.

"I thought you were in Italy," I say awkwardly in the
silence that follows Carol's less than gracious apology.
This isn't the direction I want the conversation to go in,
but I'm powerless to stop it. These words tumble out of
my mouth without bidding. They're more thought bubbles popping.

"We were," he says. "We cut our trip short. My assistant forwarded your postcard to us in Capri."

Emotions that I had pushed safely behind police barri-
cades elbow their way forward to the crime scene. First

his great leap of faith and now this—a holiday cut short on my behalf. "Thank you," I say softly past the lump in my throat.

"I couldn't miss this." He looks around again—at the couch, at the table, at the light, at the pillows. "Your mother would be proud."

"I know," I say, my eyes bright with unshed tears. They have to be bright—I can feel the water pooling.

Sensing that for once he's said exactly the right thing, Dad capitalizes on his gains. "I'd like to buy the couch."

The look of dismay on Carol's face is so comical, I giggle. It's an unusual sound and oddly childlike. Dad winks at me.

"But, Joseph," Carol says, "it doesn't go with anything in the apartment."

Dad shrugs off his wife's protest. "We'll redecorate."

"The couch is yours," I say. "I want you to have it—as a gift." It's one-eighteenth of my inheritance but it's a small thing compared to this fleeting feeling of having a father.

"Redecorate?" Carol wrinkles her nose. "But we just redid the apartment before the wedding."

"No, I insist on paying." Dad takes out his checkbook. "It's bad business to give away products for free, and I didn't raise my daughter to be a bad businesswoman. How much? And don't give me a discount just because I'm your father."

"But it's too big. Where will the entertainment center go?" Carol asks.

"All right," I say, the tears falling unchecked down my cheeks. I can no longer hold them back. I have gone through so many emotional storms in the last twenty minutes that I can't hold anything back. "That'll be five thousand dollars. Please wait six to eight weeks for delivery."

"Hear that, Carol?" my dad says, only amused by her predicament. This is why he's able to live with her: He thinks her ugly traits are funny. "You've got two months to buy a smaller television." Dad signs the check, tears it off and hands it to me. "We should get going. We've come straight from the airport and we're both tired. But perhaps dinner tomorrow?"

"Oh," Carol says, "but aren't we having dinner with the Prestons tom—"

My father sends her a quelling look and she hushes up immediately. The events of this afternoon have spiraled out of her control. First she is returned early from Italy, then she is called ridiculous and now she is forced to suffer dinner with a plagiarizing wild child rather than the Prestons. But Carol is savvy and knows not to say anything. She won't encourage the building of a bridge between father and daughter, but neither will she wield the wrecking ball. She's quite willing to let it self-destruct on its own.

"Tomorrow night?" I say. There are several excuses at my fingertips. There are several dodges and evasions that I keep on tap for situations precisely like this, but I'm suddenly hesitant to employ them. In the wake of today's tremendous leap of faith, I'm reluctant to say no to my father.

"We'll celebrate your success," Dad says, trying to make the invitation as alluring as possible. He's still not sure what he did wrong. He still thinks he's been the ideal father, but he recognizes progress when he sees it. He recognizes a breakthrough when it stands before him crying, and he doesn't want to backslide.

There is so much hope in his eyes that I have to turn away. I look at the starburst on the wall and at the throw pillows on the couch and at Carol's absentminded half smile. She's certain I'll say no. In her head she's already telling the Prestons about the charming little villa they stayed at on Capri. In her head I've already destroyed the bridge. No, she won't be the one to wield the wrecking ball. She won't have to.

With tears running slowly down my face, I say yes.

7

Hannah drops by the booth just as I'm gathering my things to go home. Her look has returned to normal—no prosthetics, no awful metallic blue eye shadow, no frizzy *Charlie's Angels* wig. She gives me a cheeky, triumphant smile—obviously her interview with *Entertainment Weekly* went well—and asks about my afternoon.

I fluff pillows and give her a full account. She's horrified and appalled, and I've barely gotten to the good part—the part where my father swoops down like a superhero with a cape and saves me—before she starts plotting Marcos's downfall.

"Don't worry," she says, taking a seat on the couch and flattening the recently fluffed throw pillows. "I'm on it. I already have a few ideas." She leans back, draws her eyebrows together and deliberates silently for several long moments. Her gaze is steady and fixed and directed at me, but I ignore her and straighten brochures. After a moment, she looks up. "Does he have a washing machine?"

"What?"

"Does Marcos have a washing machine? I can do some serious suds damage with a Maytag and a bottle of Era Plus."

This isn't what I'm expecting from her. It's simple and straightforward and involves hardware. Her plans are usually convoluted and insane and require things that don't quite exist. "I don't know. Maybe," I say, thinking of all the appliances he charged to the company over the years. "Probably."

But Hannah is already shaking her head. She's driving past the washing machine scheme. "No, that's just a childish prank, something any good ol' boy in a frat house could do. Marcos deserves a punishment tailored especially for him. It should fit the crime."

I laugh at the determined edge in her voice and the way her eyes narrow with concentration when she's trying to come up with a truly diabolical idea. "Trust me," I say, "punishment isn't necessary. I'm really okay with this."

Hannah leans forward and stares at me as if I'm some rare and exotic foreign species: Tallulahcus Accepticus Lying-downicus. I'm supposed to be raging against Marcos. I'm supposed to be wailing at the injustice with my fist in the air, not fluffing pillows. "Lou, he ripped off your designs. He not only ripped off your designs but he tried to convince your father that *you* had ripped off *his*. He can't get away with this."

"He won't. Cheaters never win and winners never cheat," I intone wisely, and at this moment I believe it. At this moment, I'm convinced that the new Marcos line will wither and die without my inspiration. Next season he'll be making trash cans again.

Hannah rolls her eyes. Karmic justice doesn't count. "I know," she says, inspiration striking now like always. "I'll give my contact at the *Post* a call and get a short Page Six item in tomorrow's paper." She takes out her cell phone and taps it against her hand. "Now, who shall I be? Someone with a tenuous connection to industrial design but well placed enough to have the inside scoop. A cleaning woman who comes into the office every night at six-thirty? She would have seen you working at the computer." Hannah shakes her head slowly. "No, we need someone with greater understanding of what goes on in a design office," she explains, demonstrating the skill that invented Geri Webster and the Duchess of Nottingham. "Someone who flies under the radar but still has access. Like an intern." Hannah looks at me eagerly. Even though I've been quiet, she thinks I'm in the war room with her. She thinks I'm sitting across from her studying logistical maps and satellite photos. "Does Marcos have interns?"

I try explaining again why punishment isn't necessary—Tallulahland still stands and for a few seconds this afternoon I had a father—but Hannah doesn't get it. Where she comes from anger isn't tempered by outcome. In Hannahville, all that ends well is not necessarily well.

Seeing her blank stare, I sigh heavily and submit. "Yes, two interns each semester, usually from Parsons."

"That's perfect. There's no way Marcos will remember names and faces. I'll be Jean Stuben, a junior. You know, now that I think about it, this is the best solution: It'll raise your Q rating, sell more tables and exonerate you of any wrongdoing," she says, listing the everyone-wins benefits of her new scheme. Then she rests her forehead on her hand and closes her eyes. She looks as though she's about to fall asleep, but I know what's really going on: She's creating a character. Jean Stuben—smart, funny, good at drawing freehand, Wisconsin-born, likes swimming, hiking and quiet nights in front of the television with her boyfriend.

I watch her quietly for several minutes more. Hannah's way of doing things doesn't make sense. It doesn't follow a reasonable formula or respect any of the laws of nature, but it works. She is always on the next rocky ledge looking down at me. She's always marching forward to the "Battle Hymn of the Republic" while I'm huddled in a foxhole hoping the next shell won't cause too much damage. It isn't right.

"I've got to go see Nick," I say abruptly, deciding I have to do something and I have to do it right now. Bravery is a broken-down car. It's a rusty, old Mustang with an engine that only works in spurts and if I don't act now it will stall. "Here." I toss the keys at her. "You take the rental."

Hannah's eyes open wide and she stares at the keys with something like amazement. I've managed to surprise her. This is rare. "Why?"

The answers are nonsensical and rambling—because I don't always know what everyone is thinking, because sometimes you have to take a risk, because I'm a landowner—but Hannah doesn't know about any of that. All she knows is that she has the keys to the Pathfinder in her hand. "A cab will be faster. I don't want to spend an hour looking for a parking spot," I explain, before grabbing my shoulder bag and running out of the convention hall.

The line for taxis is short but few drivers make it this far west and I'm forced to wait for five excruciating minutes while the out-of-towners in front of me argue about where they're going to eat dinner.

I curl my hands into fists and close my eyes and try to relax. The blood is pounding in my head and the desire to run back inside the Javits Center and hide in Tallulahland is almost overwhelming, but I refuse to succumb. This has to be done now. It has to be done today. It has to be done in the waning shadow of my father's revelation. Tomorrow will be too late. The comet will have zipped by and I will once again be inert.

I climb into a heated cab and try to stop shivering but

I can't. This is nerves. This is too much adrenaline traveling through narrow veins. I lean back against the cushion and try to plan the scene—my knock, my hello, my
explanation of why I'm there—but I can't. All I can do
is replay old footage—the cup of coffee by the fire, the
Science section on his lap, the look of relief on his face.

No, I remind myself, you don't know what he was
thinking. You only think you do. That look of relief—it
could have been disappointment wearing the Townsend
mask of mild good humor. It could have been regret slipping into the dark blue overcoat of the diplomatic corp.

*You think you have all of us figured out, but you don't have
a clue.*

The cab pulls up in front of Nick's apartment building
and I hand the driver a twenty-dollar bill with shaking
fingers. I try to get change but his money is wadded into
a ball in his hand, with singles buried deep inside, and I
can't wait. I climb out and shut the door and stand on the
sidewalk wondering if this is really going to happen. Am
I really going to do this?

The building door opens and a short woman with pink
hair steps out. She pauses a moment to hold the door for
a friend and then lets it swing close. I run and catch it before it shuts completely. It's better this way. I can roam the
halls without committing myself. I can turn around and
flee without his ever knowing I was here.

But this is just wishful thing. Epiphanies are one-way
streets and you can't leave the way you came in.

Nick lives on the fourth floor. He's forty-eight steps from the street and I stand on each one fighting the impulse to be the other Tallulah—the one who doesn't deal with things. But I don't give in and when I get to his door, I take a breath. I take a deep, calming breath, close my eyes and tell myself Mom would be proud. This is Tallulah West, inert landowner, trying to be brave. I knock loudly and firmly. Nick answers wearing a sweat-stained T-shirt and running pants. He isn't surprised to see me.

"Hey," he says, holding the door open for me to come in.

But I don't want to come in. I want to say my piece here on the threshold, where I can make a quick getaway. I open my mouth to speak but I'm struck dumb. There are no words or sentences. There are no greeting-card sentiments waiting to be recycled. There is only a void. Bravery is a worn-out clunker that sputters and dies in the middle of a busy intersection.

I take another deep breath. This isn't the hardest thing I've ever done. This isn't Mom and a white emergency room and a doctor who will not resuscitate. It's only a freshly painted hallway and Nick staring down at me with curiosity and a faint smile. It's his look that calms me. It's his familiar grin that gives me the courage to jump-start the bravery engine and lean forward. I lean forward, put my arms around his neck and press my lips against his.

Nick doesn't pull back immediately. He doesn't push me away in disgust or ask me to leave. He just sighs softly and wraps his arms around me. His grip is solid and tight and constricts my breathing, but I don't care.

One kiss turns into a constellation of others and before we know it, we're necking and groping and getting carried away like teenagers on a porch swing. But we aren't adolescents. We aren't hormone-driven creatures with only one thing on our mind. At least Nick isn't and after a while he pulls away. He raises his head, looks me in the eye and says we have to talk. Then he runs a hand through my hair and kisses me again.

"Later?" I ask.

He nods, but his agreement is short-lived and he steps away from me. He pulls free of my grasp with a determination that's so resolute, it seems as though he has to reach deep within himself to find it. "No, now. We're going to do it right this time." He shuts the door to the apartment and points me to the couch. "First we sort out our problems. Then we behave foolishly. Got it?"

I nod.

"Good. Now let me get changed and we'll go get a bite to eat," he says, taking off his stained T-shirt and disappearing into the bedroom. "We won't get a thing said if we stay here. And while we're eating, you can tell me all about Marcos and your father."

I laugh, amazed by the calm I feel. Here it is: another still point. "I take it Hannah called."

"She was worried about you," he calls from the other room. "She claimed you handed over the keys to the

SUV without even flinching—it kinda freaked her out. She also told me to let you know that all systems are go." When he comes out again, he's throwing on a clean T-shirt. "The duchess wouldn't tell me what she was up to but she promised you'd give me all the sordid details."

"Sordid is the word for it," I say, recalling her outrageous scheme. I can see it now: Hannah on the telephone with the *Post* relating a shocking tale of theft and innocence wronged, her voice equal parts fear (Jean Stuben cannot afford to alienate one of contemporary design's high chieftains) and anger (but nor can she stand idly by…). It won't work. Too many forces have to align. Too many pieces of the Marcos puzzle have to slip into place for him to get the pillorying he deserves, but that's all right. Dad came to the show. He cut his trip to Italy short and stood at the gates of Tallulahland fending off invaders. And then there's Nick—pulling on jeans and grinning foolishly and saying we have to talk when there are other things he'd rather be doing.

Feeling peaceful and happy, I close my eyes and picture Mom in the Sloan-Kettering cafeteria. She's holding my hand and looking into my eyes and assuring me with all the strength she has left that I'll be all right without her.

For the first time ever, I believe it.

Fashionistas

Lynn Messina

Vig's Things To Do List

1. Pick up dry cleaning.
2. Transcribe interview with Jennifer Aniston's hairstylist's assistant.
3. Research up-and-coming designers.
4. Drinks at the Paramount.
5. Take part in devious plot to depose evil editor in chief.

Vig Morgan's got what it takes to go places in the fashion-mag world. The trouble is, she might have to engage in a little backstabbing to get where she wants to go.

Conniving and treachery aren't really her strong suits. But can she do it just this once? Let's just say that the world outside her cubicle is about to get a whole lot more exciting....

At *Fashionista* magazine, all is fair in fashion and war.

RED
DRESS
INK
™

Visit us at www.reddressink.com   RDI0303R-TR